JACK RONDER

The Lost Tribe

W. H. ALLEN · London
A HOWARD & WYNDHAM COMPANY
1978

PRINTED IN GREAT BRITAIN BY
FLETCHER & SON, LTD., NORWICH
FOR THE PUBLISHERS
W. H. ALLEN & CO. LTD., 44 HILL STREET, LONDON, WIX 8LB
ISBN 0 491 02326 x

BOUND BY RICHARD CLAY (THE CHAUCER PRESS), LTD.,
BUNGAY, SUFFOLK

AUTHOR'S NOTE

The Lost Tribe is based on the life of my grandfather. The occasional foreign words I have spelt to indicate the sound of Lithuanian Yiddish modulated by East Lowland Scots.

Although I have used some characters and events outside their proper times to satisfy my 'Writer's Truth' about the story, no character represents any person now living, apart from some pieces of myself in David.

J.R.

GLOSSARY OF YIDDISH TERMS:

Afikomen: At the Passover meal, a piece of matzo set aside to be eaten last.

Alevasholoum: 'Rest in peace'

Alkies: Matzo-meal and egg, made into balls and dropped into boiling chicken soup. (Called 'Knaydlach' by Jews from other parts, but we called them alkies)

Ballibostie: An expert housekeeper.

Barmitzvah: The 13th birthday (according to the Jewish lunar calendar) of a Jewish boy. He sings his portion of the Law and an excerpt from the Prophets in front of the congregation in the synagogue. Afterwards there is much rejoicing among relatives and friends, and a big social do, if father is wealthy

Charoushes: a traditional dish on the Passover table, made from apple and cinnamon, almonds and wine. It symbolises the mortar used to bind the bricks without straw, but it is such a sweetmeat that I never believed that; I thought they were kidding me.

Chazan: the Cantor of a synagogue.

Chazzer: Pig (the most taboo animal of all)

Chazzerai: Rubbish, especially things to eat: things that are a waste of money but could be good for a giggle.

Cheder: Night classes for all Jewish children to learn Biblical Hebrew.

Der Heim: the homeland.

Fleischekky: containing meat or meat products.

Gefilte fish: chopped fresh fish, onions, eggs and matzo-meal, highly seasoned, made into balls and boiled.

Gelt: money

Goy, Goyim: Gentile, Gentiles.

Haggadah: the book containing the family service on the first two nights of the Passover.

Kaddish: praise of God pronounced by a mourner.

Kiddush: The consecration of the Sabbath. The ritual prayers, usually sung by the head of the house, on Friday night when the candles are lit and the men are home, and the bread is tasted and the wine is drunk.

Kind, kinder: child, children.

Kosher: ritually clean for eating.

Lignor: liar.

Locksher: home-made vermicelli for chicken soup.

Machotonim: family friends and relatives of relatives.

Maerev: the evening prayers.

Matzo: unleavened bread.

Mazel: luck.

Mazeltov! congratulations and good luck!

Mensch: A man who does a deed for the good of others. One who can hold his head high.

Meshuggie: mad.

Mezzuzzah (plural Mezzuzzim): An oblong metal box 2–3 inches long by about $\frac{1}{2}$ an inch square. The box contains certain texts from the Law, about the Unity of God and the command to love God: and the commands to affix these commands to the doorposts of one's house. Thus the metal boxes have a flange at each end pierced

7

with a nail-hole. Every door in a Jewish house except the lavatory door must have a mezzuzzah fixed to it. Certainly the front door must have one, and this is a sign to friends and enemies that a Jewish family resides within.

Mitzvah: a good and holy deed.

Nedan: dowry.

Nu: Well? or So . . . or anything in between, depending on the intonation and accompanying gesture.

Pesach: the festival of the Passover.

Phoont: pound-note.

Rov: the Rabbi.

Seder: prayer-book

Sefer-Torah: Scroll of the Law.

Shabbas: the Sabbath (Saturday)

Shah!: Say nothing!

Shein: beautiful one; said with impatience.

Shegets: a male non-Jew who is thick-witted, poor and without taste.

Shidduch: wedding-match.

Shiker: scornful word for a drunkard.

Shiksie: a non-Jewish girl, poor and stupid but with a glitter of attraction for Jewish men; applied also to the maid-servant in the house, and to the non-Jewish wife of a mixed marriage, to derogate her further.

Shlemiel: a stupid drip of a person.

Shmuous: a pleasant chat about this and that and old times.

Shool: the synagogue.

Shtiber: a shilling.

Shveig!: Shut up!

Simcha: an occasion for rejoicing.

Succus: the harvest festival of Tabernacles.

Tallis: prayer-shawl.

Tephillin: two small black leather boxes with long leather straps. The boxes contain the same texts as do mezzuzzim, with the injunctions to put the words about loving God on one's heart and on one's head and between one's eyes. During morning prayers, every male Jew goes through a ritual, tying one of the leather boxes round his head, and one on his left arm and hand. The straps form mystical patterns of numbers and letters, and I did it every morning for about a year after my barmitzvah, and then got bored with it and stopped.

Torah: the law of God revealed to Moses.

Tsimmus: a long-cooked carrot mixture.

Tsubrennte: burnt.

Tsitsis: a square of material with the middle cut out to put one's head through. Dangling from the material fore and aft are fringes: 'Put upon the fringe at each corner a cord of blue: and it shall be unto you for a fringe, that ye may look upon it and remember all the commandments of the Lord, and do them.' The trouble was that they were looked upon by other non-Jewish little boys and laughed at.

Tsorris: Sorrow and trouble.

Yamulkeh: skull-cap, worn always by male Jews because they are always in the presence of God, but more usually only in the home or the synagogue.

Yom Kippur: Day of Atonement.

Yortseit: the anniversary (by the Jewish lunar calendar) of the death of a close relative.

Zorg: worry.

9

Introduction

It is forty years since I was in a synagogue. The shock of that statement comes not from any guilt about my religion, for I have none, but from the span of time. My boyhood is gone yet it is as clear to me as if I were living it now.

The sounds and smells of the synagogue, the mutterings, the melodies, the voice of the Chazan, and of Rabbi Dr Daiches with his little hand-clutchings and arm-gestures and high, flat-topped, black velvet hat; and the old men swaying, beating their hearts with their fists, shouting the words in a babble – regulars in their rose-pine wooden seats with the white name-strip on the back; woollen tallises, silk tallises, the smell of sweat on crowded festival days, the bleak stained glass in loving memory. And that swish of tallises halfway through the final song, everyone packing up with No Decorum at all, hurrying to get out and home for lunch or a smoke, or a blether at the corner of Salisbury Road where we spilled out from the pavement on to the roadway: the Goyim didn't do that, not on a busy Saturday anyway.

I was an easily scandalised boy. The behaviour of my friends and relatives often embarrassed me, as if they were screaming out to the normal people of Edinburgh, 'Look at us, we're *Jews*!' and including me by association. All my friends were Jews, apart from at school, but in all my school-days I didn't bring more than two non-Jewish boys home. And when I did, there was a certain formality about it. With Jews now, you knew their fathers and aunties and everything. I don't remember ever meeting a formal Jew.

Looking back, I don't remember ever meeting a formal Glaswegian either, but I lived in stiff Edinburgh where society mattered.

The irreligious behaviour of the previous generation shocked me immensely. They obeyed *some* of the laws; they ate kosher food *most* of the time, they smoked on Shabbas round the corner from the shool, they drove cars on Shabbas, they missed out on prayers, some of them even worked on Shabbas and did a little business on Yom Kippur. I reasoned that if you were a Jew, you believed in an omnipotent, omnipresent God, and you were very puny in comparison with God, and when you communicated with God, as in prayer, it was a huge, unthinkable, frightening magnificence: how could anyone dare not to carry out the laws and the commandments to their tiniest detail?

I didn't question in those pre-barmitzvah, pre-pubescent days that I myself never turned up for the Shabbas morning service till about ten o'clock or later, when the reading of the law was well under way. That was the time my pious mother got me ready, that was the time that most other people turned up. I didn't question my own kind of praying, which was to say the Hebrew words I found easiest, or whose tunes were singable, and to skim over the others in a random mutter. Not that I knew the meanings of even the words I said, except the most obvious and most repeated. And yet by the time I was twelve I had learned in the Hebrew classes to translate English into Hebrew at the speed of the teacher's normal voice. Somehow saying the prayers needed too much effort; their translation, when I tried, had not enough meaning.

I sat from the age of six in the seat beside my grandfather, two along from the beamie (the red-carpeted rostrum with the velvet-covered reading table on it). I stood by him and sat by him, and had my place in the book pointed out by him. I could never follow his own praying because he muttered it in a kind of breath-prayer and I believe he was tone-deaf: none of his tunes had melody or rhythm or sounded like the chant of the Chazan, and they were nothing like any tune I had been taught. And yet he knew it all. He never broke a law. He had fled from Lithuania in order to live as he lived. A small-bodied, bent old man with a stubbly white beard, high cheek-bones and slanting hooded eyes, very large ears, yellow stumps of teeth when he talked (which was rare), and a smell of snuff and Turkish tobacco. There were smellier old men in the seats behind, so I was glad to get my parents' permission, when I was twelve, to move right to the other side of the synagogue, to sit beside my friends. My grandfather was saddened by the move, and kept peering across at me to make sure I was there, and praying rather than talking with my friends.

He was not an endearing man to me. In an age of conformity for Scottish schoolboys I was ashamed of his foreignness. When my sister and I went to tea at his house in Summerhall Square, he would carve wooden moulds from the top of our grandmother's broomstick, and pour molten lead in them to make spinning tops with Hebrew letters on the side, but the game was a dull one, not as good as dice; and my grandmother was left complaining that her broomstick was too short to use. Grandpa also boiled alarm clocks and put them in the oven to dry. They went very well afterwards. When I grew up and heard respected people praise him for his learning and humanity, I was amazed.

Judaism for me as a boy was a conflict between the awesomeness of God and the ordinariness of His Chosen People. It was exemplified more than anything by the sound of the shofar, the ram's horn blown in the synagogue on the Festival of the New Year and on the Day of Atonement. The chazan couldn't blow it.

Dr Daiches would trot from his seat on one side of the Ark, round to the beamie, mount and stand by. The chazan, Mr Ordman mostly, would fish for the ram's horn under the velvet cover of the reading-desk, bring it out, warm it, wet it, wet his lips, signal he was ready. Dr Daiches would call out the command 'T'kiyoh' in a sing-song, and in the

13

packed, expectant synagogue poor Mr Ordman would huff and puff and squeak and raspberry and maybe get a sound from the shofar, and end up with blood on his lips. The effect on me was a mixture of scorn, and prickles rising on the back of my neck. It was a ludicrous sound, considering that it was supposed to symbolise atonement and repentance and the call of the Almighty, but it was also an ancient sound. I could easily visualise those priests leading the Children of Israel seven times round the walls of Jericho, and, when they blew that sound, the walls falling flat.

I

In the small synagogue at Ravelets in Lithuania there was silence. Snow outside, a dozen men inside, in their praying shawls, heads covered with skull-caps, listening.

In December 1885, Lithuania is the Lithuanian Jewish Pale of Russia, and the Jews are waiting for the sound of soldiers. Eyes on the window where the snow has drifted round the wooden frames. White inside, white walls, white praying-shawls. The red curtain over the ark, the crimson cloth on the reading-desk, and the glow under the wood stove are the bright colours in this house of God. The wooden benches are varnished brown, with the separate seats at the back for the women; but no women are here today.

The Reader stands at the desk, wearing his black velvet hat, head to one side, listening. Another man stands beside him: he has been called to the reading of the law, and he stares down at the open scroll on the desk, seeking comfort from it, courage rather than hope, as he listens for gun-fire.

In the front row sit three boys in their late teens, heads covered with their praying-shawls, eyes fixed on the window, watching, waiting. They are the brothers Kaydan.

A noise of shouting from outside. The Reader starts, twitches. The man beside him clears his throat and says the first blessing before reading the law.

— *Borachu es-adounoi ham'vouroch.*

The men, and the boys, taut with fear, eyes squinting at the window, respond automatically to the ritual.

— *Boruch adounoi ham'vouroch l'oulom vo'ed.* Blessed is the

Lord who is blessed for ever and ever. The black lines woven into the fine wool praying-shawls above the fringes move with the swaying of the men. The page in each small wood-bound prayer-book on the ledges in front of the men is turned by a finger. Blessed art thou O Lord our God, King of the Universe, who chose us from all the peoples, and gave us His Law. Blessed art thou O Lord, Giver of the Law.

A silence. The Reader looks round at his small congregation. He turns again to the window: snow and silence. He shrugs, holds out the silver stylus that hangs by a chain from his wrist, finds the place in the lambskin scroll and chants the ancient Hebrew.

– *Va'y'dabair adounoi el-Moshe* . . . And the Lord spake unto Moses saying, speak unto the children of Israel that they turn and encamp by the sea –

He has his back to the door of the synagogue but he knows it has opened. He turns. A Russian soldier stands there with a grin on his face. For the three Kaydan boys, fear turns to terror. The soldier throws open the door to its fullest with a crash of wood against wood. Long boots, leather greatcoat, rifle over his shoulder, bayonet on it, fur cap on his head, he strides in, and behind him comes a file of other soldiers. In time to their stamping feet they shout, 'Jews, Jews, Jews!'

And a bayonet digs into the youngest Kaydan: 'Get up, sonny! Get out of it!' The boy backs somehow over the wooden stall and the one behind.

The Reader stands in his place, legs planted apart under his gown. His hat is knocked off, the butt of a rifle in his ribs knocks him sprawling from the dais.

'And what's this?'

The scroll of the law is lifted from the desk, one end unwound; another soldier lifts that and pulls: it rips apart. A moan of terror and sickness rises in the synagogue and continues through the stamping and kicking and laughing. Bayonets remove prayer-shawls and wave them in the air.

16

An old Jew lies flat on the floor and a boot on his face leaves him bleeding at the mouth. They bend a thin one over a stall and a heavy boot in the rump heaves him over on his head.

'Well kicked!'

The first soldier reaches up to the velvet curtain across the ark and rips it down. He opens the dark doors and surveys the old scrolls inside. He lifts one out and throws it as a streamer across the room. 'Wheeeee . . . !'

To the Kaydan boy watching from the cover of the back stall, it is as if God is hurtling through the air to the whoops and yowls of the soldiers.

A boot, tired of kicking men, catches the door of the stove and opens it, and hot coals cascade out. Another kick sends them flying. The Kaydan boy clutches his prayer-shawl and book, and dives for the door as the house of God goes up in flames.

Outside there is packed snow. He runs through the short lane, past the tethered horses, past windows with frightened faces, stops at the square because there are more soldiers, runs back and round the market hall to the patched one-storey shack that is his home. The door is locked. His two brothers arrive panting.

There is gunfire now, and the crackling of flames from the burning synagogue, and a child screaming. Shouts, more gunfire, as the boys open a window and climb in. They shut the window and lift their farm-coats down from the pegs. They take the bread from the tin box and break it into three lots. The youngest boy, Moshe, is the only one who has brought his prayer-shawl and book. He takes a towel that is hanging up to dry, puts his bread and prayer-shawl and book in it and ties it up. The others put their bread into their coat pockets. They listen at the window. Only shouting now, and wailing. The oldest boy kneels down by the hearth and presses the end of a floorboard. A corner comes up and he raises the board and brings out a box. The second boy takes the lid off. Inside are three slim bundles of bank notes. He gives one to each of the others and puts the lid back on the box. The oldest boy replaces it and puts the floor-board down.

They stuff their money inside their jackets. The oldest boy takes a pencil from the dresser, and a used envelope. He looks at the others. It is forbidden to write on the Sabbath. But to fly for your life on the Sabbath is allowed: you can't keep the Sabbath if you are dead. He writes, for their mother to read, in Hebrew characters and Yiddish words: GONE TO AMERICA.

He leaves the envelope and pencil on the dresser. If the soldiers go away and their mother comes back from hiding on the farm, she will know that they've done what they said they'd do, all those months ago when they sat at their fireside and decided that life for a Jew would be better in a new country.

The middle boy opens the window and they all three climb out. Moshe turns back to lift his bundle out and to close the window. When he turns round again, the other two have gone, and a soldier is staring at him, gun held at the hip, pointed at his heart. Death. Slow dream.

The snow has started to fall again. A lowing of animals in the barn and a chorus of laughter. Moshe points up the street, and shrieks, 'What's that?'

The soldier takes a quick look and Moshe darts away. The soldier brings his gun to his shoulder and fires after him and the bullet pings off the corner post where the street divides.

In the forest, the three boys trudged along. The snow underfoot was soft, lying on the old leaves. There was a silence, almost a warmth in the stillness. Perhaps it was the physical warmth of their own bodies inside their overcoats. Moshe was leading, collar up, hat well down, bundle over his shoulder. He was seventeen, small, stunted almost, for life was hard and bad harvests and poor land had fed him inadequately. But he was wiry. His brothers, Shmul the oldest at nineteen, and Dovid who was eighteen, were taller than he but hadn't filled out, and were not so strong.

So Moshe was leading, the pacemaker. And when the shadows were lengthening he stopped at last, and turned. The others weren't there.

He called, gently at first. 'Shmul? Dovid?'

Snow fell from an overloaded branch. He looked up. Looked back. He shouted, 'Shmul! Dovid!'

Silence. He walked back the way he had come.

He rounded the track through the forest and looked along the open avenue into the dusk. The darkness of the forest was on each side. He gathered all his strength and shouted, 'Hoi!' Then he saw the sleigh-tracks going across his own, down a lane into the darkness. What had happened? Were they soldiers who took his brothers away? Would they come back and follow his own trail in the snow? A raven croaked and croaked. He looked up but couldn't see it, and the croaks died away.

A redness flashed over Moshe's eyes. He blinked and there was nothing but the forest and the snow, and he thought of the red curtain being ripped from the ark. He was mortally afraid. He put his bundle on his other shoulder and turned again and walked on.

The dusk became the glimmer of night. Moshe did not know which way he was going, and now only a fraction of his mind cared. He had walked past weariness, his legs had gone leaden, then numb; he had slept as he walked, and woken in the dark, under trees, still walking. His hands felt as if they were a mile away and he slithered down a bank into a ditch. He lay against the snow and closed his eyes again. To sleep. His hands clamped round the bundle, round the whole world. Just a little sleep. He forced his eyes open and stared to make out the shape of the ground in front of him.

It took a long time to untie the bundle. He put his face down on the prayer-book and shawl but couldn't feel them.

19

He rubbed his glove over his face to scrape away the snow and tried again. He felt the hard bread against his cheek, and took a bite, and chewed. If he wrapped his prayer-shawl round his head, the good wool would keep him warm and he could have a sleep. He bit again and chewed, and his belly responded and he felt he was still alive.

He took his gloves off and rubbed and rubbed his hands together and blew on them. He picked up the bread and finished it off, then wrapped up the shawl and the book and tied the bundle and climbed out of the ditch. He was on a road and he could see starlight between the trees, the same stars as the ones he knew. He headed north.

Presently the moon came up and he could see the hut on the side of the road, and beyond it another hut with a light. He stopped in the shadow. From the far hut came a soldier with a rifle; he looked up and down, stamped, leaned the gun against the wall, swung his arms, breathed as steamily as a horse, picked up his gun and marched up and down twice, looked around again, lowered the gun and went back inside.

Full of fear, Moshe backed round the side of the dark hut. He could see that the roof was half in. His mind was clear and he was possessed now with anger, anger at the hut, and anger that his legs and guts were giving way. The door leaned sideways with the hinges rusted and broken. He moved round it without a sound and looked at the great-coated figure sitting inside. But the man didn't move: he sat with shut eyes, perfectly still. Moshe's foot scraped some rubble. The man didn't heed.

Moshe stared hard for signs of life but there were none. He laid his bundle carefully on the bench beside the figure. He opened his own coat and untied his trousers and squatted down and, staring always at the corpse, opened his bowels on the frozen mud floor of the hut.

When that was over, and clothes tied and buttoned again, Moshe went out to look at the far hut. It was still lit up and he could just make out the gate across the road, by which he knew he was at the frontier. He looked up at the black hills on each side of the road. He went back to get his bundle for he had to try to cross the border. The figure in the hut was as still as before and his own stench was foul and sharp to him. He took off his gloves and laid them on the bundle so that he would know where they were. He unbuttoned the man's coat, then his jacket underneath. The man moved, but as one rigid body. Moshe felt for the inside pocket and brought out the man's papers. He held them to the moonlight but his lips were too cold to mouth the Russian that he could make out. He put the papers in his own pocket, found his gloves and put them on, lifted the bundle and made his way out of the hut.

He walked steadily, willing himself to live. As he drew near the gate his legs refused to obey and he stopped. From the lit doorway he could hear the sound of humming. He walked on to the gate, his whole body trembling, his teeth rattling together. He closed his mouth firmly, pushed his chin up with his hand.

The soldier was sitting in the porch of the hut by a glowing brazier. He looked up.

'Ay-ay?'

Moshe stopped. The soldier got up and took his gun and came out. He spoke in Russian.

'Where are you going?'

Moshe opened his mouth. 'Memel.'

The soldier pursed his lips, looked him up and down. Moshe took out the papers and handed them over. The soldier studied them in the light of the storm-lamp in the porch. He handed them back to Moshe and motioned him forward with his rifle.

'Cold night.'

'Not so bad,' said Moshe.

He ducked through the gate and gave a wave behind him, and walked on. He was out of Lithuania, in Memel Territory: beyond the soldiers, beyond the bullets, beyond the raids and whippings, beyond starvation.

2

The harbour office on the quay at Memel was a stone building with a rough paved floor. There was a big wooden counter sloping back for writing on and leaning on. There were
pigeon-holes stuffed with papers and ledgers and books of
dockets. The clerk, a sharp-faced man with gold-rimmed
spectacles, sat on a high stool writing shipping orders in
triplicate on a printed pad. Two kerosene lamps hung from
the rafter above him and bathed him in a figure-eight of
light.

The stove blazed. Beside it, on a rickety bench, sat a
bearded seaman smoking his pipe. He lifted the top of the
stove, poked with the poker, slid a block of wood in from
the pile at the side, took his pipe from his mouth and spat
on top of the wood, and replaced the lid. A pendulum clock
on the wall ticked loudly enough to be heard above all this
activity, and the wind and breakers outside. It was half
past seven in the morning.

The clerk tore off the sheet of paper he'd been writing on
and laid it on the pile beside him and put the pile into a
pigeon-hole. He took another rough paper and started to
copy the details on to his pad.

The seaman cleared his throat.

Without looking up, the clerk said in guttural English,
'It is yours now, Mr Cole.'

The seaman put his pipe back in his mouth, and the
clerk wrote on.

The door opened. They both looked to see the muffled
figure who came in.

Moshe Kaydan shut the door behind him against the wind. He stood not knowing what to do. His collar was up, his hat pulled low, he was hiding inside his coat. Only his eyes were alive. He had walked through the night because there was nowhere to lie down. He had had nothing to eat since the bread and his whole body had the numbness of fatigue.

The clerk said, '*Da?*'

Moshe came to the counter, and the clerk looked away, then down at his papers again and continued writing.

Moshe said, '*Amerika.*'

The clerk looked up. He spoke in Russian, 'Are you alone?'

Moshe understood but didn't answer. The clerk repeated the question in German.

Moshe gave a half-nod.

The clerk spoke to the seaman in his guttural English. 'Meester Cole?'

The seaman, Cole, was listening. The clerk went on, 'Here we have a Jew –' He looked at Moshe and spoke in German, 'Are you a Jew?'

Moshe kept still. The clerk went on. 'I speak to him in German. He speaks Yiddish, which is a kind of German, so we understand. *Ja? Sind Sie Juder? Aus Litau?*'

Moshe retreated into his greatcoat. There were Enemies here; he turned to catch sight of the other one, the bearded seaman.

The clerk spoke on in German: 'Aren't you afraid? You've come from Lithuania?'

Moshe turned back to him. He was certain sure that this was Memel Territory, a free land. He gave a nod.

'So, and you want a ticket for America.'

'*Ja,*' said Moshe.

The clerk spoke to Cole, the seaman.

'Meester Cole, he is a Jew from Russia, from Litau, Lithuania. We have many, many – this year, last year, because –' he became respectful, 'the Tsar of all the Rus-

23

sias, God save him, he say, all the Jews in Russia to divide in three. One – two – three –' He made three cutting gestures with his hand. 'One third to become Christian, in the Russian army. One third to die. And one third –' he indicated Moshe with his other hand, 'to emigrate.'

Cole took his pipe out, cleared his throat and spoke with a pleasant Scottish lilt. 'Is that so? He's a Christian, the Tsar?'

The clerk flashed him an icy look. 'He is Christian.' He turned again to Moshe and inspected what showed of the boy's face: half-hooded dark eyes, big cheek-bones, almost a Mongolian slant to the eyebrows. 'So this man, it seems to me he ran away from to be put in army. So he go from Lithuania, into –' He gestured at his own office.

'Memel,' said Cole.

Moshe caught the word and looked round again.

The clerk continued, 'And he ask to go from Memel to the land of gold.'

Cole said, 'America.'

Moshe caught that, too. He asked the man, '*Amerika?*'

'Right,' said Cole.

'We will now see,' said the clerk, 'if he has money. *Haben Sie Geld?*'

Moshe retreated again inside his coat.

'You can't go to America without money,' said the clerk in German.

'*Ich hob,*' said Moshe. He had money.

'*Ich hob,*' mocked the clerk. 'He has money.' He reached to the pigeon-holes for a book of dockets.

Cole got up and came to the counter. He was an easy-going man.

' 'S a great place, America,' he said, 'I go back and forward myself. In my ship. I'm going to America, son. In half an hour, when it's light.'

Moshe was staring at him. '*Amerika?*' he asked.

Cole said, 'That's right. It's no' a luxury-ship but you don't look as if you want that. Make the boy out a ticket.'

'*Das Geld*,' said the clerk.

Moshe said nothing. He wasn't even sure if he was awake, but he knew he didn't have the strength to walk out of this office. '*Amerika?*' he asked once again.

Cole said, 'America, son. Land of freedom.'

'*Das Geld*,' the sharp-faced clerk insisted.

Moshe unbuttoned his coat, then his jacket, and brought out the roll of notes. He kept tight hold of them and leaned over the counter and tapped the clerk's docket.

'*Shreib!*' he told the clerk.

The clerk looked at the seaman.

'Do what the boy says,' said Cole.

So the clerk made out one single steerage ticket to America from Memel, to travel on the ss *Clydebank*, and the money was handed over and counted, and shrugged over, and divided out. Then Cole put his arm round the boy and the boy hugged his bundle and they went out of the office into the wind and spray, over the ropes and fish-boxes to the gangplank where the little coaster bobbed against the quay.

Down in the hold were baulks of timber stacked high, and in the hollow in the middle, casks of tallow. It was dark and smelly, with sea-water swilling above the keel so that the pumps were kept busy. Moshe lay on the top of the timber, just under the hatch, buried in a bed of sacking. He had fallen asleep to the grinding and juddering of the engines, and now woke when the hatch above him was raised by a deck-hand.

Cole was there, with two food-cans, and he stepped down on to the timber.

'Are you awake, boy?'

Moshe sat up, felt for his bundle, rubbed his hair and face and ears.

Cole sat down carefully beside him and laid the cans on the wood. 'You've had a good sleep. I've got your dinner.'

Moshe sniffed at the steam rising from one of the cans. It was a meaty stew. He looked and shook his head.

'No?' said Cole. 'What's wrong? I've just had mine, it's good and hot.' He scooped up some in the spoon and held it out to feed Moshe. But the boy withdrew his head.

'*Treif*,' he said, which was the Yiddish word for unclean. The food was from an animal, perhaps blemished, maybe even pig, but he couldn't tell the man that. '*Treif*,' he repeated.

Cole got it wrong. 'Trifle?' he said. 'It's a stew!'

Moshe gestured that, for himself, he was forbidden to eat what was in that can. He had already looked at the other can and knew he wouldn't starve. He nodded vigorously at it. Boiled cabbage and a hunk of bread was all right. He took the can. He found his cap in the sacking and put it on: God had understood why he had not said the blessing for the bread he had eaten while walking to Memel, but now it was different. Moshe turned away from Cole and held the can and said the two Hebrew blessings, one for bread and one for vegetables. He started to eat, scooping up the cabbage with the bread and his fingers.

Cole watched him until he was nearly finished. 'A Jew, eh? You'll have to get used to the ways of the world. I mean, you cannae live on bread and cabbage in America.' He eyed Moshe's bundle. 'What's in there?'

He lifted it. Nothing much. Moshe took it from him and put it behind his back.

'A' right, a' right,' said Cole. 'It's yours, you keep it.' He watched the boy wiping round the tin with the last crust of bread and wondered how old he was. And no English. 'Who're you going to talk to in America? Buffaloes? I hope you can find some other Jews there.'

Moshe ate on; the man's words were incomprehensible to him, apart from the one word, America.

'Sonny, you can walk about,' said Cole, 'you don't have to sit here a' the time. Have you been on a ship before?

It's no' the warmest place, is it? That's why I think you should have your stew.'

Again he held out the meat, and Moshe, his appetite whetted by the bread and cabbage, eyed it, then turned away, nauseated by the thought of pork.

Cole laid the can down. The boy was gazing at him. 'You may ask,' said Cole, because he thought the boy was trying to fathom him, 'why I am a sailor, suffering on the cold sea with a load of pit-props. You may well ask. Well, it's preferable to sitting at home with my wife. She's a good woman, but –' He stressed the last word and left it as the end of his statement. 'You think I'm a blether,' he said to Moshe, discerning a look on the boy's face as if the boy had summed him up. 'Well, I'm no'. If I could talk your language, I'd shut up and you'd do the blethering.' He got to his feet. 'I'll leave it with you.'

He climbed up through the open hatch. '*Hai*,' said Moshe. Cole turned back and the boy handed him the stew-can. He took it and left.

Moshe took out his prayer-book and read the Grace after Meals, all of the full Grace even though he was on his own.

Later he climbed out through the hatch and stood at the rail and watched the grey sea and thought about his two brothers. Where were they? Had they died in the snow, were they shot by soldiers, or forced into the army? Did they get back home? Why wasn't he at home with them now, saying the morning prayers, playing cards with his mother, bringing firewood from the meadow, potatoes from the hut in the back yard?

The ship's crew called him down to the galley and shared their tea and bread and thick marmalade with him. They offered him cigarettes and he smoked, but he kept his distance and ate only what he knew was clean.

Down in the darkness of the hold again, he cried into the sacking. Where had his mother been when the soldiers came? Had she gone to the farm? Was she dead in this pogrom, or from hunger? And the girl, Rivka, and the promises? He tried to put those thoughts away for later, and dreamed and woke sorrowing. What would he find in America, '*Die Goldener Amerika*'? That's what the weekly Yiddish paper in *der Heim* had called it. How would he live there? The only work he had done was labouring on the farm in Ravelets, and he also knew his Torah and was learning the Talmud – a real scholar, they said. God was the God of loving-kindness and mercy: that he knew.

After a voyage of four days and four nights, he awoke in the morning in his nest in the hold, and realised that the engines were silent. There were shouts from far away. He got up shivering, found his cap and his bundle and opening the hatch, he saw grey buildings and other ships. He climbed on to the deck. A cobbled quay, barrels being rolled along it. The ship was tied up and the mate was in the wheelhouse directing the ship's derrick, unloading the deck crates on to the quayside. An engine puffed along with bumping, rattling trucks and gave a hiss and a screech of metal on metal as it turned the corner.

From the long grey building came Cole with a document-case under his arm. He called up, 'Come on boy, you're here!'

Moshe came to the gangplank. Cole walked up it.

'That's it. Voyage over.'

Moshe was incredulous. '*Amerika?*' he asked.

Cole made an expansive gesture towards the quay. 'A great country. Come on now, your ticket's up, anyway.'

He took the boy's arm and together they went down the gangplank. The boy stumbled on the unyielding ground.

'Steady now.'

An old woman leading a donkey with a fruit-barrow came into view. She had a ragged coat tied with string and the remains of a flowered hat pulled down to her eyes. She called out to the men in the warehouse and on the deck, 'Apples! Potaties! Leeks!'

'See here,' said Cole as the barrow passed them, 'is this good to eat or is it trifle?'

'*Ist gut*,' said Moshe.

Cole spoke to the woman. 'Give's a couple of apples.'

'Couple o' pun?' asked the woman.

'No, a couple of apples, hen,' said Cole. He had no intention of buying the boy two pounds of apples. 'Here.' He brought a penny out of his trousers pocket.

The woman picked out two apples and exchanged them for the penny. 'They're awfy guid the day. You're frae the Baltic, eh?'

'Ay,' said Cole. He gave Moshe an apple.

Moshe said the blessing for fruit and took a bite and chewed appreciatively.

'Good?' asked Cole.

'*Gut*,' said the boy and pointed to the other vegetables on the barrow. '*Gut, gut, gut* –' He pointed to the coconuts. '*Vos?*'

The woman said, ' 's a coconut, son. Here, he's no' seen a coconut. Have you no' seen a coconut?' She held one out to him. 'Penny to you.'

Moshe backed away. '*Nein, nein.*'

Cole explained to the fruit-wife: 'They don't grow in his country.' He turned to the boy and said in tones of significance, 'Well, they grow here. On telegraph poles. Coconuts.' He patted the boy's back. 'Have a good time, son. Get rich, that's the thing.' And he went up the gangplank to his ship.

The woman took the donkey's bridle and pulled it along. Moshe walked alongside, listening to the babble of her voice.

'Where you going, son? You speak English? What you here for? Whaur ye staying?'

Moshe munched his apple and looked around the quay. He could hardly believe it. He caught up with the woman and with big gestures to make his meaning plain said, '*Ich Yid. Jud.*'

She stopped the donkey. He spoke on in Yiddish, asking where he could find other Jews, because he had to find

Jewish homes. The woman watched his mouth and his eyes. 'I dinna ken what yer talking aboot, son.' She had caught one word. 'Yood? Jute, d'you mean?'

Moshe held on to the word too. 'Jute, Jute.'

'What do ye want wi' jute? Tae buy it like? Well, this is Dundee, we get lots o' jute here. Go into that shed, see, and find a man heaving bales o' jute. Ask him. I dinna ken.'

Moshe shrugged. The woman wanted him to try the shed. '*Yid, Yud,*' he said.

'Ay, jute,' said the woman.

Moshe asked her, '*Doss ees Amerika?*'

Her face was blank. 'America? No, 's Dundee!' She trundled on; she had her fruit to sell.

The shed was long and there were men heaving bales on their shoulders and rolling crates along on hand-trolleys. A tall red-bearded man with a notebook seemed to be in charge. Moshe went to him, and spoke with intensity.

'*Ich bin Yid.*'

He was a Jew, he had to find Jews. He was asking the man to tell him where he could find Jews. He felt the man's eyes staring at him as he spoke slowly and loudly in Yiddish. 'This is a big town, there are Jews, I know there are Jews here.' He stopped to let the words sink in.

The foreman said, 'Eh? Have you come off that ship?'

'*Yid'n,*' said Moshe, '*Yid'n.*'

The foreman spoke to the man with the bales, then went out to the quay. 'C'm 'ere,' he said to Moshe.

Cole was supervising the unloading of the tallow barrels from the hold. He looked down at Moshe. 'Are you still here?' he shouted.

'Who is he?' asked the foreman. Cole shrugged.

'Hi!' said the foreman.

Cole waved the story into thin air: the boy was a Jew he had picked up in Memel, who couldn't speak a word of English. As he signalled for the placing of a barrel, he shouted to Moshe, 'Away into the city, find yourself some gold!'

'Gold?' said the foreman.

'He wants the land of gold, so I brought him here. What better place than Scotland?' He took his pipe from his mouth and spat into the green harbour water. 'Follow the road through the gates, boy, and you'll see the people.'

Moshe stared up, sick in the stomach with apprehension, stammering incomprehensibly, 'Have you cheated me? Where have you brought me?'

'Go on!' said Cole in reply to the gibberish. 'You cannae stay here, you'll need to earn yourself some money to buy your bread and cabbage with.'

And the foreman said, 'I'd better get the polis, eh?'

That worried Cole. 'Eh, no. Can you no' find him a job humpin' bales?'

The foreman looked at Moshe. The boy was small, if he carried a bale he might fall down.

Cole asked about Jews in Dundee. The foreman had never heard of any. Why couldn't the boy speak right?

Cole then remembered that the boy understood German. Did the foreman speak German? The foreman spat over the quayside. No, he didn't.

And Moshe stood, uncomprehending; then turned and walked away along the quay, leaving the two in sarcastic debate about whether or not a Russian Jew could go to a German Consul, and, anyway, who said that there was a German Consul in Dundee?

Moshe walked out through the port gates, past the chandlers' shops and shuttered pubs. He turned into a narrow street of two-storey houses, a long unbroken row on either side. Horses with carts passed him, milk-carts, coal-carts, people walking. Each house he passed might be a Jewish house. He went to one and stared at the right-hand doorpost. The mark was only a cut in the wood. He came away.

He walked along the neighbouring street, with the port

sounds fading, and children now, laughing and screaming. He came to a row of tenements, grey high houses with spaced-out doors, and a dozen brass handles outside each one. Pushing one of these doors open, Moshe went into the dark lobby. He climbed up the stairs, pausing at each door on each dark landing to run his hand up and down the right-hand doorpost. Nothing at any door.

He spent the whole day walking round the streets of Dundee, looking at people and at doorposts, and in the evening he made his way back to the quay. The ship had gone. There was an open cart-door into the shed, so he walked in. Cold and hungry, he climbed on to a bale and started to say his prayers but fell asleep.

When the foreman opened the big door in the morning, a shaft of sunlight fell on Moshe. 'Hey!' he shouted, 'you again!'

Moshe woke and almost immediately spoke a torrent of Yiddish: he needed a job, he needed to work, to earn money to buy some food; he had been cheated but he would still work; he was a very good worker and all he needed was a chance. The foreman stopped him, angrily waving him away because there was a lot of stuff to shift and the gaffer was coming.

The boy jumped up, took a bale on his back and nearly fell.

'What in the name of hell do ye think ye're doing?'

Moshe recovered himself, staggered along with the bale, and the foreman waved his arms and directed him to the cart outside. He made it.

The foreman took his cap off, scratched his head, and said, 'Ay, go on well.'

With silver coins jingling in his pocket, Moshe bought rolls and milk from a milk-cart, kippers from the smoking-shed behind the quay, and apples and carrots from the wifie with the donkey. And always he said the blessings, and slept at night on jute-bales. The foreman learned his name.

32

'Mowshie!' he called, 'there's two bales here for yon coaster, get them shifted!'

He shifted bales through the day; in the evening after work he went up and down the streets of Dundee looking for a sign. Three weeks of bitter weather came, with sleet and an east wind that blew through his bones. He knew all the mean streets by now and was walking along a street of bigger houses that stood on their own, with garden walls round each. To see their front doors he had to hang over railings and peer round bushes.

As he was coming away from one, a plump lady carrying parcels shouted at him. She'd had to step round him to get past.

'Vy can't you look vere you're going?' she said. She opened the next garden gate and stamped up to the door, raised the latch and went in. Moshe watched her shut the door. On the right-hand doorpost, at head height, there was a diagonal black box about the size of his finger.

He opened the gate and went in, and fingered the mezzuzzah, the sign, the little case that surely had the writing inside in sacred letters, 'Hear O Israel, the Lord our God is one Lord.' And the commandment to love God with all your heart and all your soul and all your might.

He kissed the mezzuzzah. Then he knocked on the door.

Footsteps inside, and the plump lady opened it.

'Vot do you vant?' she said. 'Go avay!' And she shut the door as Moshe shouted excitedly, '*Bist du Yid?*'

There was a pause. The door opened again, but only a crack. She had put the chain up. Moshe asked again, gently, '*Bist du Yid?*'

The lady replied tentatively, '*Bist du Yid?*'

And Moshe poured out a flood of Yiddish at her: that he'd come from Lithuania, in a ship, that he wanted to go to America, that he'd bought a ticket for America, and paid for it, but the sailor had brought him here and put him off; that he didn't know where he was or what to do and that he couldn't speak to anyone.

33

All this, while the lady shut the door to release the chain, then opened it again and said, '*Shah! Genug!*' ('Shut up! You've said enough!') She invited him in, turning to call to her husband, 'Hymie! Come here!'

3

The Brombergs had been in Dundee for five years. They had come from East Prussia because of the uncertainty there, and because things might have been better, and because their friends were taking a chance so they took a chance. They sold up, took their money and their best furniture and made their way where thousands and it seemed like millions of others were going: to Hamburg and thence by ship to Grimsby. The other travellers continued westwards to Liverpool, bound for the New World. Mr and Mrs Bromberg went north to their British relatives in Leeds, the ones who'd been writing to them that there was a good living to be made in that city. Then they went further north to Glasgow; looked round them; then joined the little Jewish community in Dundee.

Their house in Dundee was comfortable, with a separate dining-room and a good fire burning. Hymie Bromberg was thirty-five now, a well-fleshed man with a trim beard and moustache and fierce eyes and a well-tailored suit. He had been in the kitchen playing with the baby when his wife called, and now he stood on the hearth-rug with his back to the fire to question the small, thin, ragged youth who had found his house. Mrs Bromberg took her hat and coat off and sat at the table, lifting the baby on to her knee. The baby banged with a spoon upon the table. They had an older child too, a two-year-old who kept running in from the kitchen, screaming 'Da-da' and running hysterically out again.

Moshe stood facing them and was content to be tested.

The Brombergs' pronunciation of Yiddish was a little more guttural than his, but it was the same language.

'What's your name?'

'Moshe ben Zvi, Kaydan.'

Mrs Bromberg repeated, 'Moshe'.

Bromberg said, 'Moshe Kaydan, where do you come from?'

'Lithuania.'

'Where, where?'

'Near Ravelets. A few hours from Vilna.'

'So it was bad.'

Moshe recounted his memories of the soldiers: they had taken his cousin into the army and shot his uncle, so he and his brothers had prepared. When the soldiers came again they kicked in the *Shool*, tore the *Sefer-Torah*!

The Brombergs tut-tutted their shock at this desecration of the synagogue. And when Moshe described the tearing-down of the curtain and the breaking of the Ark, Mrs Bromberg rocked in her seat and wished a plague on the soldiers.

The story of the walk through the snow, the losing of his brothers, the finding of the dead man and the removal and use of his identity papers were accompanied by such gestures from all three that the two-year old came and stayed to watch in amazement.

As for Moshe's thinking that Dundee was America, this dissolved the tension in laughter, and Mr Bromberg explained it all over again to Mrs Bromberg and even Moshe managed a little wan smile. He opened his bundle to show them his *tallis* and the *seder*. His prayer-shawl and prayer-book were all that he had now.

Mr Bromberg went to the cupboard and brought out a bottle of Scotch whisky and two glasses. He poured out, handing one glass to Moshe.

'Vos ees dos?'

'Visky.' Bromberg raised his glass to Moshe. *'L'chaim!'* To Life! He tossed back the whole glassful, rolled it round his mouth and downed it.

Moshe did the same, grimaced, then swallowed. He shut his eyes, stood still, then as the spirit of Scottish life spread through his whole being, he started to smile, from his lips to his ears and the tears in his eyes, and his head nodded to and fro in appreciation.

They sat down at the table, with the babies in high chairs, and the maid brought the supper that Mrs Bromberg had prepared. Blessings were said; all was eaten and praised.

Then Bromberg looked at the young man: then at his wife, who looked back at him and nodded. It was time for business.

'Can you sew?'

Moshe was surprised. Mrs Bromberg made the action of sewing. 'Yes, he can sew,' she said, 'everyone can sew.' She offered him the ornately painted bowl which was full of oranges and apples and bananas.

Moshe gestured that he was full up.

'Go on, enjoy it!'

Moshe took a banana. He'd eaten his first banana that same day, bought from the donkey-wife. It was delicious but his belly was full to bursting now. He laid it on the table-cloth for later.

So it was settled, he would do sewing for a living.

Mrs Bromberg broke into English. 'Ve have to teach him English.'

Moshe said, 'English?' Bromberg asked him in Yiddish whether he knew the word, and Moshe said yes, he did, it was the language of England. Was this England?

Mrs Bromberg's bosom swelled. 'No,' she said with pride, 'dees ees *Scotland*!'

Moshe slept that night in the bed in the spare room at the Brombergs. They knew a *mensch* when they saw one: Moshe was obviously a decent, responsible human and they had invited him to stay. He had scrubbed himself with soap and hot water, and put on an old nightshirt of Bromberg's and

37

said his prayers and crept with wonder between the linen sheets loaded down with blankets. The mattress was a hard, hair one because the Brombergs had brought only one big feather-mattress with them from East Prussia, and that was on their own bed. But it didn't matter to Moshe. He was safe. There were mezzuzzim on all the doors, it was a Jewish house where he could eat anything that was laid before him. God had kept him alive, and had nourished him, and had brought him to enjoy all this.

Mr Bromberg had promised to get him *tephillin*, the two little black-leather boxes with leather straps, one for his arm and hand, the other for his head. With his tallis draped round him, his morning prayers would then be complete, as they had been in Lithuania; Moshe would be loving God with all his heart and praising Him with his mouth, and doing His Law. He fell into a deep sleep.

In the morning he woke early and came downstairs to watch the children being washed and fed by the maid, whom the Brombergs called the Sheeksie. She was a pimply, shiny-faced, mouse-haired girl of about his own age. He marvelled at Jews employing a non-Jewish menial and having her live in the house, even if it was only in the attic room above the scullery. She blushed and giggled at him but he kept his distance.

After morning prayers and a breakfast of hot porridge, a boiled egg, and strong sweet tea, he went with Bromberg to the shed on the quay to collect the money owing to him. Bromberg in his top hat explained to the foreman that Moshe had found a new job; the foreman nodded and directed him to the tiny office. Then, as Moshe turned away, the foreman held out his hand. Moshe hesitated, but took it. The foreman gave him a warm handshake, the first Moshe had ever had from a *Goy*.

The money collected and pocketed, Bromberg and Moshe went by dock streets and lanes, behind the tall chimneys of the jute-mills, past the carters and the cow-byres and came to a short alley. Stone stairs on all sides led to upper storeys from whence came sounds of hammering and sawing. At street level, beside one of the wicket doors that had recently been a stable entrance, was a painted wooden notice board.

Bromberg paused there and smirked at it as he always did. What a pity the boy couldn't read the words:

H. BROMBERG

WATERPROOF GARMENTS

ENQIRE WITHIN.

He pushed open the door and beckoned Moshe in to the dim brick and stone shed. Little high windows spilled light over the benches and tables, where men sat cross-legged stitching coats and hats. There was an open range with irons heating on the hob, and a man was ironing the finished seams on a table, and then hanging the coats on a rail. Another man was standing at a side table, cutting out shapes for arms and pockets and hats. One end of the shed had big rolls of oilcloth in grey and brown.

If the men had been talking when Bromberg came in with Moshe, they were silent now, concentrating on their work. Bromberg made a little speech about the boy, asked them to welcome him, showed him a place on the front table where he could sit cross-legged, and gave him a needle and a bobbin of thread, and a sleeve to sew up.

Then Bromberg went into the office just inside the front door to mark up his orders. Moshe the farm-worker sewed a few stitches and smelled the smell of rubber, and smoke and sulphur from the burning coal, and he thought that this was an easier life. Working slowly and carefully because he couldn't see very well in the dim light, the only sounds that came to his ears were the rustle of material and irregular coughing. When he looked up, a tall, very thin and ragged man, who leaned on a sweeping brush, was staring at him from hollowed eyes. The man didn't look Jewish; he was another Goy, a labourer. Moshe looked round at his neighbour. No mistaking this man – long nose, dark hair, big dark eyes and large mobile mouth – who sat hunched

39

over his sewing. The man caught Moshe's look, and his big mouth slewed into a grin. He winked.

Bromberg bustled out of his office, rubbing his hands together. He noticed that the man cutting out shapes had run out of oilcloth, he took his yardstick and pulled material from one of the rolls, measuring it off with a flourish. Then he cut across it with the big scissors. He bundled the material towards the waiting man, and folded his arms. Then he came to inspect Moshe.

'Good,' he said. 'Faster!' He mimed a more energetic sewing than Moshe was doing. Moshe speeded up. It was more difficult but not so hard as heaving bales.

So through the day, eating the vorsht sandwiches the maid had given him, when the others ate theirs about noon, sewing between bites and chattering in Yiddish; telling jokes. In the late afternoon, the shed door opened and Mrs Bromberg came in. She was followed by a girl of twenty-one, dark and pretty, who shut the door behind them. Moshe's eyes, like all the other eyes in the room, were raised to watch.

Bromberg's wife tapped on the office door. It was opened and Bromberg came out. A moment's annoyance melted in a smile.

'*Nu?*' he said, 'Leah, how are you?'

The girl said, 'I am keeping fine, sank you, Uncle Hymie.'

Mrs Bromberg said, 'I meet her and I bring her. Oy, s'calt.' She made a show of shivering and moved to the fire. 'More coal,' she said.

Moshe put down his sewing and jumped off the table to tip some coal from the coal-bucket on to the fire. He was stopped imperiously by Mrs Bromberg. '*Nein!*' she said. 'Vere is de *shegets?*'

And Bromberg waved Moshe back to his place. 'De shegets?' he asked. He called, 'Hamish!'

His wife shrugged off the ridiculous sound of the name. The tall thin ragged man shambled in.

40

'Hamish,' said Bromberg, 'de fire. Vy don't you look after de fire? Vot for do I pay you?' Mrs Bromberg nodded to Leah her approval of the way her husband treated servants.

Hamish muttered, 'Sorry, Mister Bromberg.' He picked up the bucket and shook out some lumps on to the fire. He stared at Leah, who turned her back on him.

Mrs Bromberg hadn't seen the stare. 'Vos?' she asked Leah. Leah shrugged, 'De goyim.' Mrs Bromberg gave Hamish a sharp look, then dismissed him with a hand-flop to Leah. 'You can go,' Bromberg told him, and he shambled away from the fire and took up his sweeping-brush and swept up a corner.

Mrs Bromberg now felt free to talk to Mr Bromberg, but in low tones.

'You know *vy* I bring Leah?

'*Nu?*' said Bromberg.

'Tell him,' said Mrs Bromberg to Leah.

Leah had her eyes on Moshe. 'I teach de yonk man English,' she said. And Mrs Bromberg gave all the added significance of this with a triumphant nod. Bromberg stood non-committally.

'Can I speak with him?' Leah asked.

'Of course,' shrugged Bromberg.

Leah left the fire and made her way between the tables to where Moshe sat. He was sewing a laborious seam and Leah addressed him.

'How do you do?'

Moshe looked up.

'My name is called Leah Rosen. Mrs Bromberg she say you are Moshe Kaydan.'

Moshe got the last part of it. '*Ja*,' he said.

Leah looked into his eyes and liked them. 'How are you keeping?' she asked.

Moshe looked to the Brombergs for guidance. He got a smirk from Mrs Bromberg, and a hollow stare from Bromberg.

Leah went on, 'I come to Mrs Bromberg's house to speak mit you.' She hastily corrected it to '*vit* you – English – to you.'

Bromberg had had enough. He called to Moshe in Yiddish, 'Leah's going to teach you English.'

All eyes in the room turned to the young pair. Moshe bobbed where he sat in embarrassed thanks. '*Danke.*'

Leah translated for him: 'Tenk you.'

Bromberg looked up at the windows, consulted his watch. ''S getting dark, *ve dav'n Maerev.*' It was time for the evening prayer.

Mrs Bromberg called, 'Coom, Leah' and swept to the door.

She waited there with the young woman, until Hamish got the message and opened the door for them. They swept out; Hamish shut the door.

'*Maerev!*' called Bromberg.

There was a rustling and sighing and everyone put their work aside and jumped down and put their hats on. Bromberg fetched his top-hat from the office and put it on. He waved at Hamish; 'Out, out!' Hamish leaned his brush gently against the wall and withdrew.

Bromberg turned his face to the wall.

'*V'hoo rachum y'chapair ovoun* . . .'

And they responded and swayed to the evening prayer.

The next night, after Moshe had come from work and after he had dined with the Brombergs and the maid had cleared away, there was a knocking at the outside door. The toddler rushed shrieking to beat on the door and the maid opened it to Leah. She came in carrying a large hand-bag. Mrs Bromberg welcomed her and admired her coat and helped her to take it off; the maid was left in the hall to hang it up.

In the dining-room, Moshe had been primed by Bromberg, it was essential to speak good English before he could advance in the world of business. And this was an exceptionally nice girl.

Leah came in and Mrs Bromberg remarked how nice

Leah was looking tonight. Moshe stood at the table; Mrs Bromberg took Bromberg by the hand and led him out. The door was shut.

Moshe was blushing and he knew it. And when he looked, he saw that she was, too.

'Sit,' she said.

Moshe remained on his feet. She showed him what she meant by sitting at the table.

'Sit.'

Moshe sat opposite her.

'Say "sit". Sag "sit".'

'Sit,' said Moshe.

'Good.'

'Good,' said Moshe.

'My name is Leah Rosen. You say!' And she gestured.

Moshe said, 'My name is Leah Rosen.'

She giggled. 'No – *my* name is Moshe Kaydan.'

'My name is Moshe Kaydan,' he echoed.

'Good.'

'Good.'

She undid the straps and buckles on her bag, and opened it.

'Bag.'

'Bag.'

She brought out a school slate and laid it on the table. Then a newspaper. She fumbled in the bottom of the bag and found the slate-pencil. She laid it on the slate and put the bag away. She looked at Moshe in fond anticipation, but he kept his eyes down.

She wrote his name, MOSHE, and pronounced it. She passed him the slate.

'Moshe. You write.'

'You write,' said Moshe.

'You,' said Leah, and pointed at him, then touched him. 'Write!' She pointed to the slate.

He took the pencil and started to copy the letters, writing from right to left, as in Hebrew.

'No, dis vay. Dis vay.'

He understood, and frowned, and copied the letters slowly with the pencil scratching the surface of the slate. Then she wrote her name, and he copied that. She made him say the name, Leah, and it gave her pleasure to hear it from his lips.

She said, in English, 'You don't know vot I'm talking about so I talk. I like you. I tink I like you very much.' Moshe was puzzled. She went on, 'So I like your – face? I like to kiss it sometime.' Moshe asked in Yiddish what she was saying.

She took up the newspaper and pointed to the banner.

'*The Courier*,' she said. She told him in Yiddish that the printing was a little different but she found for him an A, B, C, and D, corresponding to the Hebrew *Aleph, Baiz, Gimel, Daled*. She wrote them large on the slate, and passed it over for him to copy.

But Moshe didn't take the slate. Instead he brought out a crumpled envelope from his pocket. It was sealed and had Yiddish writing on the front.

'Vot ees dat?' she asked.

'Vot ees dat?' he repeated as he smoothed the crumples.

'A letter,' Leah told him.

'A letter.'

She asked him in Yiddish who the letter was for. '*Meine Mutter*,' said Moshe, hesitantly, fondly. She translated it: 'My muzzer.' He passed it over to her. He wanted her to write, in English, for the postman to understand, the word 'Lithuania.'

4

The lessons continued. Moshe's sewing improved. On Saturdays, when the factory was shut for the Shabbas, he went to the little *shool* in a room in another house and took his part in the rituals that he knew so well. He praised God and was reassured. In the afternoon he walked, sometimes to the seashore, where the grey sea came in white waves to break over the rocky beach. He watched, and raised his eyes to the horizon. He was very sad, but he didn't cry.

The man with the big mouth who sewed next to him was called Yankel. He was thirty and he had been five years in Dundee and eight years in Glasgow before that. His speech was a blend of the two cities and his native Polish-Yiddish. He and Moshe would converse when Bromberg had gone out of the factory, for Yankel was an enquiring man.

'Did ye have another lesson last night?' he would ask Moshe.

'Yes.'

'At de Brombergs?'

'Yes.'

'Mit Leah?'

'Yes.'

'Are you going to keep staying mit dem?'

'I'm looking for a room,' said Moshe one day in reply to this.

Yankel threw him a look. 'Have they told you to go?'

45

'No,' with a shrug and a frown.

'Vy you going?'

Moshe concentrated on his sewing and didn't reply.

'You're daft, Moshe,' said Yankel. 'Stay on mit dem. Leah's a nice girl. You get on all right?'

'Yes.'

'So, she's Mrs Bromberg's niece.'

'*Shveig!*' said Moshe.

But Yankel didn't shut up. 'Meester Bromberg's a rich man. He's a German Yid, he brought his gelt mit him. No' like you 'n me, Moshe. So vy ye goin'?'

'I can go,' said Moshe, 'I got money.'

Yankel looked at him in surprise. 'Yer vages?' He shrugged the idea away. He dug Moshe in the ribs. 'Leah's father's anodder German Yid. Mit his hardvare store, eh? Ye're a' right dere, Moshe.'

'*Shveig!*' said Moshe again, and Yankel broke into a raucous laugh that subsided into a chortle. 'Mind you,' Yankel said when he'd wiped his eyes, 'maybe ve should all leave Dundee. Because it's no sae guid here.' And he recounted the latest news of the stones that had been thrown at Jews in London. He'd read it in yesterday's *Jewish Chronicle*, so it was true. 'Von in hospital,' he said, 'a Cohen voman.'

Moshe had stopped sewing. He said, 'Dey don't trow stones in Dundee.'

'No' yet,' said Yankel. He gave a wave of his hand. 'Dey'll trow stones in Dundee.'

A chill gripped Moshe; where was there to go, where they didn't throw stones at Jews?

Yankel knew. 'De Highlands,' he said. 'Up dere. A trebbler. Ve save up and buy hairpins and ribbons and votches and ve trebble up to de Highlands. I'm telling ye, man, dey've never seen a Yid, dey von't trow nae stones.'

Moshe sewed in silence. A traveller would be safe. Would Bromberg travel?

'Bromberg'll no' need to trebble,' said Yankel, 'cos he's

getting naturised.' It was a new word to Moshe. Yankel explained: 'He writes his papers and dey make him British and nobody trows nae stones at de British.'

'But he's a Yid,' said Moshe.

Yankel dismissed that with a hand-flop gesture. They sewed on. Moshe wondered if there was a new rule to stone-throwing: a Yid was a Yid but maybe a British Jew wasn't.

He thought if Bromberg could do it, he could do it. He said so to Yankel, but Yankel knew what you had to do to be British. You had to have lived in Britain for five years; Moshe had only been here for three months. He, Yankel, could do it. He might, if the stones came. He climbed down to lay his finished coat on the heap for ironing and brought another unfinished one back to the table. He stretched himself and asked if Moshe had had a letter from Ravelets.

'No.'

'So you don't know how your mother is?'

'No.'

Yankel sighed and tut-tutted. 'And who else? Have you heard from your brothers?'

'No.'

'And your cousins?'

Moshe tensed, and sewed on.

Yankel said, 'Moshe, you've never told me. Did you have a girl?'

Moshe didn't answer, and Yankel climbed back to his place.

'Eh? I tink you did.'

'I have a girl,' said Moshe.

Yankel said ho-ho, and pressed Moshe for her name.

'Rivka.'

Yankel savoured it. 'Rivka . . . And you don't know how she is?'

'No.'

The workshop door swung open and Bromberg swept in, resplendent in his hat and frock-coat.

47

Yankel called, 'Good morning, Mr Bromberg!'

'Good morning, good morning,' said Bromberg and there was a chorus of replies. Bromberg went into his office.

'D'you see?' said Yankel, breaking off his thread, 'He's got a new lum-hat.'

The letter was waiting for Moshe when he got back to the Brombergs that night. Mrs Bromberg was sitting in the easy chair in front of the fire, and handed it to him. He stared at it.

'*Nu*, it's for you, open it!'

He told her it was his mother's writing on the envelope.

'*Nu shein!* Open it!'

He opened it and took out the letter and read it, while Mrs Bromberg folded her arms and waited.

Moshe told her, in English: 'She got my letter . . . My brodders, Dovid and Shmool, are in America.' He looked towards Mr Bromberg and gave a nod-shrug of relief, and blinked a who-would-have-thought-it? 'She got a letter from dem. Dey vork, in Noo York, for Yid'n, a lot of money.' Mrs Bromberg smirked. 'De golden country!' She felt the triumph of Moshe's brothers.

But Moshe's other uncle was dead: the soldiers came and broke his arm and he died. Mrs Bromberg wished a plague on them.

Moshe reread his letter. 'Dey still come mit de horses, and dey burn de rye.' He paused for reading. 'And Rivka she ask for me.'

That was all. He looked at Mrs Bromberg and she rocked from side to side in sympathy. Moshe folded the letter up. Then he unfolded it and started to read it again. But his tears welled up and he sat at the table and put his head on his arms and sobbed.

Mrs Bromberg got up. She caressed his heaving shoulders.

'*Nu*, Moshe,' she comforted. '*Nu-nu.*'

Moshe got up and went out. She called after him, 'Vere you going? Listen Moshe, Leah's coming!' But Moshe opened the front door and went out and pulled it shut behind him with a bang.

He walked in the streets, oblivious of where he was. He neared the harbour, passed children bouncing a ball between their legs and against a stone wall, one-two-three-a-leerie, children hopping along boxes chalked on the pavement, kicking the lid of a boot-polish tin with a metallic scrape. He leaned against the wall but saw nothing. He was filled with the same terror for the people he had left behind him in Ravelets as he himself had felt when the arm pulled down the curtain across the Ark.

He found himself staring down into the green, oily mirror of harbour water. He sat on a fish-box. From round the corner there came towards him a man in his middle years, with flapping coat and tacketty boots and a sideways cap, with wispy, sandy whiskers around a mouth full of broken teeth. The mouth was smiling a beatific smile, and the eyes above it were dancing. The whole man was dancing an elegant soft-shoe minuet, and as he advanced on Moshe, he sang: 'Heederum, hoderum, hi-diddle-diddle-i, Hooderum, hoo-diddle hoderum –', the variations of his own mouth-music. He was a drunk, and a Dundonian, softly dancing his invitation to Paradise.

He swayed round Moshe, waking him from his tragic trance. Moshe didn't know what to make of it.

'Hi-deedle-eedle-eedle, hum-dum-deedle-um, hoo-hoo-hoo-hoo –' sang the man. He wanted the boy to join with him in song and dance, to experience the shared joy of it.

Moshe was half scornful and half afraid. He got up and backed away, the man following with beseeching gestures and heederums. Moshe backed against the wall, the drunk had him cornered. Moshe ducked under his arm and ran clattering away down the quay. The drunk stopped singing and dancing. Once more he held out his arms to the departing Moshe.

'A wis only bein' frien's,' he pleaded.

Running up the quay, Moshe swerved to avoid the don-

key, and stopped to get his breath back. The fruit-wifie
said, 'Whit's wrang son? Whit's the ma'er?'

'Nodding,' panted Moshe.

'Ye want an orange?'

'No.'

'Penny.'

'No.'

'Banana?'

'No.'

'Whit's wrang?'

Moshe walked away. 'Nodding.' He turned back, adding
politely but nearly crying again, 'Tenk you.'

The drunk hove into view, and the old wife called out
'Leeks . . . potaties!' Moshe walked home.

He asked the men in the shool on Shabbas and they spread
the word around. He was offered a room with a Mrs
Kepple, a Jewish woman whose husband had died on the
boat. So she'd come to Dundee because her brother was an
auctioneer there. Greying and sorrowful, she asked no questions of Moshe, which was better than the Brombergs anyway.

Moshe had a bare room with a bed, a little table and a
wooden chest on the floor. Mrs Kepple brought him his
meals on a tray and he ate in peace, reading the Talmud
and marvelling at it. He stumbled through paragraphs of
the *Jewish Chronicle*, which was all in English, at the factory
whenever Yankel pointed out something of interest in one
of the old copies that Mrs Bromberg used to leave there.
Sometimes there was an issue of *Der Yiddisher Amerikaner*,
all the way from America, and all in Yiddish. They took
it in turns, and when it was Moshe's night to have it, he
almost didn't sleep and almost didn't say his prayers.

He still saw Leah, but not for lessons, only at functions:
a wedding, or a barmitzvah, or a funeral, or a talk by the
rabbi from Edinburgh. Of course, every Saturday she was
in shool, in the women's place at the side. Always she talked
to him afterwards, and he walked her home.

On Friday nights he made *Kiddush* for Mrs Kepple, and ate with her off her white tablecloth with the two Shabbas candles. They exchanged news from letters, because Mrs Kepple had also been born not ten miles from Ravelets.

When Bromberg's cutter left for a position with his wife's brother-in-law in Leeds, Moshe took over his job. He was good at marking out with chalk round the wooden template, and he cut with no waste. He kept count of the pieces for Bromberg and never made mistakes.

He let his beard and moustache grow, black and downy they were, but he did not get any taller.

One day, egged on by Yankel, he knocked on the office door.

'Ye-es?' said Bromberg.

He went in. Bromberg stood at his high desk among his ledgers and papers on spikes.

'Mister Bromberg.'

'Yes, Moshe.'

'I am your cutter,' said Moshe, 'and I do de counting.'

Bromberg eyed him. 'So? You go up in de vorld. You come to ask for more gelt?'

Moshe stayed silent.

'De honour, de position, ees not enough?'

Moshe said, 'I vould like more money.'

'A man in my position, and mit de state of de business,' said Bromberg, 'I can't give. I vish I could give it. You're a nice boy, you're doing vell.'

'I vant more money,' repeated Moshe.

Bromberg grew angry. 'No, Moshe! You vant more money, you go and vork for de goyim!'

In the workshop, they had gathered round the office door to listen. Hamish sniggered, 'The goyim, the goyim!'

'Shut up, Goy!' said Yankel.

Hamish said, 'Who's a goy?'

Moshe came out of the office crestfallen. They made way for him and went back to their places. Moshe looked at Yankel. Yankel shrugged back.

When he resumed his cutting, Hamish swept under his feet, jabbing with the brush. 'There's a rat, a rat!' he shouted.

Moshe said, 'Dere are no rats here,' and Hamish guffawed.

Bromberg came out of his office.

'Listen, Moshe,' he said, 'you come home to my house tonight.' But it wasn't *Pesach*, or *Yom Kippur*, and Moshe said so.

'No,' agreed Bromberg, 'but you come home. Leave your room, we'll have a good fire, and soup and meat, I'm sure. You come? And ve'll hae a *shmuous*.' He handed Moshe the workshop keys. 'After maerev, after you lock up, see everyting safe, you come.'

'All right,' said Moshe, and as Bromberg went out he nodded his satisfaction.

Hamish jabbed with the brush at the door. 'A rat! A rat!'

'*Shegets!*' said Moshe.

'Bloody Jews,' said Hamish.

All the eyes in the factory glared at him and he bowed his head and muttered into his ragged shirt and swept dust meekly into a corner.

At the Brombergs, they had a discussion. Bromberg stood with his back to the fire. Mrs Bromberg sat in the armchair, and Leah was at the table.

'He vants a rise,' said Bromberg, 'I give him a rise mit a condition.'

'Vill he do it?' his wife asked.

'It's all right. I'll also tell him Leah's fadder vill give him a hundred pounds.'

'Did he say so?' asked Leah incredulously.

'I know he vill,' said Bromberg. 'So Moshe vill take de money, and put it into my business, vit me, and I'll' – he thought about it – 'I'll give him a share of de business.'

Mrs Bromberg said, 'Oy.'

Bromberg went on, 'He's a nobody but I'll give him a share of de business.'

Leah said, 'He's not a nobody.'

'It's a vay of speaking,' said Bromberg.

Mrs Bromberg leaned forward. 'Listen, Leah, if your muzzer vos alive, *alevasholoum*, she vould be doing dis for you. Mind, I don't know vot she vould advise, but if you like Moshe, dat's half de battle.'

Bromberg shrugged that off.

'Hymie,' said his wife, 'I've known vorse. He's a good boy.'

'Ye-es,' agreed Bromberg without enthusiasm, 'he's a good Jew.'

'So? Vot more do you vont?'

'It isn't me dat vonts,' said Bromberg, 'it's Leah.'

Mrs Bromberg looked piercingly at Leah. 'You're sure?'

Leah looked straight back. 'I'm sure.'

'No more to say,' said Mrs Bromberg, and went on to say it. 'Vit Leah, he vill do very well.'

'True,' admitted Bromberg. 'True.' He consulted his waistcoat pocket watch on the end of its chain.

Leah said, 'You'll leave me alone with him?'

The Brombergs were scandalised.

'No!' said Mrs Bromberg.

'Please?'

Bromberg shrugged with both arms. 'How can you be alone vit him for dis?'

'I can. To talk.'

'Alone here?'

'Please,' Leah pleaded.

'Vell, after I talk –' The front door knocker banged twice.

'Before you talk,' said Leah. 'Please?'

The Brombergs looked at each other. 'Go and let him in,' said Mrs Bromberg.

While Bromberg went out to open the front door, Mrs Bromberg spoke urgently to Leah: 'All I vont is your happiness.' They heard the men speaking in the hall and Bromberg's voice saying, 'You go into de kitchen, de kettle's on de fire, you can vosh.'

'I voshed.'

'You have been home to your place?'

Mrs Bromberg divined something from this conversation. 'He knows,' she whispered loudly, 'he knows!'

Bromberg brought Moshe in. Moshe was indeed pink and shiny, with his hair plastered down and his boots clean.

Mrs Bromberg put on a huge smile. 'Moshe how are you?'

'Fine, tenk you. How are you?'

'I'm fine.' Her shrug added, but of course she was!

Leah said, 'Hello, Moshe!'

'Good evening, Leah.'

Mrs Bromberg got up. 'I go into de kitchen to see to de *alkies*. Hymie, I vont to talk to you.'

'Vos?' asked Bromberg.

Mrs Bromberg nearly jerked her head off. Bromberg got the message and went out.

'Leah,' said Mrs Bromberg by the door, 'give Moshe de seat by de fire, and don't eat de figs because I got a good meal for you.' She went out and shut the door behind her.

Leah and Moshe shared the silence.

Leah said, 'Hello.'

'Hello.'

'Sit.' She indicated the seat by the fire. 'Please . . .' said Moshe, meaning that she should sit on it. Leah sat on an upright chair at the table. Moshe took another upright chair, pulled it back from the table, and sat down.

Leah said, 'How are you?'

'All right. How are you?'

'All right.' She thought hard, and ventured, 'So?'

He shrugged, nodded.

She asked, 'Have you had another letter?'

'Yes.'

'How are they?'

'Not good,' said Moshe.

'Can I read?' asked Leah.

Moshe hesitated. 'No,' he said.

'Please?'

He shrugged to indicate a private sensitivity. So she left it.

She said, 'I meet you in shool on Shabbas, and I don't see you any other time.' Moshe had a reply ready. 'Mr Bromberg, your oncle, makes me vork hard. And I learn.'

'English?'

He shrugged to indicate that no, he was not learning English.

'The Talmud?'

'Yes,' said Moshe, 'is good.'

'It's all you talk about.'

'Yes.'

'And you haven't been outside of Dundee?'

'A little.'

'In two years.'

It wasn't quite two years but he let that go. She regarded him steadily and he lowered his eyes.

'Uncle Hymie says he give you the day off on Sunday.'

Moshe looked up in surprise. 'For vot?'

'A holiday. We could go . . . in a train . . . to Broughty Ferry. We could take bread and . . . salt-beef, you know . . . and if it rains, you aren't short of a waterproof.'

A joke; he acknowledged it with a grin. 'No,' he said.

'So?' It was a question.

Moshe shrugged. 'All right. Who else?'

'Nobody else,' she said.

Moshe gave her a long look. She held it. She said, 'We must be strong, Moshe. We must . . . keep together.'

Moshe thought about this. As Leah watched him she let love come into her eyes. She said, 'I like you, Moshe.'

He said, 'Tenk you.'

She said, 'I'm fond of you.'

This time he didn't answer. He found himself unable to.

Leah stretched out her hand to him, then laid it on the table. Moshe looked at it.

'Moshe?'

'*Yoh?*'

She had caught him out. 'You mean yes.'

He grinned; it was all right. 'Yes.'

'Stand up!' she commanded.

Wonderingly, he stood. She eyed him roguishly, then she stood up also. '*Kish mir,*' she said.

Moshe did not know how to react to that command.

Slowly she walked to him, leaned forward and kissed him full on the lips. Then, still kissing, she embraced him. She pulled her head back, breaking the kiss, and looked into his eyes. He looked questioningly into hers. She put her face to his again, and this time he responded and they kissed and he put his arms round her.

Mrs Bromberg came in.

'Oh, I'm *so* sorry . . . ! Oy!' She went, hastily shutting the door again.

Moshe broke off the embrace in agitation. 'Not to say! Not to say!' he told her.

'Why?' she asked, aglow with the physical contact.

'Please not to say!'

A rattle at the door-handle, and a coughing, and the Brombergs came back.

'Vell?' beamed Mrs Bromberg.

'Well?' replied Leah, composing herself and patting her hair into place. 'I help you with the soup.' She went out, taking Mrs Bromberg with her.

Bromberg took up his place by the fire. He extolled the virtues of his niece, mentioned that her father was comfortably off financially, and implied in a roundabout way the possibility of the hundred-pound arrangement.

Moshe nodded to this.

'So it's a *shidduch?*' asked Bromberg, with the pleased smile of a successful marriage-broker.

Moshe was confused. 'No,' he said. 'I don't vont.'

Bromberg was thunderstruck. 'Vot you mean, vot for you don't vont?'

Moshe looked at the carpet.

Bromberg went on, 'She's a nice girl. She's beautiful. You should have de *mazel*!'

Moshe stayed silent, and Bromberg became irritated. 'You get a share in de business, vot for you don't vont! Let me tell you von ting, Moshe, you don't deserve Leah. She's too good for you, Mrs Bromberg say so. I say so. Who are you, Moshe Kaydan, from a hen-house in Litau?'

Moshe was provoked into a reply. 'De Kaydans are good people, my fazzer vos a *Talmud Chochom*.' (A man made wise by study of the Talmud.)

'Listen,' said Bromberg, dismissing this argument, 'you ken your Talmud, dat's good, but marriage is a different ting. You need more dan de Talmud to feed a family.' He caught sight of his top-hat, which he had laid earlier on the sideboard for saying the blessings at the supper. He jerked his finger at it. 'You try to make dat from de Talmud!'

Moshe stood turning over his thoughts; his reason said one thing, his feelings another. Bromberg was still asking him, so vot did he vont, a nice girl, a business? – Bromberg had to be told, but where to begin? 'I vont to be naturised,' said Moshe.

Bromberg goggled.

'Naturised? You can't be naturised.' He corrected himself, 'natur*a*lised.'

'Vy?' said Moshe.

'Vy? All of a sudden, he vonts to be British! Listen, Leah is naturalised, she's already British, she stay British if she marry you or not marry you.'

Moshe asked urgently, 'Vy can't *I* be naturised?'

Bromberg came forward and thumped the table. 'Because you haven't been staying in dis country for five years! Talmud Chochom!'

Moshe went on, 'Soon I vill have twenty-von.'

Bromberg calmed down. 'Vot for you vont naturalised?'

'To go back to *der Heim*.'

'Litau?' asked Bromberg incredulously. 'To go *dere*? You're *meshuga*. Have you read? In de *Jewish Chronicle*? Dey kill you.'

'If I have a passport,' said Moshe, 'dey leave me alone. No?'

Bromberg gave a big shrug, which was to say that he wouldn't bet on it.

Moshe said, 'I must go home.'

Bromberg suddenly saw it from the boy's point of view. 'You had another letter?'

'Yes.'

'Bad?'

'Yes.'

'Vot you do ven you go?'

'I marry Rivka and I bring her.'

This took some time to sink into Bromberg – the fact and its implications. But he understood.

'Oy . . .' he said, quietly.

Moshe said, 'You can be natur-alised ven you have tventy-von.'

Bromberg automatically corrected him: 'Ven you *are* tventy-von.'

'Tenk you.'

Bromberg asked him, 'Who said?'

'I read,' said Moshe, 'is called special.'

Bromberg ran his eye, benevolently now, over his young apprentice. 'Rivka. Your letter vos from Rivka.'

'*Yoh*.' said Moshe. 'Please?'

Bromberg breathed in and then out with a great sigh. 'My vife vill give me hell.'

He opened the door and called out, '*Nu?*'

The ladies came in with the soup on trays, all of a twitter, Leah pink. So Bromberg explained, waiting only till the soup was safely on the table. He was as brief as he could be. The ladies sat as if turned to stone. Tears rolled down Leah's face and she kept saying, 'I understand, I understand.' Then she left without touching a drop of soup, seen out by Mrs Bromberg. After a few minutes Mrs Bromberg came back saying that she had a headache, excused herself pointedly to both men and retired to bed.

Mr Bromberg and Moshe covered their heads and said the blessings, but the soup was cold.

5

In time for Moshe's twenty-first birthday according to the Jewish reckoning Bromberg had made all the necessary enquiries, had filled in the papers, and Moshe had signed his name many times in English. He had to do what he had to do; there was no choice for him in the matter. He could no more abandon Rivka to be desecrated and killed than he could curse Almighty God; he had thought about both these things because they were connected in some way, but the thoughts were brief. Anyway, he loved Rivka, or had loved her, and the picture in his mind made him love her again.

So Bromberg gave Moshe the morning off and loaned him his second-best top-hat and the top of a morning suit. He himself put on a new frock-coat and his shiny new top-hat and accompanied Moshe to the Dundee Branch of the Home Office.

It was a stone building in its own dank garden. They were admitted by a policeman, their papers were read by a sniffing clerk, and after no more than half an hour they were ushered by a young man with a monocle into a high room that shone and smelled of waxed wood and linoleum.

Mr Grant was sitting behind a leather-topped desk on a square of carpet. Small and sixty, with white whiskers, his way of thinking had not changed in the least since he had received his education at the Edinburgh Academy for the sons of lawyers. Mr Grant was of a very sound mind.

He studied the assorted sheaf of papers that Moshe had handed in at the front door.

He said, 'Moash Kaydan,' and looked up. 'Which one is Moash Kaydan?'

'Me,' said Moshe.

Bromberg gave him a dig in the ribs. 'Sir,' added Moshe.

Grant read from a form that Moshe had filled in. 'Moash Kaydan, of four, Cowgate, Dundee, care of Mrs J. Kepple, born twelfth July eighteen sixty-eight in Ravelets, a Russian National, resident in Dundee since January ninth, eighteen hundred and eighty-six.' He looked up. 'Which is three and a half years.' He read on: 'Sewer and cutter for H. Bromberg, Waterproof Garment Maker of sixty-three, West Port, Dundee. Is that correct?'

'Yes,' said Moshe.

Bromberg dug him in the ribs. 'Sir.'

Grant riffled through the other papers.

'Hyman Bromberg?' he said.

'Yes, sir,' said Bromberg, speaking in a hushed voice to match the gravity of the office.

'You are a British National?'

'I am naturalised since two years.'

'President of the Dundee Hebrew Congregation?'

'Yes, sir. Since last – *Succus*? – October.'

'How big a congregation is it, Bromberg?'

Bromberg said, 'Ve have forty families, about.'

'Really?' said Grant, interested. He made a note, then read on. 'I certify that Moash Kaydan is a good and honest worker and deals in a true way with British customers. Hyman Bromberg.'

'Yes, sir, he is very good.'

Grant turned a page, to the English language test. He could make out the backward-slanting words that Moshe had laboriously written: *The quick brown fox jumps over the lazy dog.* And on the next sheet: *Benjamin Disraeli is the great Prime Minister of Great Britain. He is a Jew.*

Grant looked up. 'Kaydan, Disraeli's been dead for eight years. I believe he was baptised.' He laid that page aside too. 'Certificate by the Chief Rabbi of Vilna about date of birth, Translated and Attested by Rabbi Abraham Rabino-vitch of the Edinburgh Hebrew Congregation.'

He looked piercingly at the young applicant. 'Kaydan, you understand that a foreign national such as yourself has to be not only twenty-one, but resident in Great Britain and Ireland, or in some part of the Empire beyond the seas, or in territories under the gracious sovereignty of Her Majesty the Queen, for a continuous period of five years, before applying to be naturalised as a British citizen. It is a great privilege and an honour to be a British citizen. Do you understand that?'

Moshe nodded. 'Yes, sir.'

Grant then asked why, in that case, he was applying after only three and a half years.

Bromberg dug his elbow into Moshe. 'Say.'

Moshe said, 'I vont to go back to my country for von month.'

'Why can't you do that?' Grant asked. 'Have you broken the law there?'

'No, sir, I am a Jew. Read de papers please?' He indicated the pages taken from the *Jewish Chronicle* that they had added to the application forms.

'I saw them,' said Grant. 'I'm sure His Majesty the Tsar wouldn't harm you for a month.'

'He vould harm me,' said Moshe.

Grant studied the two men. He tapped his fingers on his waistcoat.

'Why do you want to go back?'

'To see my muzzer.'

'Is she ill?'

'Yes, sir, very ill.'

'And your father?'

'He is dead, killed.'

'Killed?' asked Grant.

'Yes, sir, a long time ago.'

'Who killed him?'

'Stones killed him,' said Moshe. 'Trowing stones.'

Grant thought about this, picked up his pencil, almost started to write, then put it down again.

'There have been a number of you, Kaydan, in the last few years, settling in Britain.' He paused. He eyed the two men in their carefully respectable rig-outs. 'Do you understand Scots?'

'Yes, sir,' said Moshe.

'Tell me,' said Grant, 'would you understand it if I said "lang may your lum reek?" '

The faces of Moshe Kaydan and Hyman Bromberg went blank: they didn't know the way to wish people a long life in Scots.

Grant opened his desk drawer and took a form out. He shut the drawer and picked up a pen and dipped it into the inkwell.

The two men watched him.

Grant wrote on, then laid the pen down and dried the wet ink. He opened the attaché case beside his desk. He brought out the morning's copy of the *Dundee Courier*.

'Read this,' he said, holding it out to Moshe and pointing.

'De Courier. Dundee, Vednesday, July fifteenth, eighteen eighty-nine,' read Moshe.

'And this.'

'Notice of naturalisation. I Alberto Marco –'

Grant was satisfied. 'Follow that wording, with your own particulars, for three consecutive weeks in the *Courier*, and come back here. If no one has come forward with any knowledge as to why you shouldn't be naturalised by special dispensation, I'll put it through.'

They thanked him five times and went out into the Dundee sunshine.

Bromberg put the notice in the *Courier*, and took it off Moshe's wages.

Three weeks later, the workshop door flew open, and Moshe and Bromberg came in. All the men looked up.

Bromberg said, 'He is British!'

There was a silence, then Yankel said it first: '*Mazeltov!*'

63

Then they all shouted their congratulations and good wishes and put their work aside and came to shake Moshe by the hand. Moshe said, 'Tenk you' over and over again with modest smiles. Then he became aware of Leah standing in the doorway of the little office. The hubbub died. The men went back to their places.

'Go in,' said Bromberg.

Leah retreated into the office. '*Nu?*' said Bromberg to Moshe, and waved him in after her. He shut the door on them, and turned to his workers, who stood with their eyes popping with curiosity. '*Nu-u?*' he said.

In the office, Leah sat on the high stool at the desk, trying to look resigned, but inwardly in a state of despair.

Moshe laid his top-hat on the desk.

Leah said, 'No trouble?'

'No.'

She drank him in with her eyes as he faced her. She asked, 'When are you going?'

'Soon. Ven I have a passport and a ticket.'

'To see your mother.'

'Yes.'

'And Rivka.'

Moshe's heart missed a beat and he shrugged that the answer to her question was yes, and what could he do about it, and the answer was yes, yes, yes.

There was a silence between them.

'I'm sorry,' said Moshe.

'Yes.'

Moshe added, 'I like you.'

'I know.'

'In anodder time . . .'

Leah looked for the end of that sentence. But Moshe didn't have the end.

She got off the stool and held her arms out. He went to her and embraced her and she embraced him. They kissed a long kiss.

'*Ich liebe dich,*' said Leah.

64

His embrace tightened and he kissed her with passion. She broke away and burst into tears. She turned away, fumbled for her handbag and her gloves and went past him sobbing to the door and out.

Moshe stood at the desk, leaned on it and put his head in his hands.

Bromberg came in and surveyed him.

'Vell, she got to cry. Is natural.'

Moshe looked up. He was crying, too. He tried to go past Bromberg and go out.

'Listen,' said Bromberg. 'Sit.' He commanded Moshe to sit on the stool.

'So vot's dis? You change your mind?'

'No.'

'You cry for Leah?'

Moshe shrugged that he supposed so and turned his face away.

Bromberg said, 'You haven't seen Rivka for four years nearly. You've forgotten her, so forget her.'

'No,' said Moshe.

Bromberg searched for wisdom in his beard.

'So here's anodder idea. Don't decide it now. You got enough money for your return ticket to Litau, and Rivka's ticket to here.'

'Yes.'

'Vy not spend de money on a ticket for you to go to America?'

Moshe looked up: this idea had also crossed his own mind. Bromberg went on, 'For a few years. And den you decide.'

'No,' said Moshe. 'Rivka vill be my vife.'

Bromberg gave up with a shrug that went from his waist to the tips of his fingers. '*Gey, gezunt-heit. Gey mit mazel.*' He picked up the top-hat. 'And you can keep de lum-hat. You suit it, so take it, not as a loan, as a present from me.' He put the hat on Moshe's head, and gave it a tap to the best angle.

*

Moshe applied for his passport and got it, and then, wearing his lum-hat, he went down to the quay. He found the fruit-seller with the donkey.

'Apples, oranges, bananas,' she chanted.

Moshe asked, 'How much de coconuts?'

'Thrippence.'

He chose the biggest coconut, shook it to hear if there was milk in it, put his hand in his pocket and counted out three pennies to give to the wifie. 'Tenk you,' he said.

He went with all the Brombergs and Leah to a photographer's studio, and posed behind a rustic bench, first alone and then with them.

'Put de hat on,' said Bromberg.

Moshe emptied the coconut out of his hat.

'Put von foot up on de bench,' said Mrs Bromberg, 'It's nice.'

Bromberg put the new suitcase on the bench beside him. 'Smile, Moshe,' said Leah.

So he was photographed in the top-hat, holding the coconut. When he had collected the finished print, mounted on thick card with rounded edges, he pushed it into the back of his wallet to show them in *der Heim*.

He took a train to Leith, changing at Edinburgh, and there boarded a small steamship for Memel. He thought about Leah and what might have been, but he thought more of what he would find when he arrived home. He became so tense with excitement that it pained him. Saying his prayers helped, but he drifted many times from praying to dreaming.

At Memel he reported to the British Consulate, then took a train to Vilna. Rivka was there to meet him, with her black hair hanging down to her waist, her lovely face and full red lips, brown eyes full of life and wisdom and laughter, eyes that she shut when she laughed properly. She had lost the plumpness of sixteen and was shapely now. Her family had taken her to Vilna for safety, and to await Moshe, for they had received his letter.

66

Moshe's mother had gone with them but had died only the week before he arrived. Moshe went with Rivka to the grave and said *Kaddish* for her, and wept.

The wedding took place in the side-hall of the great Vilna synagogue. They had remembered each other with love; now they knew each other, loved each other. In the morning they went together to the Consulate in Vilna, where Moshe's passport was endorsed for his wife.

Back to Memel, and then on a tramp steamer that called at Copenhagen, Bremen, Amsterdam, Middlesborough and finally Leith. The train from Leith brought them to Dalry station, Edinburgh, where they got off and made their way on foot to the Dalry synagogue.

Isaac Caplan met them. He was a second cousin of Bromberg's but he had a much bigger waterproof-garment factory. Moshe became his chief cutter and joined the Dalry Jewish Community, renting a one-roomed house for himself and Rivka in the street of houses and factories known as Fountainbridge. Rivka was nineteen years old when she made a home for Moshe, and became pregnant for the first time.

6

Three children made their way home from school. They were barefoot and happy, a girl of ten in a shapeless brown dress, a boy of eight in a jersey much too small for him and short trousers that were much too big, and a little girl of six in a ragged cardigan and skirt, chasing each other over the broken cobbles in the afternoon sun. Sometimes the smells of Edinburgh halted their game: they peered down through a grating at the dark basement below to see the new-sawn wood; they skirted a broken drain-pipe with sewage leaking out; and put their noses into the steam from an open hatch where biscuits were baking. They stopped to shout a greeting into the open crammed doorway of the Jewish delicatessen on the corner and then pressed their noses against the window, longing for the good food inside.

Then across the broad avenue of South Clerk Street with the whirr of the cable-cars. A driver clanged the bell at them and they hurried to the pavement, rounded the beer-shop corner with the sawdust spilling out, and into Cross-causeway. High old gables jutted overhead; horses stood below, pulling where they were tethered to the iron rings, their carts leaning back and good for climbing over.

Sarah and Solomon and Lala had a drink from the iron cup chained to the fountain beside the horse-trough, then turned in through the tenement door. It was dark inside but they knew their way well enough and started to climb the stairs. Sarah pretended to run away, Solomon and Lala chased after, then Sarah turned to face them and there was a screeching confrontation that bubbled over into giggling and Sarah, the eldest, turned and ran up another flight.

The stone treads of the stairs were worn in the middle and sloping down. The old green and brown paint on the enclosing wall was hacked out with letters and symbols. Sarah passed her name that she had scratched the month before: Sarah Kaydan 1903.

Halfway round each flight a broken, grimed window gave only a grey light on this sunny day, for the space outside was narrow. On each landing were two opposing doors of flimsy, ill-fitting wood. Between them stood a zinc sink with a dripping cold tap above, and above that, a gas bracket on the wall with a broken mantle.

As the children ran up to the top, a voice shushed them loudly. They looked up alarmed, pressing against the wall. Above them, framed in their own open doorway, was their mother, Rivka, and their elder brother, Zelek. Rivka's squarish face and dark beautiful eyes were composed in a look of warning. She had a black shawl round her shoulders and her feet were bare on the stone landing.

She nodded at the opposite door, and the children looked. It was being opened, and through it came a small pine coffin, borne easily by two men. The children shrank against the stair wall as the men came down and passed them. Following the coffin was a gaunt woman in dark clothes carrying a thin bunch of irises, and a carrot-headed boy in his Sunday best with a black band round his arm. They walked down the stairs past the children in a trance of disbelieving grief. Behind them came a man and two women, each carrying a small bunch of flowers.

Rivka was saying, 'So sorry . . . so sorry . . .' and when the cortège had passed to the landing below, the three children climbed up and turned to hang over the broken railing and stare down with their brother Zelek.

'Oy,' said Rivka, full of sorrow, 'Oy. Coom.' Her hair was smooth and jet-black, tied behind her head and falling down her back; her lips were full, though not as soft as they'd been when she married.

She enfolded her three youngest children to her, and ushered them into the tenement. She exchanged a look of understanding with Zelek and he followed them in and shut the door; their neighbour's child was dead.

The home of Moshe and Rivka Kaydan contained two rooms. The front door opened directly into the larger one. Dark paper hung from the walls and was torn off at child level. The floor had some worn linoleum over the rough boards. The furniture was a table, a bench, two chairs, a dresser, and a bed in a recess with faded curtains. Over the open range was the mantelpiece with the two Shabbas candlesticks on it, and a clock, a small candelabrum and a blue tin box with the letters JNF on it. And there, too, was the tea-caddy and a china hen sewing-box. Two water-colours in gilt frames hung on the door to the other room.

The children had rushed to the window to peer down at the funeral below. This was their aperture on life, the three panes that had glass in them; sagging cardboard covered the broken one. They knew everyone, man, woman, child and horse; every stone, drainpipe, window and chimney-pot in Crosscauseway. Now they knelt on the bench, with Solomon and Lala standing on it.

'Where, where?' asked Solomon.

'Wait,' said his big brother Zelek, 'they haven't come out.'

'Will they put the box in that cart?'

'Ay.'

'Was that Mabel from next door?' piped Lala.

They all knew it was. Even little Lala knew, but they had to be sure. Zelek pronounced that it was Mabel and that she was dead. Solomon reminded them that he had said the same thing.

There was another person in the room, a dark girl of fourteen, with lank hair, lying in the bed-recess – this was the Kaydan's eldest girl, Chaiki. She called, 'Ma?'

Rivka padded over to her, bending below the towels and trousers and knickers hanging up to dry. 'Poor soul, she's at peace, she von't cough now.' She took Chaiki's hand.

Chaiki thought of the girl next door. Mabel, fancy . . .

Rivka knew her thoughts. 'Ven somebody gets so bad as Mabel vos, it's good to be at peace.'

'She was a Goy,' said Chaiki.

'De Goyim also have peace.' She scanned Chaiki's face. 'You're getting better.' She willed herself to say it and say it cheerfully, with conviction, and to believe it. She turned to the others, crowded at the window. 'Vot vos de school today? Shlomo?'

'What?' said Solomon, answering to his Yiddish name, still staring down to the street. 'There they are!'

'Lala, coom avay!' commanded Rivka. She left the bed and gathered up her youngest and took her to the cot in the smaller room. Lala screamed her rage.

In the street below, the little coffin was carried out, then lifted on to the hearse, a black-painted open cart, drawn by one black horse. The flowers were laid on the coffin by the two bearers, then they climbed up in front. One took the reins, looked back to see if the mourners were ready, and tugged. The horse set off. Mrs Urquhart and her son James, and the uncle and the two aunties stepped out after it, the procession winding away over the bumpy cobbles. All this the children watched with open mouths.

A private cab pulled in to the space left by the hearse. A middle-aged man alighted, wearing spats, a checked frock-coat and a top-hat. He carried a bag. He waited respectfully till the funeral procession turned the corner, then he looked up at the tenement.

Sarah reported him from the window, but Rivka was still in the small room, holding the sulking Lala.

'Shah,' she said to her littlest. 'Here's de cards.'

She pulled open the top drawer of the chest of drawers and brought out a worn pack. Lala knocked them flying.

71

Her mother made to slap her but Lala shrank back and was silent. Rivka gathered up the cards from the floor.

'Where's Mabel gone?' asked Lala.

'She's gone avay.'

'Gone away,' Lala corrected her. 'Why do you say gone avay?'

'Dat's how I say it.'

'Where's Pa?' Lala knew where her Pa was, sewing good tweed jackets for Mr Levinson, in Levinson's tailor's shop. Rivka sighed. 'Vorking.'

'Why?'

'Vy, vy, vy!' returned her mother.

Zelek called from the other room. 'Ma, the man's coming up!'

'Vos man?'

Chaiki called from the bed-recess, 'Ma?'

Rivka came through to the main room. 'So he'll coom.'

Chaiki asked who it was, and her mother assured her it would be a *mensch*. Rivka took a quick look down at the street and saw the cab: certainly it would be a *mensch*. She went to the bed and straightened the blankets.

'Shlomo, put coal in de bucket.'

'Why me?'

'Because I said you. Here.' She handed him the bucket from beside the range, and he sighed and began to fill it with coal from the bunker inside the front door. Rivka quickly took the broom from the cupboard and swept the floor and put the dust in the ashpan below the range. 'And behave,' she said, 'and say how-do-you-do.'

Chaiki watched this activity and wondered what was happening.

Zelek announced an important point: 'He's not a Jew.' Rivka asked how he knew. The fact that Zelek had never seen the man before was proof enough.

'If he's no' a Jew,' said Sarah,' he's no' coming here then.'

'You'll see,' promised Rivka.

'Has he come to see Pa?' asked Zelek.

'He's coom to see you.' Zelek was astounded.

Solomon pooh-poohed this, and gave it as his opinion that the man was coming to see Ma. Chaiki's eyes searched her mother's face.

There was a knock on the door. Solomon dumped the coal bucket by the range with a clatter, and raced Sarah to the door and opened it with coal-dusty hands.

The man stood there, tall, distinguished.

'Doctor,' said Rivka, 'is good of you.' She told the children to stand aside and let Doctor Harris come in. They stared at him, and Sarah shut the door behind him.

'Mrs Kaydan, is it?'

Rivka crinkled up her face, smiling in acknowledgment. She had left a message with the greengrocer and it had been delivered and now the doctor was here.

'Coom in to de fire – Sarah, bring a chair.' She put another lump of coal on the fire. 'A cup of tea?'

Dr Harris politely refused the offer, noticing the marks of damp rivulets down the peeled wallpaper.

'No cup of tea? Vait.' Rivka lifted the china hen lid from her sewing box on the mantelpiece, and felt for the coin. She brought it out, a half-crown. She held it out in the palm of her hand and said what it was, low but clear.

Dr Harris eyed the coin. He knew medicine didn't work unless it was expensive.

Rivka took his hesitation the wrong way. She said, 'I could owe you.'

Dr Harris took the coin and pocketed it. 'Thank you.' He turned to Chaiki in the bed. 'Is this the patient?' Chaiki's eyes were wide in wonder.

Lala came and stood in the doorway between the rooms and whispered loudly, 'Is it a doctor?'

'We'll see you in a minute, young miss,' said Harris. He asked Chaiki her name.

Solomon shouted it: 'Chaiki!'

Chaiki anglicised it to the name she was called by at school, Annie – which was really Hannah, which was really

73

Chaiki. The doctor understood. 'When were you at school last?' Chaiki didn't remember, but she had left school now being fourteen.

The doctor tested the temperature of her brow and took his thermometer from the bag. 'Slip this under your arm, Annie. How are you feeling?'

'All right.'

'No' all right,' said Rivka. 'A fever, hot.'

'When did it start?'

Rivka shrugged. 'Four days, five days.'

'Coughing?'

Chaiki said, 'Not much.'

Rivka said it wasn't like the cough the girl next door had. 'No,' said Chaiki, 'not a cough like hers.' She corrected herself, 'Like hers *was*.'

Harris asked if that was the girl whose funeral he had seen.

'Ay, sir,' said Rivka.

'When does Annie cough? In the night?'

'Not much.'

'Is this where you sleep?'

'No,' said Chaiki, 'I sleep next door.'

The doctor asked to see her pillow, but Rivka pointed to the pulley above him. She had washed the pillowcase.

'Did you notice any marks on it?'

Rivka's heart turned over. 'No,' she said. Chaiki's eyes were round.

The doctor asked if she had any pains, and she had – in her arms and legs, especially the elbows and knees and ankles. He sat her up, removed the thermometer and read it. He took out his stethoscope and knocked at her chest with his fingers and listened while she breathed and said 'Ninety-nine'. He pushed and felt in her abdomen, but she didn't have any more pains. He covered her up.

'Has she had a cough for long? Or at any time in the past, a bad cough?' Rivka told him they'd all had coughs, always a cough in the family.

74

The doctor asked where she was from, and she told him it was Lithuania. He asked how long she had been in Scotland, and they calculated it from Chaiki's age, fourteen-fifteen years. Dr Harris seemed satisfied.

'Who's next, then?'

'Zelek,' said Rivka.

Her eldest son was surprised. Lala shouted from the doorway that it was her turn, but Rivka assured him that the little girl was fine. Harris went through to the smaller room. He felt Lala's brow.

'What's your name?'

'Lala.'

'How old are you?'

'Six and a quarter.'

'Any coughs?'

'No!' said Rivka.

'Any pains?'

'No!' said Rivka.

'I have so,' said Lala.

Dr Harris asked where the pains were and Lala showed him her ear and her nose and her toes and her bum and laughed and laughed. The doctor said that he believed the little girl was all right. Then he asked who slept where.

Chaiki and Sarah slept in the bed in the small room, and Lala slept in the cot. Rivka and her husband slept of course in the bed-recess.

Dr Harris asked Zelek where he slept.

'They sleep up,' answered Sarah.

'Up?' asked Harris. 'Where's up?'

Rivka interrupted. 'Doctor, de von I vould please like you to look at, my eldest son.' She pushed Zelek forward, her beloved, her handsome one. 'I keep him off school today.' She smoothed down the back of Zelek's head.

Harris ran his eye over the tall thin boy before him. He asked what his name meant, but there was no anglicised form of Zelek.

'How old are you?'

Solomon gave the answer, 'Nearly barmitzvah.'

'What?' asked Harris.

'*Shah*,' said Rivka.

But Solomon did not shut up. 'Next month,' he told the doctor, 'he has to sing.'

Rivka explained. 'Is being Jewish – ven a boy is tirteen, he sing, in de synagogue.' And she smiled with pride.

Harris said, 'You become a man.'

'Dat's so. How you know?'

'And you wear a praying-shawl,' said Harris. Rivka looked at him in wonder. 'A tallis,' she confirmed. How could a Goy, even though he was a doctor, know these Jewish things?

Harris asked Zelek if he was a good singer, and Solomon exploded with a farting sound of mirth. Rivka said defensively, 'Zelek has a fine voice!'

The doctor went about his profession. 'What's the trouble, Zelek?'

'Tell him!' said Rivka, 'tell him de pains!'

Zelek said, 'Just the usual,' in his diffident way.

'Arms and legs?' asked Harris.

'A bit.'

Dr Harris told him to sit on the bed and pull his jersey up. Zelek was reluctant and his mother gesticulated at him. 'Ven de doctor's here, vy shouldn't he see to you, you need to be barmitzvah!'

Zelek sat on the bed and the others crowded round. The doctor sounded him and tapped him and prodded him. Then he went back to the bigger room.

'Where's the water? I'd like to wash.'

'Shlomo,' said Rivka, 'de basin.'

Solomon fetched an enamel basin from the open shelves above the coal bunker, and put it on the table. '*Nu?*' said his mother to him, as though to an idiot, 'Put some cold in, oddervise de vasser in de kettle vill be too hot.'

Solomon shrugged and took the basin out to the landing to fill it at the tap.

'The cold water's outside?' Harris asked.

'Yes.'

'And down the walls when it rains?'

Rivka found it hard to admit. 'Is not so bad. Ve're used to it.'

'Where's the lavatory?'

'Lavatory? Vasser-closet, is down in de green. Is not so nice. But ve have – you know.' He could see the you-know under the bed.

Solomon came back, carefully carrying the basin which he had half-filled with cold water. Rivka told him with a finger to put it on the table.

'Ah'm putting it,' said the little boy.

His mother brought the kettle from the fire and topped up the water and tested it so that it should be not too cold and not too hot.

'And soap,' she said to Sarah, 'and towel.'

Sarah brought the soap in a tin, and a folded towel from the shelves.

Harris said to Solomon, 'What's your name?'

Sarah replied for him, 'Shlomo.'

'Solomon,' shouted the little boy, 'Solomon Kaydan!'

'Before I wash, Solomon Kaydan, show me where this "up" is, where you sleep.'

Solomon pointed upwards. Harris looked at the broken ceiling inside the door, by the shelves. The laths hung loosely round a jagged, dark hole.

'How do you get up there?'

Solomon dragged the high stool from the table, jumped up on it, then using the open shelves as a ladder, he climbed through the hole and disappeared. His head peered over the edge.

'I'm up.'

Harris asked, 'Can I have a look?'

'No, Doctor,' said Rivka, who was growing worried by this inquisitiveness, 'dere is no need, nodding up dere.'

'Just a look,' said Harris. He mounted the stool and was

77

tall enough to see into the loft. He found he was looking under the eaves of the tenement. The floor was not made up; there were rough joists, with here and there some loose, warped boards for walking on. The roof-tiles above were loose and displaced, and daylight filtered in through the gaps and lit up the cobwebs and some orange boxes in the corner. By the chimney stack was a straw palliasse with a crumpled blanket on it.

Harris spoke to the crouching boy.

'Where do you sleep?'

'By the chimney. It keeps warm.'

'I can see where the rain comes in.'

'Just there an' there.' The boy pointed.

Dr Harris jumped down into the room. He handed his thermometer to Sarah. 'Can you wash this, very carefully, under the cold tap? Don't touch this end, and don't break it.'

Sarah took it gingerly and went out. Harris washed his hands in silence. Rivka watched him. Chaiki watched him from her bed, Zelek from the doorway, Solomon from above, as if it were a magic ritual before the unfolding of the truth.

The doctor said, 'I want to talk to your mother alone. We'll go through there.'

Sarah came back with the thermometer. He dried his hands, put the thermometer in his bag and went into the smaller room. Rivka followed wonderingly, fearfully.

'*Das kind?*' she asked.

'Lala, go to the other room,' said Harris.

'Not too near de fire.'

Lala hopped out of the cot where she had been playing with her wooden spoon dolly, and went through.

'Sit please, doctor.'

Harris sat down on the chair beside the window.

'You vont more money?' asked Rivka, her brow furrowed.

'No,' said Harris. 'Sit you down, Mrs Kaydan.' Rivka sat on the bed and folded her hands to listen.

78

'D'you have a husband, Mrs Kaydan?'

'Oh yes, a good man,' she told him, 'he coom ven he finish vork.'

'What does he work at?'

'A tailor,' Rivka shrugged.

'Does he make a living?'

Rivka modified the shrug to add an affirmative but that it depended what you meant by a living, but yes, it was a living.

'Does he earn enough to move out of here, to a house that doesn't leak and has some more air and light?'

Rivka didn't understand the question, it seemed so unreal. She stared at him through narrowed eyes.

'Your eldest daughter, Annie,' said Harris bluntly, 'has rheumatic fever. She can pull through that, if you look after her, but it's from the damp, and it'll come back. That's one thing I'm afraid of. The other is, if the girl next door died of consumption, it's on the cards you'll get it here. It's the kind of house for it, Mrs Kaydan.' He watched the effect of his words on her, to see if she had understood. When he saw that she had the gist of it, he added, 'Not just Annie but the others, too.'

Rivka stared and stared at him, seeing behind his face the people she had known, in *der Heim* and here, who had died young, of consumption. She forced herself to ask the question, 'Now? Already?'

'Annie could have. There are signs.'

It was the worst news of her life; she was benumbed.

Harris went on, 'She certainly has acute rheumatic fever. It needs careful nursing. When the fever goes, fresh air would be the thing. Fruit, green vegetables.'

'Chicken?' An automatic thought.

'Of course.'

He looked at this bare-foot woman and he knew that she couldn't do what had to be done. Rivka knew too, but her mind balked at the knowledge.

'Are you going to write a medicine?'

'A medicine, yes,' he said. He opened his bag and took out his prescription pad and his pen. 'The boy also has a touch of rheumatic fever.'

Rivka sat in silence, willing it not to be.

'Just a touch,' said Harris.

'Zelek, I keep him off school.'

Harris considered as he started to write. 'You'll have to be very careful with him, too. It affects the heart, you know.' He wrote in silence, then added, 'They've probably all had it, or they'll get it.' He wrote on.

At last, Rivka asked him, 'His barmitzvah?'

'When is the ceremony?'

'A month.'

'It depends if he gets better or worse. Does he sleep – up?'

'De two boys,' nodded Rivka.

'Change that, Mrs Kaydan. Annie should sleep by the fire meantime.'

'Mit me.'

'With you.'

Rivka worked out that her husband would sleep in the small room, with Zelek. And Sarah would go up, with Solomon.

Harris finished writing out the long prescription. 'The pills are for the pains. The bottle's for the cough. Three times a day. After meals. One teaspoon.' He tore off the paper and handed it to her. She glanced at it and put it in her bosom.

The doctor said, 'Pardon me, Mrs Kaydan, but I see you aren't wearing a wedding ring.'

'It vos tight, so I took it off.'

'Let me see.' He took her hand. 'There's no sign of tightness.'

'So vot you vont me to say?' said Rivka. 'I took it off!' she repeated.

'I'm sorry, Mrs Kaydan,' said Harris, 'none of my business.'

'Ve have de ticket for it,' Rivka told him with candour, 'so is all right!'

'Good . . .' said Harris in embarrassment. 'Now let me have a look at you.'

'Me? I'm fine, tenk you.'

'You're pregnant.'

'Vell, so . . .' She had been pregnant before.

'And well on the way?'

Rivka shrugged. It made no difference how far she was on the way.

'About eight months gone?' he pursued.

'Doctor, de bairn vill coom ven it cooms.'

He fastened his bag, then he stood up. The medical examination was over.

Rivka stood. 'Zelek . . .' she said.

'Look after him.'

'He's a good boy.'

'I can see that,' said Harris.

He went through to the main room. Solomon, Sarah and Lala scattered from beside the doorway where they had been listening. Zelek sat at the corner of the bed, beside Chaiki. The doctor bade them a cheery goodbye, Solomon opened the door for him, and he left.

Rivka tried to concentrate on making soup for Moshe's supper. The children went to the window and watched for the doctor to appear in the street below. He did; he mounted his waiting cab and drove off.

7

In the empty tailor's shop, by the light of a gas-lamp, Moshe Kaydan sat sewing. He'd taken in the back seam of the jacket and now it should fit across the shoulders. Mr Levinson pushed open the door. He was fat, grey-haired, and wearing his overcoat.

'Moshe! Go home!'

Moshe said, 'Please, Mr Levinson,' without looking up.

'You're burning my gas! Go home, use your own!' He came over to Moshe and turned off the gas. Moshe sighed and said, '*Ich hob nisht gas.*' He said it nearly every night. He got down from the table in the dark and felt for his coat and hat.

Levinson said kindly, 'Time to go home, Moshe, is late.'

He walked home up Potterrow, then turned left along the broken pavement of Crosscauseway, past the single lamp-post with its yellow hissing light. He had his bowler hat down to his ears, the brim casting a shadow that moved across his small black beard and moustache. His coat was ragged over his waistcoat and he carried a sack.

He paused outside his own tenement door, where the row of bells had been pulled out and sold for its brass, leaving broken holes. His body was tired and his soul was weary; bringing up children in poverty in a city had left its ravage-marks. He pushed open the door and went in.

Up the dark staircase to the top, his own door. He opened it. Rivka sat in the chair she had pulled up to the fire, asleep. Moshe gently shut the door behind him. He laid the sack on the floor, then took off his coat and hung it on the back of the door. Then his hat. Under it he wore his *yamul-keh* his skull-cap.

Rivka stirred. Without looking at Moshe she got up, took the table-candle to the fire and lit it and put it back on the table, where it flickered, then burned clearly. She stirred the pot on the fire. She took the kettle from the hob and added hot water to the basin of cold that was on the table.

Moshe pushed up his sleeves and said the blessing for washing the hands: God had commanded it. He rinsed his hands in the warm water and Rivka reached up and pulled a towel down from the pulley. Moshe dried his hands.

'*Nu?*' he asked.

'*Nu-nu.*'

He gave her the towel and pulled his sleeves down; she laid the towel over the basin.

Moshe went over to the bed and looked down at Chaiki. She opened her eyes, saw him and smiled.

'Sh, Chaikili . . .' He kissed her brow. He went through to the smaller room and had a look at his children there, and came back.

Solomon stuck his head down through the hole in the ceiling.

'Pa.'

Moshe looked up.

Solomon said, 'Yer coat.'

Moshe went to the peg and handed up his coat to the little boy, who took it and disappeared again.

Rivka removed the covering cloth from the bread on the table. Moshe sat in the chair at the head and brought out his pocket-knife, he opened the blade and cut a hunk of bread. He held the bread up and said the blessing, '*Hamout-see . . .*' God had brought forth the bread from the earth.

He took a bite and chewed and it was good. He uncovered the stone jar beside the bread, dipped into it with his fork and brought out a pickled herring. he dangled it above his mouth and lowered it in, chewing. When he had swallowed it and let the sharp savour go, he nodded that he was content with his lot. He looked up at Rivka.

'*Nu?*' This time he was asking her a question.

'I got a doctor.'

Moshe stared, indicating Chaiki with a movement of his head. Rivka came to the table and sat beside him. She whispered, 'Rheumatic fever.' Moshe questioned her with his eyes. She went on, 'And Zelek . . .'

'*Vos Zelek?*' An urgent whisper.

'De fever but he's fine. He'll be all right.'

She felt between her breasts and brought out the prescription. She laid it on the table beside Moshe. He studied it.

Rivka went to the pot, stirred it, ladled out the bean and barley soup into a bowl and brought it to the table.

'Pa?' said Chaiki.

He turned to her. 'Vos?'

'Have you brought me trousers to sew?'

Moshe nodded. Being a full-fledged tailor now – well, as Levinson's assistant – there was some money to be made by bringing work home.

Rivka said, 'Tomorrow.'

'Play cards, Pa,' said Chaiki.

'Yes.'

'Ven he's had his supper.'

She watched him eat his bread and soup, this man she had married, this provider. 'Ve need money.'

'How much you pay de doctor?' Rivka shrugged. 'A *shtiber*. De medicine . . .' Moshe wiped a splash of soup from the prescription.

Rivka said in a low voice, 'Ve need to take Chaiki . . . all to a new house.' That was it, that's what the doctor had said.

Moshe stared at her, then round at Chaiki, who smiled back at him.

'*Vos machs du?*' he asked how she was.

'Fine, Pa.'

Moshe returned to his good thick soup. A house . . .

'Gae to Levinson,' said Rivka, 'he pays you notting, he's got money, he'll lend you.'

'No, he vouldnae.'

'Ask. Ask again! Tell him!' But she knew it was hopeless. She put her hand over Moshe's. 'Have your soup. Ve need money for medicine, and clothes. Shoes for vinter. Ask at shool, somebody must have old shoes. An old voollen anyting, I can undo it and knit. Ask.'

'All right.'

'You mustnae pawn your coat!'

'No.'

'Ask Levinson for more, dat's all ve need, a few shillings more.'

There was a sharp bang. They started a little as they always did. 'A mouse,' said Chaiki.

Moshe finished his soup and got up. He opened the cupboard door.

'Is it dead?'

'Is dead.'

'Is its neck broken?'

'Is dead.' He brought the mousetrap out and shook the mouse into the ashes of the fire.

'Did he get the cheese?'

'No, he didnae get the cheese.' He resprung the trap in the candlelight and took it to the cupboard again. On his way back he brought the sack.

'Is that trousers?'

'Ay.'

Rivka caught Moshe's eye and there was a long look between them. Moshe lifted the blue tin box from the mantelpiece and rattled it. 'Tree fardings in it,' said Rivka. Chaiki said, 'That's for planting trees in Palestine, you can't have that.'

'Orange trees,' said Rivka, 'in Palestine.'

Moshe returned the blue box to its place. The letters on it stood for Jewish National Fund. They'd had it since the

Fund was established two years ago in 1901. A collector emptied it once a year and they couldn't take their farthings back from the JNF box.

Rivka took a trouser leg from the sack.

'De doctor,' asked Moshe, 'vos mit de bairn?'

'Ay, de bairn.'

'Ven?'

Rivka shrugged, 'Next veek.' Then suddenly she couldn't dam her tears any more. She clenched her fists and pummelled her knees. 'Oy! Oy . . .' She got up quickly and opened the cupboard door and stood behind it so that Chaiki couldn't see her, and she suppressed the noise of her sobbing. One must live, live on.

Moshe stood helplessly. 'If I gae to Levinson, he'll give me a present of a shilling, and dat will be dat. He'll no lend me notting.'

'Cards, Pa.'

'Ven I finish.'

'You've finished.'

Rivka wiped her face on her apron behind the cupboard door, and tried to say, 'He hasnae said his prayers.' Moshe went to her and embraced her in helplessness. They rocked back and forward.

Rivka said, 'You need to leave Levinson. If you vait till he gives you a share you'll vait fifty years.'

Chaiki called out to know what they were doing. Rivka kissed Moshe on the forehead and came out, sniffing. Moshe stared at the empty shelves of the cupboard. He looked out from the cupboard to the room, at his wife, at his firstborn. He retreated again out of sight. His mind raged, he could beat his brains out against the wood of the shelves. He screwed his face up to God and mouthed his agony, 'Aie . . . !' Then he took control of himself and came out.

Rivka had brought down the china hen and was picking out a needle and thread. She prepared to start sewing the trouser leg.

Moshe rinsed his hands again in the basin and dried them.

There was a hard glint in his eyes now. He sat at the table and said the shorter grace after meals. '*Boruch atoh adou-noi . . .*' As he mouthed the prayers, his eyes wandered round the squalor that was his home. He looked at Rivka, sewing. He got up and walked around the room, still praying. He took down the two framed pictures. Rivka watched him.

He used his knife to remove the backs of the pictures, took out the paintings and replaced the backs. He took the clock from the mantelpiece and stood it on the table. He took the china hen and emptied its bric-a-brac on to the table. He wrapped the lid and base separately in the Yiddish newspaper from the dresser.

He emptied the sack completely on to the floor, and put the china hen in, then the clock and the picture-frames.

'De pawnshop vill give you two-tree shillings de lot.'

Moshe paused in his prayers. 'Not de pawnshop. I sell dem. Vere's de ticket?'

'Vot ticket?'

'For de vedding ring.'

Rivka heard her own heart beat loudly; the ring was for pawning, not selling. What would be left then? She searched among the contents of the china hen, found the pawn ticket and gave it to him.

He put it in his waistcoat pocket, and resumed his prayers. He laid the sack near the door ready for the morning. He finished his prayers, bowing to one side and to the other, and in front, asking peace from the Giver of peace, for themselves and for all Israel. '*V'imroo omain!*'

'Omain,' chorused Rivka and Chaiki.

8

Miss Ross sat at her desk on the dais. The windows of her classroom at James Clerk's School were high up on the blank wall behind her. In front of her the children's desks and benches were screwed indestructibly to the grey wooden floor.

Miss Ross was twenty-five and wore her auburn hair in a tight bun at the back of her head. She was a good-hearted woman, and as hard as she had to be.

Her sixty pupils had filed in with whispers and scrapings of boots and only a few scuffles, and had climbed over each other to find their places. They were mostly in tatters, aged from eight to ten, the boys sitting to her right and the girls to her left. Few of them had washed, because soap cost money; some of them hadn't breakfasted.

But a huge fire of life burned in the fireplace behind the criss-cross wire guard, and they all looked into it from time to time and were given comfort.

'Are we quiet then? Are we?'

There were some shuffles.

'Don't let me bring out the Black Man.'

There was silence. The Black Man was thick and two-pronged and when Miss Ross swung him across their hands the stinging lasted a long time.

'Thomas and Donald now!' She held up a warning finger, lifted her desk lid and brought out the leather strap and dangled it. Total silence.

Solomon in his row concentrated hard. Sarah in her row sat with her hands folded neatly on the desk. She moved her feet, scraping her too-big boots against the iron strut of her chair. She grimaced. Miss Ross gave her a warning look but put the Black Man away.

A girl put her hand up and snapped her fingers.

'Yes, Jean?'

'Please Miss, it's my turn for the fire today,' said the little ginger-haired girl with the white face.

'All right, Jean, have you been good?'

'Yes, Miss.'

'Move then.'

Jean came out and moved to the end of her row, which was the seat nearest the fire. All the other girls in the row moved along one.

'Quiet now, quiet!'

Sarah wriggled her body.

'Sarah Kaydan, stop fidgeting.'

Sarah controlled herself.

Miss Ross was satisfied. 'Let's do our weather now. Quiet, Robert! Our weather.'

She stood up and stepped down from the dais and went to the easel and blackboard, lifted the heavy board off, turned it round and placed it back again. On the other side was a calendar of squares, each square for a day of the week, half of which had been filled in with different colours and emblems. Miss Ross took her wooden pointer and pointed to the next empty square. 'What day is it today, children?'

The class read it off. 'Tuesday,' they chanted.

'Tuesday,' repeated Miss Ross. 'And the date is the –?'

'Tenth,' they chanted.

'Tenth of –?'

'October.'

'Tuesday the tenth of October. And what's the weather?'

There was a forest of hands with snapping fingers.

'What's the weather, James?'

James Urquhart sat next to Solomon Kaydan.

'Grey, Miss,' he said.

'Grey,' said Miss Ross. She shaded in the top half of the square with a white chalk, making it a black-white mixture.

'What else? Sarah?'

Sarah said, 'Cold, Miss.'

'Cold,' said Miss Ross, 'so we'll put on our gloves.' She drew a pair of gloves in the lower half of the square. 'There we are. Now children, take out your slates.'

There was a great rattling as each child fished a slate up from its slot at the back of the desk.

'Quiet!' shouted Miss Ross, 'Quiet!' The class gradually settled again, apart from a few tinkles from slate-pencils in the pencil-grooves.

'Solomon!' said Miss Ross. 'What is the matter with you!'

Solomon was wriggling. 'Nothing, Miss,' he answered, squirming. His neighbour, James Urquhart, explained, 'He's wearin' brown paper, Miss.'

The class laughed.

'Stand up, Solomon,' said Miss Ross.

Solomon stood. He was wearing big boots like his sister Sarah. Miss Ross made her way between the rows to his desk. She looked down at the little boy, where his too-short jersey showed the brown-paper vest underneath.

'What's this?'

'A vest, Miss.'

The class laughed again.

'Quiet! Brown paper.'

'It's crinkly, Miss.' Another laugh.

'Do you not have a bigger jersey?'

'No, Miss.'

Miss Ross lifted up the jersey. There were revealed two fringes dangling at the front, and two more at the back. She pulled the front ones, and the back ones disappeared. She reached for the back ones and pulled them down again, and the front ones rose to where they had been.

'Solomon, what is this?'

'Ma tsitsis, Miss.' Miss Ross had pulled the fringes that his father said he must wear always.

The class laughed and laughed. Sarah sat with her head bowed in shame. Miss Ross let the laughter subside.

'Sarah Kaydan, what's your brother wearing?'

'I don't know, Miss.'

Miss Ross looked down at Solomon. 'Whatever it is will hardly keep you warm.' This time the class laughter was dutiful.

'Are you a silly boy, Solomon?'

'Yes, Miss.'

'Can your mother not do better than this?'

'No, Miss.'

Miss Ross made her way back to her desk.

Solomon said to her retreating back, 'She's having a baby, Miss.' Miss Ross stopped. The class tittered.

'Sit down. Take out your slate.'

Solomon did so.

'Stop wriggling. Solomon?'

'Yes, Miss?'

'If you're a good boy, you can sit at the end of the row tomorrow, by the fire.'

Solomon looked up at her in open-mouthed joy.

On Shabbas, on the top landing outside the Kaydans' home, the tap dripped into the sink as it did on every other day. Sarah Kaydan opened the door and came out. She crossed to the opposite door and knocked.

James Urquhart answered. Sarah said to him, 'My Ma says, if your Mammy's up will she come and light the fire?'

James bawled back into his house, 'Mammy! Will you come and kindle their Saturday fire?'

Mrs Urquhart answered from within, 'Ay, I will.'

Sarah waited politely. Her father and her mother said that God made the world in six days and rested on the seventh, so His chosen people must do no work on that day, and certainly must not kindle a fire.

'Can I come?' asked James. Sarah shrugged her uninterested consent.

Mrs Urquhart came out shuffling in her bauchles, her old, worn shoes, with a shawl wrapped round her. She shuffled into the Kaydan house and the children followed, and shut the door.

Rivka lay on the bed in the recess with her newborn baby. Chaiki lay beside her.

The cot had been brought through from the smaller room and stood in front of the dead fire. Lala was sitting up in a corner of it playing with the wooden spoon, re-wrapping the rags round it to make the shape of a dolly.

On the table was half a loaf of bread; beside it, a jar of apple jelly and a battered milk can. Dirty plates and cups stood in the basin.

Moshe and Zelek were dressing in the smaller room. Mrs Urquhart went to the fire and started to rake out the old ashes.

'How are you this morning, Mrs Kaydan? Aw, the bonny bairn.' Carrot-haired James stood and stared.

Rivka said, 'Fine, tenk you, Missus. It's awfy good of you to do de fire.'

''S a' right,' said her neighbour. 'Have you got a name for her yet?'

'Kveenie,' said the proud mother.

James gawped. Mrs Urquhart hadn't heard properly. 'What?'

Sarah repeated the name: 'Queenie.'

'Oh, what a nice name!'

Chaiki said, 'Queenie, Queenie,' as she fondled the baby's head and cooed to it.

'Are you up and about yet? I havenae seen you.'

'I'm fine, de children do de shopping.'

Moshe came into view in the doorway between the two rooms, without trousers, in his long shirt, trying to do up the stiff collar. He shouted, 'Shlomo!'

Sarah was embarrassed. 'Pa! Mrs Urquhart's here.'

Moshe became charming. 'I am sorry. Shlomo? Time to go.' He retreated to the other room to finish dressing.

Solomon's head appeared in the hole in the ceiling. James looked up and gawped. 'Oh, there you are, Solomon.'

Solomon came down. 'Where are you off to this morning?'

'Hush, James,' said Mrs Urquhart, 'they're off to their church.' She got up from the fireplace and went to the bunker inside the front door. She gathered up sticks and paper there.

James asked in surprise, 'On a Saturday?'

The Kaydan children had turned away to snigger at the mention of church, and now Rivka corrected it. 'Synagogue,' she said.

'Shool,' said Solomon.

'Shool?' echoed James. Solomon's mirth exploded in a raspberry.

Chaiki explained: 'We call it shool, the synagogue.'

'And handy, too,' said Mrs Urquhart for them. 'That's it, the next block, isn't it?'

'That's right,' said Chaiki.

Mrs Urquhart, bringing the heavy coal bucket from the bunker, gave her a nod. 'You'll not be going, though?'

'No,' said Chaiki.

Rivka said, 'Just de boys, and Sarah.'

'Zelek, is he well enough?'

'I hope so, tenk God. Zelek?' she called. Zelek answered with a grunt from the other room. Moshe appeared with his trousers on. 'He's ready.'

'Mind you,' said Mrs Urquhart, laying the fire, 'when our Mabel went, passed over – it's a month, God rest her soul –'

James repeated it loudly and firmly, 'God rest her soul.'

Rivka said, '*Omain.*' All the Kaydans repeated that.

'We had to take her all the way to Newington,' Mrs Urquhart went on. 'It's downhill but it's a long way. You've got yours in Braid Place, I've noticed that.'

'Handy,' said James.

Rivka said, 'God forbid!'

They were all silent, except for Mrs Urquhart, laying the

93

coals on the wood and paper. She took the box of matches from the mantelpiece, struck one, and held it to the paper.

James asked, 'Why do we make your fire every Saturday?'

'It's their Sunday,' said his mother.

'Oh, I see,' said James, who didn't, but was thinking it out. 'You'll not have had your porridge, then?' His questions had a sing-song lilt to them.

Solomon took up the sing-song. 'No-o,' he said, going up an octave on the vowel.

James didn't notice. 'Are you going to church without your porridge?'

'We're going to church without our porridge,' mocked Solomon.

Rivka rebuked him. 'Shlomo!'

'What?' said James, looking at his opposite number. 'I see you've had bread and jelly though.'

'So we have,' said Solomon gravely.

'James,' said Mrs Urquhart, 'that's enough talking. He's never done asking questions, that boy, drives you daft. There's your fire then, it's drawing.' They all looked to see if the fire would win and stay alive.

'There,' said Mrs Urquhart, satisfied.

'Tenk you, Missus. Could you put de pot . . . ?'

'Yes, there you are.' Mrs Urquhart put the pot of potatoes that Rivka had peeled yesterday on to the infant fire. 'Is there salt in it?'

'Pa?' asked Rivka. Moshe said, 'Is got salt.'

Mrs Urquhart straightened herself. 'Are you all right then? Anything you want, give me a knock, aw the wee darling! Queenie, eh? Looks like you, doesn't she?'

'Vell,' said Rivka with a happy shrug.

Chaiki said, 'I don't think so.'

'Eh?' said Mrs Urquhart wonderingly. 'You look after yourself now!'

'I will,' said Chaiki.

Mrs Urquhart went to the door, opened it, then turned. 'Come, James!' She went out.

Moshe said, 'Zelek, Sarah, Shlomo – get your caps.' He lifted his bowler from the peg on the door.

James asked, 'Why does he wear a wee hat in the house?'

Moshe answered him, direct, 'Is de house of God.'

James gawped. He pointed at Zelek. 'Why doesn't he wear a wee hat?'

'He vill. Next veek.'

'When he's barmitzvah,' explained Solomon.

'What?' said James.

'Please God,' Rivka breathed.

Solomon explained to James: 'In shool. Barmitzvah.'

'Shool's yer church.'

'Ay, so it is.'

'What do you do there?'

'*Keesh'n tochas*,' said Solomon. His mother tut-tutted at him. 'Shlomo!'

'What?' asked James, looking sideways to see and hear better. 'What does that mean?'

'It means, how are you keeping?'

Moshe said, 'Vos he say? Vos you say? Shlomo?' Sarah told. 'He's sayin' *Keesh'n tochas*.' Moshe threw up his hands and took up his prayer-book from the dresser.

James echoed the words doubtfully, '*Keesh'n tochas?*'

Sarah, Chaiki and Lala giggled. Zelek went close to James and whispered in his ear. 'It means, kiss my bum.' James was startled into silence. Is that what they did in their church? His mother called from across the landing, 'James!' and he scuttled out, wide-eyed.

Moshe said, 'Coom.'

'Zelek, must you go?' asked his mother.

'Yes, I'll be all right.'

'Next week, haw-haw,' said Chaiki from the bed, 'you're for it.'

'Ay.'

'*Nu shein!*' said Moshe in exasperation. He marched out, and Zelek, Sarah and Solomon followed.

'Shut de door!'

Solomon came back and shut the door.

Rivka and Chaiki and Lala listened to their footsteps on the stone stairs, till they could hear them no more. Then Rivka swung her legs out of the bed. The baby woke and grinned. She undid her woollen jacket and put the baby to her breast, looking into the burning fire.

Chaiki asked, 'Will I be able to go to Zelek's barmitzvah?'

'*Lieber Gott.*'

'And me?' piped Lala.

'And you.'

'And Queenie?'

'And Kveenie, if she don't cry.'

'And my baby?' Lala held up the spoon-dolly.

'All, everyone. And ve'll all get strong, and vell, and Pa vill make some more money, and ve'll have a new house, mit rooms to sleep and rooms to eat, and meat, and fish, and bread and vine, and candles,' She looked down at the suckling baby, 'and milk and honey . . .'

9

Next day was Sunday, and in the afternoon, the Kaydans sat round the table playing rummy with the two dog-eared packs of cards. Lala did not have a hand of her own but was helping Rivka. Moshe sat at the end of the table taking an alarm clock to pieces with his knife. There were two other clocks on the table beside him. He had bought all three for a penny from a rag-and-bone cart.

Sarah took a card from the stack and laughed.

'No, no!' pleaded Zelek.

'And kings,' said Sarah, 'and I'm out!'

Lala shouted, 'Rummy!' and Rivka said, 'She's out.'

Solomon reached for another card.

'Stop it! Count!' demanded Sarah.

'I'm just seeing.'

Zelek had counted his hand. 'I've got fifteen.' He was the scorer and he wrote it down. 'What's Chaiki got?'

Chaiki laid down a fistful of face-cards. She sighed a deep sigh.

'Bed, Chaikili,' said her mother.

'But what's she got? She's just going to bed because she's got a big score.'

Rivka helped Chaiki up and away from the table.

'What you got?' Zelek asked her.

'Count it.'

Rivka comforted Chaiki at the bedside. Chaiki was laughing at her own helplessness.

'Vy you laugh?'

'I don't know.'

'Pa,' demanded Sarah, 'what's Chaiki got?' But Moshe was too intent on the clock interior. Zelek took Chaiki's cards and counted. 'Fifty-three. She's out the game. Shlomo?'

'Five,' said Solomon.

'Let's see!' Sarah grabbed his cards and was surprised to find a two and a three. Solomon put his tongue out at her. 'There, see!'

Zelek said, 'Lala?'

'What?'

'How much have you got left?' He took her cards and counted.

The baby cried from the other room, and Rivka went through. The top drawer of the chest of drawers was open and inside was Queenie, wrapped in a shawl. '*Nu shein?*' Rivka picked the baby up and cuddled it.

Round the table the cards had been gathered and Zelek was shuffling them. Chaiki had subsided in the bed-recess.

Solomon asked his father, 'What are you going to do with the clock?'

'Ven it goes, I sell it.'

Sarah looked sideways at Moshe at work. 'Have ye found out what's wrong wi' it?'

'Is dirty.'

Zelek started dealing another round. 'Pa, I'm saying all these blessings on Shabbas. *Boruch atoh adounoy*, blessed art Thou, O Lord – what's God look like?'

Moshe didn't look up from his clock. 'God looks like us.'

The children stared at him. Chaiki sat up in her bed.

Zelek said, 'How d'you mean?'

'De Torah says, God made man like himself. So ve look like God. God looks like us.'

Zelek went on dealing.

Chaiki said from the bed, 'Pa, what happens to the mice?'

'Vot mice?'

'In the trap. I mean, Mabel Urquhart went to the cemetery at Newington, where all the Goyim are.'

Rivka came through from the other room, having quieted the baby. 'Ve put de mice in de bucket.'

'I know, but do they go to heaven?'

'Vot heaven?' asked Moshe.

'You know,' said Sarah.

'Do they?' Chaiki pleaded.

'Pa, she vonts to ken.'

'No, dey don't go anyvere.'

Zelek said, 'But we kill them.'

'Yes.'

Sarah said, 'Doesn't God? – I mean – he made the mice.'

Moshe looked up and saw all eyes upon him. 'De Torah says, God gave man dominion over de animals.'

They were satisfied. Zelek asked who was playing, and they picked up their hands.

Sarah said, 'Shlomo's got a Bible from school' They sorted out their cards in silence.

'Show me,' said Moshe.

There followed a ritual they had seen for each one of them. Solomon rose, climbed up, put his hand through the hole in the ceiling, and brought down a small cloth-bound Bible. Moshe reached out for it, and Solomon gave it to him.

Moshe inspected it, flicked through it. God had given him dominion over his family, to be decisive, to protect them. He stopped at the New Testament title-page. He laid it open on the table. He took his whetstone to the fire, put a drop of water on it from the pot and brought it back to the table. He ground his knife-blade on it, round and round and to and fro until it was razor-sharp. He wiped it on a leaf of newspaper. He grasped the entire New Testament section and cut it out with the knife. He went to the fire and threw the wad of pages on to it. The blaze was watched by the whole family with satisfaction.

Next day in the classroom, Miss Ross stood over Solomon.

'Show me what you were doing!'

99

Solomon sheepishly kept his head bowed.

'Stand up!'

Solomon got to his feet.

'Show me!'

Solomon uncovered his Bible, which he had hoped to hide under his slate. He waved it in the air so that the loose back cover flapped over the gap.

The class laughed.

Miss Ross took the Bible from the little boy and inspected it. She couldn't make out what had happened, then she understood and was startled.

'Who did this?'

Solomon didn't answer.

'Where's the New Testament? Solomon Kaydan, what's happened to this Bible!'

'My Pa cut it away.'

There was a silence in the room.

'Why would anyone do a thing like that?'

'Ah'm a Jew.'

A rustling and a whispering in the class. Miss Ross eyed her pupil.

'A what? But Jews – that was the New Testament . . . that was the word of Our Lord. That was a very, very wicked thing to do. . . . What do you mean, a Jew?'

Solomon couldn't answer that one.

'You're Scotch, aren't you? Aren't you?'

'Yes, Miss.'

'There are no Scotch Jews,' said Miss Ross.

Solomon looked up at her in wonder and fear. But she left him the Bible and walked back to her desk, upset for much of the morning.

On their way home from school, Solomon and Sarah walked past a knot of their schoolfriends lurking in an alley. They quickened their pace, as the others came out and started to throw stones. Solomon and Sarah ran for it, and James Urquhart threw one that hit Solomon on the leg.

*

On the Thursday night, Zelek did a practice run for his barmitzvah. The table candle was lit, the fire burned brightly. Rivka sat in the chair beside the fire and Chaiki listened from the bed-recess. All the others were gathered round the table.

Zelek stood at the end of the table with two books open, one for the blessings and the other for the portion of the Prophets that he would sing. Moshe sat next to him, watchful for mistakes. Zelek chanted his way tunelessly through to the end, wearing his prayer-shawl as well as his yamulkeh for the sacredness of it.

'*Yisborach shim'cho b'phi col chai tomid l'oulom vo'ed; boruch atoh adounoi, m'kadesh hashabos.*' Blessed was the Lord, the Sanctifier of the Sabbath.

There was a silence after he finished, then Rivka sighed and said, 'Verra gut. Zelek, vot a mensch.'

Sarah asked, 'Have you got the tune right?'

'No, I haven't,' replied Zelek.

Moshe shrugged, 'Tune –!' and gave a dismissive gesture.

Zelek asked his mother, 'Have I, Ma?'

'Vell, dat doesnae matter.'

'It does so.'

'Zelek, is your barmitzvah on Shabbas, and you'll be dere, in shool. God has cured you, he has given your healt and strengt, your *gezunt* . . . I love you.'

Solomon said, 'But the tune's no' right.'

'So,' said Rivka. 'Pa taught you, and he doesnae ken von tune from anodder, so how can you sing, who expects it? Is beautiful, Zelek.'

Moshe grinned in embarrassment, but he didn't really mind. 'De song . . . is vot you say.'

'Dere's only von ting I miss,' said Rivka, and she hummed an old melody that she'd heard at every other barmitzvah. 'So ve'll hae von barmitzvah mitout it. Is money,' – she waved her arms expansively – 'if ve had de money, you vould gae to de cheder and learn from Rabinovits, he can sing. But Pa knows de vords and you say it –!' She kissed her fingers at the sweetness of it.

Moshe opened a tin on the table. It had some loose tobacco in it, and papers, and he rolled himself a cigarette.

Zelek was in the sulks. 'It's not as if I understood the words.'

Moshe pointed to the Book of Prophets. 'Dere's de translation, in English. Read.'

'I don't understand it. Do you?'

They looked at Moshe.

'In Hebrew I understand.' He licked the gum on the cigarette paper and sealed it.

'I'm not Hebrew,' said Zelek, 'I'm Scotch.'

Solomon quoted to the air, '*Sh'ma Yisro'el* means Hear O Israel.'

Moshe took the prayer-book and flicked over the pages and found the *Sh'ma*. He thrust the book at Solomon. 'Read. Dere. Tell me vot you don't understand.' He lit the cigarette at the candle and puffed, and the smell of the Turkish tobacco filled the room.

Solomon read without much punctuation, 'And thou shalt love the Lord thy God with all thy heart and with all thy soul and with all thy might. And these words which I command thee this day shall be upon thine heart and thou shalt teach them –' He stumbled.

Sarah took the book and read fluently: '. . . diligently unto thy children and shalt talk of them when thou sittest in thine house, and when thou walkest by the way, and when thou liest down and when thou risest up. And thou shalt bind them for a sign upon thine hand, and they shall be for frontlets between thine yes. And thou shalt write them upon the doorposts of the house and upon thy gates.'

'That's the mezzuzzim,' said Chaiki.

Zelek said, 'I understand that, but what about the former rain and the latter rain? I ask for that twice a day and I don't want it. If it comes, it'll run down the walls and I'll get rheumatic fever again.'

Moshe puffed in silence.

Rivka said, 'Is not God, is Pa; he cannae make enough money to move to a house vit a roof dat doesnae leak.'

Was it Moshe's fault? Zelek came back with, 'Why do we wear fringes?' It was a more fundamental question.

Sarah said, 'Shlomo's stopped wearing his.'

Moshe looked sharply. 'Vos? Vy?'

Sarah told. 'Because in the class Miss Ross pulled them and everybody laughed.'

'You don't vear dem?'

'No,' said Solomon defiantly.

Moshe jabbed his finger at the place in the *Sh'ma*. 'Read!'

Solomon looked at the words: 'And the Lord spake unto Moses, saying, speak unto the children of Israel and bid them that they make a –'

'Fringe,' said Zelek stonily.

'Fringe upon the corners –'

Moshe said, 'In Hebrew! Dere!'

Solomon stumbled through the Hebrew on the opposite page. '*V'osoo lo'hem . . .*'

'*Tsitsis,*' said Zelek.

'*Tsitsis,*' echoed Solomon, '*al . . . al . . .*'

Moshe poked at the word on one page, then the other. 'Fringe. *Tsitsis*. God says.'

Solomon had had enough. 'Tsitsis-pishkies,' he said.

Moshe gave a shout of anger, '*Dos ees de sh'ma!* Learn!' And he slapped Solomon a stinger across the ear that knocked the wee boy and his stool tumbling to the floor.

Solomon cried all night because of his sore ear. Rivka kept him off school the next day and sent a message for the doctor. Dr Harris came in the afternoon and examined the ear.

'What do you say happened?'

'It vos an accident. His fadder hit –'

Harris said, 'I'm afraid his ear-drum's broken, Mrs Kaydan.'

Rivka was sitting on the bed nursing the baby. Chaiki turned to look at the doctor.

Harris went on, 'There's a perforation, a hole, inside here.'

Rivka nodded. 'Medicine?'

'No, put the bandage back on.' He tied a ragged grey scarf round the little boy's head. 'The pain should go in a day or two, but he won't hear again in that ear. I mean never. It doesn't grow again. He's deaf.'

Rivka let Queenie down from her breast.

'He vos making a mistake in his lesson. Dat's all.'

'I see,' said Harris. 'Well, there it is. He has the other ear, haven't you?'

'Eh?' said Solomon.

'Good boy. What's your name again?'

'Solomon.' He had heard the question.

Harris beamed. 'Solomon Kaydan, I remember.' He turned to Rivka and pushed the baby's nose playfully. 'Baby's doing well, I see. And how's this one?'

Chaiki smiled weakly. 'Fine, doctor.' She coughed.

Harris said, 'Fresh air, that's the thing.' He touched her brow, then felt her pulse. 'Still fevered . . .' He looked around the room while holding her pulse. 'You seem to have gained a few things since I was here last?' He meant the clocks on the table, the frames against the wall.

'Yes,' said Rivka.

Solomon pointed to the loft. 'Up there's full.'

'Shah,' said Rivka. 'My hosband he sell and he buy.'

'Is he making money?'

'No, is still a tailor. But he knows a somebody here and a somebody dere and he make an extra . . . shillings.'

'Are you going to move house?'

'Ve try, ve look. It vill take time.'

'Yes . . .' Harris supposed that it would. He scrutinised Chaiki, then laid her wrist back on the bed. He said nothing, but his lips were pursed. 'Your son Zelek, has his fever gone?'

'Oh yes, sir. Medicine for Chaiki?'

Harris felt a twinge of sadness. 'Just ask for the same again.' He changed the subject. 'Did Zelek have his initiation?'

'Vot?'

'His manhood ceremony.'

'Barmitzvah. No, tomorrow, please Gott.' She looked at him in curiosity. 'How do you ken, Doctor, about dese Jewish tings?'

Dr Harris was a student of Theosophy. He explained that the word meant 'the Wisdom of God'. It embraced all religions.

Rivka didn't believe that. 'No!' she said. There was only one God, the one she knew very well.

'Yes,' he assured her. 'There are things in the Bible that were hidden there in the days of Solomon's temple.'

The little boy looked up at that.

Harris winked at him. 'I mean, King Solomon. Do you know, for instance, about the Lost Tribes of Israel? Ten tribes were carried into captivity and then disappeared. They wandered all over the world, including here. We Scots are one of the Lost Tribes.'

Solomon stared in astonishment.

Harris continued, 'I'm interested in the Pyramids myself. Fascinating.' He collected his bag. 'Let me know any time you need me. Keep your daughter warm, the invalid. My bag, my hat. Good day.' A bright nod to Rivka.

'Shlomo.' He didn't hear. 'Shlomo!'

Solomon went to the door and opened it for the waiting doctor. Harris went out, putting his hat on. Solomon shut the door.

Rivka put Queenie back to her breast.

Chaiki started to cough.

The Richmond Street Shool was a square room with a proper gallery above for the women. Against the eastern wall was the curtained Ark, with the dais and reading desk. The men sat in rows on the wooden benches, with their praying shawls and yamulkehs. The women's gallery was packed.

Zelek wore a big new tallis that would last him for the rest of life. He chanted his portion with no tune, the Cantor standing beside him and following the words with the silver stylus. Moshe stood at one side, his tallis round his shoulders, as shyly proud as he had ever been in his life.

Rivka, sitting in the gallery above, had borrowed some feathers for her hat, and had bought a very nice pair of second-hand shoes. Beside her sat Sarah and Lala, leaning over to see, crisp and clean in their carefully contrived clothes. Rivka swayed as she listened to her beloved Zelek intoning below.

In the middle of the front row of the men, space had been found for Solomon. His ear was wrapped decorously in a clean scarf and he wore his cap on top. He stared up at his big brother.

Chaiki had not been well enough to go to the shool. She lay weakly in the bed-recess, and Mrs Urquhart was looking after her.

'The wee one's quiet enough.' She came through from the other room, and sat in the chair by the fire.

Chaiki whispered, 'She's all right.'

'Queenie, awful nice name. And Zelek's a nice boy, I like him. Having his big day, eh?'

Chaiki nodded.

'Did you have something when you were thirteen? I cannae mind.'

Chaiki whispered, 'No. Girls don't have barmitzvahs.'

Zelek had got into his stride and was intoning the final blessings. The crowded shool had picked up the emotion of it and everyone was swaying and nodding. Rivka was in tears of joy.

Moshe mouthed the blessings in time to Zelek.

'*Boruch atoh adounoi, m'kaddesh hashabbos!*'

106

And the whole synagogue shouted, '*Omain!*'

Then came the handshakes. Everyone shook hands with everyone, and said 'Mazeltov! Mazeltov!' especially over and over again to Zelek and Moshe. And there were kisses in the gallery for Rivka from all the other mothers.

And Moshe nodded and nodded his acknowledgements.

The Urquharts' door opened. James looked out. He looked over the broken banister. He listened for sounds from the Kaydans.

The Kaydans' door opened.

James turned his head back to his own house and said in a loud whisper, 'Mammy!' Mrs Urquhart came out and stood beside James.

From Moshe's house, a coffin was borne out by the same two bearers. Chaiki's coffin was small, and plain and black. The men angled it and started down the stairs.

Moshe and Rivka came out. Rivka had Queenie in her arms, wrapped in a shawl. Then came Zelek, Sarah, Lala and Solomon. All the Kaydans were in their most ragged clothes. There were no flowers. Death was stark reality.

Mrs Urquhart shook her head sadly. James stood staring in silence.

The cortège descended.

Solomon shut the door behind him. As he passed the boggling James, he said '*Keesh'n tochas!*' James stared, then grinned sideways at Solomon, and watched him go down the stairs.

Down the four flights to ground level, then along the dark close to the street and out into the daylight. The two men lifted the coffin up and slid it on to the cart. They climbed up in front, checked that the mourners were ready, then the driver tugged the reins and they set off.

Moshe and Rivka walked after the cart with their Chaiki on it and cried out loud, their shoulders heaving with sorrow. Zelek, Sarah, Lala and Solomon followed, stepping over the mud and broken cobbles.

10

The east wind in Edinburgh blows through your bones all
the year round but that November after they lost Chaiki,
it ripped the tiles from the Kaydan roof and made the loft
uninhabitable. No amount of hugging together could keep
the family warm; they all had coughs and Solomon had the
shivers, and the rain streamed down the walls and dripped
in the middle of the room too. So Moshe had to plead with
the men after Saturday night service in the shool.

The Chazan's brother knew of a flat in Summerhall
Square, two blocks away. It was only two floors up. It had,
he believed, three bedrooms apart from the kitchen, and a
parlour with windows on two sides. What a pity that Moshe
was getting so little from Levinson that he couldn't afford
the rent: may be the Board of Guardians would help him.

Moshe sold all his picture-frames to a dealer in Castle
Street and went to see the landlord of the house. He paid
two weeks in advance.

On the last day of November, with the grief of Chaiki's
death raw in their hearts, the Kaydans moved house. It
being a weekday, Levinson had asked how Moshe could do
such a thing, because it was a working day. Moshe told him
he would not be coming back, and left his erstwhile em-
ployer thunderstruck.

The Kaydan goods were brought down piece by piece:
the table, two chairs, the bench, the small bed, the cot, the
dresser and the chest of drawers, and all the rest in orange-
boxes, angling round the spiral staircase and out to a waiting cart. They were roped on and carted away in the driving

rain. Then, sobbing for Chaiki, they left their top floor and walked the ten minutes to the new house. The only one to stay dry was Queenie, wrapped in a shawl under Rivka's coat.

The new house was at least dry. Rivka got the kitchen fire going and the potato pot boiling, while Moshe nailed up the mezzuzzim he had carefully levered off the old house, together with the four new ones he had bought for all the extra rooms. True, the parlour remained unfurnished for many months, but it was a room in the house, so there had to be a mezzuzzah. The first night they all slept together in the kitchen.

Over the next few days Moshe bought for pennies old chairs and broken beds and they decided who was to have which room. So many rooms, enough to fight over! Moshe and Rivka had the bedroom at the back, overlooking the green. There they installed their *perrony*, the feather mattress that they had brought from Rivka's family in *der Heim*. The dawn chorus of birds in the trees of the back green was a joy every day to wake to, and as the room faced south there was the sun as well.

Next to their room was a little box-room that would do for Queenie when she was older. The cot was put there for her, and Lala shared a big bed at last with Sarah in the room next to the kitchen. There, and in the boys' room next door, the dawn chorus came more from the animal hospital over the square, sick sheep and cows and horses and dogs and poultry. But they got used to it, and liked that too, and appropriated the sound as part of their home.

Moshe remembered to register Queenie's birth just in time, and in the space for signing, where it said 'Occupation of father' he wrote in his spidery English 'Picture-frame dealer'. He had found a ready second-hand market in this city of artists, with a middle class who liked to frame their photographs as well as their prints and water colours.

Gradually the house was furnished, with a square of old carpet here, linoleum there, a set of old chairs and a table for the parlour, and now there was enough left over for a food-parcel to be sent to *der Heim* in response to a letter, and a penny left over for the JNF box on the mantelpiece.

The children graduated from South Bridge to Boroughmuir High School. Zelek did well in his Highers and there was talk of his studying medicine in this most famous of all medical cities. But that was beyond the bounds of possibility. Anyway, he had a gentle persuasive manner that was good for business and he became an assistant to Rivka's cousin in a haberdashery shop in the High Street. After a year there he became a commercial traveller in stationers' sundries, and made a little name for himself in picture postcards up and down the east coast. So he paid for himself; more than that, he brought money home and paid for the others.

Sarah failed her Highers – but only just, everyone was sure of it. She was apprenticed in Braverman's tobacco shop in Leith Street, and learned to make cigarettes by hand, round ones and oval ones with Turkish tobacco in them.

Then came Solomon, who was as clever as Zelek, not in his mother's eyes of course, but certainly by the standards of the Scottish Education Board. He passed brilliantly in his Highers, in the name of 'Ian Solomon Kaydan'. The additional name was because his fellow-pupils had found Solomon a good Jewish sound to chant. So he changed himself to Ian and the authorities kept both names.

There was now enough money coming into the house from Sarah as well as Zelek – and 'very well tenk you' from Moshe's dealing – to have paid Solomon's way through medical school. It was Rivka who decided against it: medicine had been Zelek's prerogative. So Ian Solomon did the next best thing; he took a job in Mr Kyle's chemist's shop in South Clerk Street, and started his pharmaceutical apprenticeship.

August 1914 found the Kaydans edging definitely into the lower middle classes. Lala became a bottle-washer in another chemist's shop with a view to becoming a dispenser, because there was security, interest and independence there for anyone with brains. Queenie, without many brains, was still at school. But Zelek was doing well and Moshe's trade widened to include anything at all that he could afford to buy, and sell at a profit. He developed a good eye for antiques and a love for the insides of clocks. The war and the pressures to enlist did not affect Mr and Mrs Kaydan. They had not left *der Heim* to bear children who might be killed in someone else's fight.

On a winter's day early in 1916, Rivka came back from shopping at the Co-op round the corner. She still had long, thick hair but it was greying now, coiled tightly in a bun under her brimmed hat. She wore a blue ankle-length tweed coat over her cardigan and skirt; her basket was full of groceries. She mounted the two flights to her own front door, then put her hand through the letter-box to grasp the string with the key on it. She pulled the key through and unlocked the door.

A voice called from the parlour, 'Ma?'

'Who's zat?'

She went into the parlour, taking off her coat and hat. Zelek sat there at the table under the hanging gas-chandelier. He was twenty-five now, tall, slim, dark, in a well-cut suit of two dark shades of brown. He wore no yamulkeh and was smoking a cigarette. He had moved the potted plant from the table to the sideboard and on the threadbare green embroidered table-cover had stacked up grey boxes of pencils taken from his suitcase on the floor. He now looked up from the notebook in which he had been doing sums, to greet his mother as she came in.

Rivka was overjoyed. 'Zelek! Vot are you doing here? You said Friday!'

'I'm making my fortune, Ma.'

Rivka cuddled his head, taking care not to disturb the black hair brushed back. She looked at the stacks of boxes on the table. 'Pencils?'

'I've heard there are no pencils up the east coast. I've got the sole agency from Levy.'

'Levy's in pencils?'

'He is now.'

'How much vill you make from dese?'

'That's nothing.' Zelek dismissed his viewable stock. 'I'm going to clear a hundred pounds, Ma.'

'A hundred pounds! From pencils?'

'I've ordered two hundred gross.' Zelek withdrew his head from her arm. 'Don't you believe me?'

Yes, of course she believed him. He was Zelek.

'So you'll stay and have supper. As long as you don't fight. Listen, Mrs Simon, she vos in de Co-op, she had a telegram.'

Zelek's heart jumped, as it always did at such news. 'Who? – Morris?'

'Morris Simon. Tventy. He rushed to volunteer.'

'Is he killed?'

'Missing believed killed. You should see Mrs Simon.'

There was a silence for the sorrow of it. Rivka picked up her basket and went to the door. 'Have you heard more about conscription?'

'Ma,' said Zelek, 'they can't *make* you fight.'

Rivka gave a troubled shrug. That's what they used to make you do in *der Heim*. She went out to the kitchen.

'Ma?' called her son after her.

'Vot?' The voice was muffled from the kitchen. 'Coom and talk.'

'I'm working out my money.'

Rivka came back through the lobby to the parlour. She stood at the door. 'Vot?'

'I saw the landlord.'

Rivka tried to remember if she'd paid that week's rent. 'So?' People got evicted in wartime, for all sorts of reasons.

'It's all right, he wants to go fifty-fifty.'

'On vot?'

'On hot water, putting hot water in.'

This was a long-standing talking-point between the Kaydans and their landlord. He tried to persuade them of the convenience; they knew he would charge them more rent.

Rivka said, 'You said no, no money.'

'I said yes.'

'Vot!'

'Hot water, Ma. A bath.'

Rivka had been in houses with a fitted bath, Jewish houses. Her face crinkled up in a great smile, and her eyes shut as they always did when she smiled. 'Vere vould you put a bat'?'

'In Queenie's room.'

She considered it. She had done so before, in secret, to herself.

'Mit a voter-closet?'

'Ay.'

'But it's his house, he should pay.'

Zelek tapped his pencil-boxes. 'A hundred pounds, Ma. Ma, he's making money and I'm making money.'

Rivka regarded her first-born son. 'But nobody asks *him* vy he's not fighting!' She put her arms round Zelek's shoulders again. 'Oy, Zelek . . .'

She was tired of people asking her why her son was not fighting

Mr R. Kyle, M.P.S., Chemist and Druggist, was in his sixties, with grey hair and a grey face but with humour on his lips. He came through from the shop carrying a letter and sat at the desk in his dispensary, below the shelves of bottles and jars, and alongside the bench with the scales, mortars and pestles, measuring-jars, bunsen burner, pill-board and pill-boxes and labels and wrapping paper and sealing-wax and pink string.

He opened the letter and read it. He called through to his apprentice in the back shop, who was rinsing bottles at the sink and putting them on the pegs to drain.

'There's a note from the Pharmaceutical Society. When

the Conscription Bill becomes law, a pharmaceutical apprentice will be an essential occupation. So you're all right.'

Ian had turned his good ear to hear. He was a tall, slim twenty-year-old, in separate jacket and trousers which were well-worn but not ill-fitting, and a brown overall on top. He stood among the carboys and packing-cases spilling their straw.

'I don't know,' he said.

Kyle turned to view him. 'You're my apprentice,' he said. 'I'll put you on the list.'

'I don't want to go on it.' Ian's voice had a pleasant quality, with the Lowland accent modified by his education.

Kyle said, 'Don't be daft! D'you want to be killed? What's the good of fighting a war if there's no chemists and druggists at the end of it? And is your name Solomon Ian Kaydan, or Ian Solomon Kaydan?'

'Ian Solomon. Why?'

'To register your apprenticeship. They want your full Christian names.'

'I don't have any Christian names.' It was always a niggling point with him when officials assumed that Christianity was universal and did not imply any particular belief. At school he had been told not to stay out of morning hymns, because Jews could sing the hymns, there was nothing specially Christian about them. Holy, holy, holy, Lord God almighty, God in three persons, blessed Trinity, he mouthed in time to the others but let no sound escape his lips.

Kyle sighed, 'All right, all right,' and filled in the names.

'I don't want to register my apprenticeship,' said Ian.

'Why? I'm not going to last for ever, somebody's got to take over. Are they after you?'

'Who?'

'Your king and country. Ian, you are doing an essential job.'

Ian looked through the barred window at the familiar back green outside. 'I've got a friend at evening classes – Harry Cochrane, you've met him. He's volunteering.'

'Can't he wait? Conscription'll be in by the end of the month. What does his master say?'

'He's not very happy.'

'Nor would I be.'

'We don't like being called dodgers.'

Kyle understood that. He had been called a dodger himself by certain customers. But he had learned to bear such things in silence: Ian was more impulsive. Kyle carried on filling in the form. 'I'm applying for you just the same.'

'No, don't,' said Ian, coming through from the backshop drying his hands.

The grey-haired chemist picked up a prescription from his desk. 'Ian, look at this. Thirty fluid drams of tolu. Dr Kerr, he's made a mistake, he means thirty minims.'

'Yes, I saw that.'

'Dr Kerr is in his eighties, he came back from retirement because all the doctors are away fighting. Ian –'

'No,' said Ian with decision.

At this point the shop bell jangled and Ian went through to serve a beak-faced woman with red cheeks and a dew-drop on the end of her nose.

'Good morning, Missus?'

Kyle watched him, troubled.

Ian walked home along South Clerk Street. A bus ground past him puffing blue smoke, and pulled out to overtake a coal-cart. The cobbles were wet with drizzle. 'Ho!' called the coalman in his resonant chant, scanning the tenement windows, but housewives were all busy making tea for the folk scurrying home. Ian saw the newspaper placard at the corner of Hope Park Terrace, and crossed to buy a paper. 'CONSCRIPTION' said the placard. Ian brought his loose change from his pocket and handed over a penny. He took his paper and opened it at the centre page, edging into the bank doorway to keep out of the rain. Conscription. It was here. Reality hit him.

In the parlour, Zelek was holding court to his mother and his sister Sarah, now an attractive, auburn, hard-faced young woman of twenty-two. Moshe sat at the end of the table with his latest batch of clocks and watches, poking lovingly at a travelling clock with his penknife.

'You know Izzy Levene?' said Zelek. 'A *shlemiel*, shop full of rubbish, he doesn't know half of what's in it – so the boys sell him everything they can't get rid of. And he's so soft he takes it from them.' A rising inflection, a shrug and an arm-gesture vividly conveyed the shlemiel and the situation. 'Under his bed, in boxes, he's got a million cards of hairpins.'

'Hairpins!' said Sarah.

Zelek went on, 'He's bought them, it's been the big laugh.'

'But Zelek –'

'Right,' said her brother. 'Now there's no hairpins in Scotland. They're not making any more. I'm telling you, Izzy Levene's a rich man. He's cornered the market. A penny card of hairpins, he's charging a shilling.'

There was a pause for wonder from the women. Even Moshe looked up.

'Get me some,' demanded Sarah.

'Go and ask him.'

'I will.' Then she looked sideways at Zelek. 'What happened to the pencils?'

'Shah!' Rivka shushed her.

Moshe, peering into his clock, said, 'Everybody's got pencils. He'll no' sell his pencils.'

This rankled with Zelek. 'It was a whim of the market.'

'Is that what you call it?' Sarah's voice had a thin kind of cackle at times.

'You'll see,' comforted Rivka, 'you'll sell de pencils. To Izzy Levene. If he's a shlemiel, he'll buy dem. Go on, try.'

Zelek thought about it. 'It's an idea.'

The outside door banged.

'Who ees dat?'

Ian, in the lobby, announced that it was him.

'Zelek,' said Rivka, 'have you ony pennies for de meter?'

'An' a shilling for me?' asked Sarah.

Zelek, the generous one, emptied his pocket. He picked out three pennies for his mother, and tossed a shilling over the table to Sarah.

Ian came in carrying his newspaper.

'Have you seen?'

'Vot? Vot's in de paper?'

'Conscription.'

'Vot?'

Zelek seized the paper from his brother and unfolded it and opened it. Sarah read over his shoulder. Moshe and Rivka sat hunched in their places, waiting.

'It was coming,' said Ian.

Zelek read on.

'Zelek? Nu?'

'It's all right,' said Zelek. 'I'm not signing on.'

Ian turned that one over. 'You mean, the bit about conscience? You'll be a conscientious objector. On what grounds?'

'No,' said Zelek. 'The bit about essential occupations.'

'Selling pencils?'

'Is dat an essential occupation?'

Ian said, 'There's a list there. No, Ma, Zelek doesn't have an essential occupation.'

Zelek studied the list. 'I'll be a medical student.'

They were astonished. Ian said, 'A what?'

Zelek was busy reading the paper. 'I got my Highers.'

'When you were sixteen!' said Ian. 'You're twenty-five!'

'They'll take me, they're short of doctors.'

There was a short silence: the Kaydans were tasting the idea.

'A doctor,' said Moshe, slowly.

'Zelek vill make a good doctor, I always said he should be.' This from Rivka, the proud mother.

'University of Edinburgh,' said Zelek, selling himself the idea. 'Best medical school in the world.'

They were beginning to nod their approval, all except Ian. 'Who's going to pay for that?'

'I'll work my way. I'll sell at weekends.'

'Zelek,' said his brother, 'I'm an evening student. I do physics, chemistry, maths, materia medica, pharmacology – it's hard.'

'I've got brains,' said Zelek.

'Oh, ay!'

Moshe confirmed it. 'He's got.'

Zelek offered Ian his packet of Black Cat. 'Here.'

Ian took a cigarette. Zelek offered the packet to his father but Moshe gestured no, he'd stick to his rolled ones. Zelek took a cigarette himself, lit up, and threw the vestas box to Ian.

'Anyway,' he said, 'I'm a Jew. You can't be a Jew in the army.'

'Yes, you can,' said Ian, exhaling and coughing at the same time. 'There's a Jewish Brigade.'

They all looked at Zelek, who closed the paper, folded it deliberately and placed it on the table. He took the cigarette from the corner of his mouth. 'I'll be a better Jew when I'm a doctor.'

Ian went to sit in the chair beside him. 'You're going to work your way for five years? That's a medical course if you pass right through.' He gave a nod at Sarah. 'Who's going to pay for her wedding? And Lala's and Queenie's?'

'I haven't been asked yet,' said Sarah. 'Nor has Lala.'

'I thought we were saving up?'

Zelek turned on him. 'What do you want me to do – save up in the army? Till I'm dead?'

Rivka said persuasively, 'Kveenie von't need anyting, she'll stay at home mit me.'

'And I see you're all right,' added Zelek. 'Pharmaceutical apprenticeship.'

Ian flicked the ash from his cigarette. 'I've asked not to be put on the list of essential occupations. I'll be conscripted.' In the astounded silence which followed, he took a deep drag on his cigarette, inhaled deeply for the pleasure of it, and coughed it out. 'What do they put in these? Sheep-dung?'

Moshe spoke first, with a face of thunder. 'You vill vot?'

'I'm going to be conscripted,' said Ian boldly. 'I'm making the gesture to fight for my king and country.'

'Du host an essential occupation!' roared Moshe.

'I can still offer to fight.'

'Shlomo,' wailed his mother, 'vot are you doing? Shlomo!'

Zelek said, 'You're mad. Read the casualty list.' He picked up the paper and slapped it down in front of Ian.

'Is dis vy ve left *der Heim*, and came here, for you to die in de trenches?'

Ian cupped his ear. 'Eh?' he said.

'Here, read the paper,' repeated Zelek.

'Eh?' said Ian. 'I can't hear very well.'

They stared at him.

Ian continued, 'I'm no' daft, folks. They won't take a man who can only hear with one ear. I'm deaf, Pa, where you battered me when I was wee. I'm only making the gesture! I'm not actually fit for the army!'

'His ear!' said Sarah, smiling. 'They'll no' take him!'

Rivka put her hand on Moshe's arm. 'Vere you *chloppied* him for no' kenning his Torah!'

And they burst out laughing in relief, and got up and crowded round Ian and slapped him on the back and tangled his hair and Rivka kissed him.

'Don't you think they'll take me?' asked Ian. 'Why not?' He straightened up and put on the tones of a sergeant-major. 'Pass the message down the line, Kaydan!' And in his own Edinburgh voice and cupping his ear, 'Eh?'

They doubled up.

'Oy veh,' said Rivka, wiping her tears. 'Oy veh – Shlomo! You fool!'

Even Moshe was laughing a little laugh. 'Dey von't take him, he's got von ear. Vell, you ken your Torah now.'

And Sarah guffawed her own haw-haw.

Ian became serious. 'That gesture will make all the difference to me.'

They calmed down. Moshe nodded and nodded and rolled himself a cigarette from his tin.

'Here,' said Rivka to Zelek, 'Give him de box.' She thrust Zelek's packet of Black Cat at Ian. 'Make your cough vorse, so ven dey test him, dey'll trow him out.'

Ian practised a cough.

'They won't take him,' said Zelek, a doctor already.

'No, dey von't.'

Rivka looked at the three pennies she still clutched in her hand. She marched to the mantelpiece and put one in the JNF box.

'A tree for Palestine.'

Ian told her, 'You're trying to buy good luck.'

'No,' said his mother. 'I'm saying, Please God, tenk you.' She put the other two pennies in as well.

11

The drill-hall was cold but sweaty, goose-pimples on arms and legs, and sweaty feet. Men stripped to the waist waited in long lines for their turn at a table where officers sat and orderlies wrote and sergeants hustled.

'Move along,' bellowed a big man in whiskers with a rod under his arm. 'I said strip to the waist!' The cowering little man he addressed had kept his grey vest on to hide his ribs; now he plucked it off and the sergeant-major eyed him and strutted off to do battle with a new crowd of men who stood bunched round the door.

Ian was in one of the queues, stripped to the waist, and talking to his friend Harry. Harry was fair and the same age as himself. There was a forced jollity to hide the tension.

'A cough mixture for Mrs Smellie,' Ian was saying, 'and her husband came to collect it. He's a wee nyaff.' And he went on to tell Harry of his dream come true. 'So *I* said, "Are you Smellie?" He said "Ay", so I said "What are you going to do about it? Bar o' soap?" '

Harry didn't believe it. 'Away!'

But Ian hadn't expected to be believed. They watched a wee man waddling away past them, trailing his clothes, harried by the sergeant.

'Other end! If you can last that long! The urinal is out-side!'

The wee man broke into a trot and went through the door at the end.

'Rejected,' said Harry. 'Too wee.'

Ian said, 'He can sue them, you know.'

'What for?'

'For building the floor too near his arse.'

Harry laughed and the sergeant bellowed in their ears, 'Move along there, all the handsome ones!'

They shuffled one pace towards the table.

Ian looked at his friend. 'You'll have to tell them about your freckles.'

'They can see them. What's wrong with them?'

Ian looked around, then whispered, 'They glow at night.'

'Shut up, Ian!'

'Next!' bellowed the sergeant. 'And you!'

Harry stepped forward to be examined.

'And you!' said the sergeant.

Ian said, 'Eh?'

The sergeant squared his shoulders and stepped round to face Ian. He put his nose very close to Ian's nose, and shouted, 'Next.'

'Sorry,' explained Ian, 'I don't hear too well.'

He presented himself to the waiting doctor at the desk, and could feel the sergeant's eyes on him. He put his hand up to his mouth and coughed. 'Excuse me. Just a cold.'

The orderly took his card and read out, 'Kaydan, Ian Solomon. Twenty years three months. Height six feet no inches. Weight ten stone and a quarter pounds.'

The doctor stood up and examined Ian visually. Then he palpated Ian and percussed him.

Ian coughed.

The doctor told him to stop coughing.

'Pardon?' said Ian.

The doctor gave him a look, then listened to Ian's chest with his stethoscope.

'Take a deep breath.'

'Pardon?' said Ian. 'I don't hear very well.' He indicated his deaf ear.

'Breathe in,' said the doctor more loudly.

Ian breathed deeply, and coughed.

'How long have you had a cough?'

'Pardon? I'm deaf in one ear. I hope it's all right.'

'I am not examining your ear! I am examining your chest! Now!'

Harry was pleased with himself. He had been examined with few questions and had been graded A-1. Now he sat on one of the benches at the end of the hall and put his clothes on among all the other chattering men.

He caught sight of Ian stumbling across from the queues, to pick up his clothes.

'Ian!' he shouted.

Ian saw his friend. He came to the benches and sank down in a tremble.

'They haven't tested my hearing!'

'That's all right then,' said Harry. 'You're through, you've passed.'

'But I'm deaf!'

'And they missed it. Cameronians for us!' He grabbed Ian by the shoulders in his joy.

Ian was nearly crying. '*Oy a cholairie* . . . !' He broke into spontaneous Yiddish to wish a shit-plague on the doctors and the sergeant and the army.

The orderly at the side desk handed a card to the sergeant. The sergeant read it and called, not in his loudest voice, 'Ian Solomon Kaydan.'

Ian looked up, took his clothes and walked across the hall to the sergeant.

The sergeant eyed him. 'You heard that, did you? Deaf in one ear, eh? I know your type!' A curling lip, almost a spit.

Ian had betrayed himself and felt sick in his gut.

The sergeant pointed to the doctor sitting alone at the side table. 'Go and see him.'

Ian went to the table.

The orderly asked him his name.

'Kaydan,' said Ian. Then added, 'Pardon, did you ask my name?'

The clerk looked at his ledger, found a card to correspond, and handed it to the doctor. 'Kaydan, Ian Solomon.'

The doctor took the card, studied it, looked up.

'Kaydan? Ian Solomon?'

Ian played his despairing game to the end. 'Pardon? I'm sorry, could you speak up? Sir?'

The doctor was silent, then spoke slowly and distinctly. 'Have you got a doctor of your own?'

Ian decided that the game was over. 'No,' he said.

'If I were you,' said the doctor, 'I'd go and see one.' He handed Ian his card. 'Your grade is C-three. We can't take you, Kaydan.'

Ian tried to read what it said on the card, but his hand was shaking so, the writing was blurred.

The doctor added, 'You've got T.B. Consumption.'

When Ian arrived home in a state of utter dejection, there was a bubbling sound that was now heard often in the house. He shut the front door softly behind him and followed the sound into the kitchen.

Rivka was asleep in the chair by the fire. Ian looked at the gleaming new copper tank in the corner above her.

'Ma?'

Rivka woke. 'So?'

'Your tank's boiling.'

He went to the sink and turned on the new hot tap. There was a whoosh of steam, then boiling water gushed out.

'So?' said Rivka.

'Waste of water, waste of coal.'

'De army?' was what his mother wanted to know.

'I'm rejected.'

He sat down opposite to her.

Rivka studied him. 'Vy are you sad? You knew.'

'It's not my ear Ma. It's my chest. They told me to see a doctor, so I've been to Dr Gibb on my way home. He says I've got consumption.'

Rivka's eyes widened with horror. 'How bad?' She believed and she didn't believe. 'Go and ask him how bad!'

'I asked him . . . He says I've got six months to live.'

There is nothing to say when your son makes that statement: Rivka sat in dazed silence as Ian got himself out of the chair and turned the water off. He went out of the kitchen, leaving her to absorb it.

Ian felt that his whole energy had been drained out of his body. He went into the boxroom and turned the tap on in the bath, and let the waste-plug down so that the bath started to fill.

Two weeks ago it had been installed. Queenie had been turned out of the room and now shared a bedroom with the other girls. In went the drains and the pipes, and then the lavvy and the bath and the basin. It had to be demonstrated, so Queenie, the youngest, was chosen for this. But Queenie was an early maturer, and bulged all over. With many screeches and bubbles and near-drowning, she had peed down the water-closet and completed her toilet in the bath. By the time Rivka dried her afterwards she had been hysterical.

But now the bathroom was taken as a natural part of the house. Ian got the temperature right, undressed, stepped in, lay brooding on his fate and fell asleep.

Next morning he got himself to work but was unable to do anything but huddle by the fire in the back shop and sip from a cup of tea. Being told he was mortally ill made him feel mortally ill; he was weary in every tissue.

The bell jangled in the shop as a customer departed. Kyle came through to the back shop and inspected his apprentice.

'Go on, then.'

Ian stifled a cough. He talked huskily. 'My sister died of consumption when she was fourteen, I was eight. The Doctor said the house we lived in was full of it. I must have had it then, and it's galloping now.' The cough burst from him and he had a long bout that doubled him up and left him wheezing.

'What exactly did Dr Gibb say?'

'He said I'm a Chinaman.'

'What?'

'He called me Wun Lung Gone. And one to go.'

'But you haven't been bad,' Kyle expostulated. 'You've coughed a bit but you've been up and about.'

'That's the way of it.'

Kyle chewed his moustache. 'Ian, you're a good apprentice to me. You're not all that sick, all of a sudden.'

'Gibb said I'm showing the signs it's starting to eat me up.'

Consumption was a killer. The chemist knew that, he had lost friends when they and he were Ian's age.

'What did Gibb recommend?'

Ian stared into the fire. 'Oh, eat, drink and be merry . . .'

'I don't believe you!'

'He said . . . if I got out to the country, maybe – how the hell can I go to the country? Pardon the language.' He felt for his cigarettes, brought them out, looked at them.

'What are you doing?'

'I might as well enjoy what's left.'

Reaching out for the packet, Kyle took it and threw it into the fire.

'Here –!' said Ian, roused at last.

Kyle said, 'I'm going to write to a friend of mine, up in Banff, in the hills.'

'Don't be daft, I've no money.'

'Muir's his name. He's got a shop, he's in his seventies, he can't get an articled apprentice there. You can't kid me you're fit for work yesterday and not today! Go and do two hours a day for him and take to your bed the rest of the day. Ian, if you want to enjoy it while it lasts, get up to the fresh air!'

Kyle wrote his letter, warmly recommending his apprentice and briefly stating the circumstances, adding that Ian was well aware of the rules of hygiene and of the need to keep his infection to himself.

Muir replied by return, saying that he would be glad of such assistance. So Ian prepared to move to the wilds of north-east Scotland. Zelek's age-group had not been called up yet, but he had applied for a place at Surgeon's Hall and had been accepted for the following September, safely and essentially occupied.

Another young man in the Edinburgh Hebrew Community, also with an eye on the future, had taken an apprenticeship with a dentist: no articles and no signing, he just watched the dentist and helped. Auburn-haired Sarah had had dental treatment from him and had taken a fancy to him.

On the day that Ian packed for leaving home, Isadore Stein came round to talk a little business with the Kaydans. The negotiations took place in the kitchen, with Zelek and Isadore the main protagonists. Moshe sat in the judgement seat and Sarah waited for the judgement. Rivka sat in her chair by the fire.

There was a bottle of whisky on the table, and glasses for the men. Ian quietly packed his suitcase on the floor beside the sink.

'Nobody,' Isadore was saying, 'gets married on credit. Sarah and me get on very well, we love each other so it's a pity not to get married.' He was a plumpish, easy-going twenty-five, with some ginger in his dark curly hair and a shrewdness which he tried to conceal.

Moshe nodded in agreement and pronounced the judgement: 'Dis is true.'

Zelek said, 'I can see that, but you can't even support her.'

'I can support her,' said Isadore, 'if I had a dental practice. You know I'll do more than support her, she'll be comfortable. With a bit of luck we'll both be very comfortable, and bring up your grandchildren.'

'Haud your horses, Isadore. There's no grandchildren yet. I hope.'

'Oh, now, Zelek . . . !' Isadore professed shock at the thought of any such behaviour.

'Stupid!' said Sarah. Isadore was a *mensch*, wasn't he? She looked at him. He was a Jewish man anyway, and not repulsive.

'I mean,' said Isadore, 'this is nothing new. It's the custom for the bride's family to provide a *nedan* for her.'

'For de right person,' Moshe stressed.

Sarah said, 'He is right.'

'Shah!' said Moshe.

'Shah!' repeated her mother.

Zelek put his elbows on the table. 'You're not a qualified dentist.'

Isadore made a deprecating series of gestures. 'Let's get it straight, Zelek. I've worked for Mr Spence for three months, I've watched him, I've taken teeth out for him, I've made plates for him. What's she wearing in her mouth?'

And Sarah flashed her upper set and lower set for them all to see.

'All I need to do is put my name up in brass, in the right place in the right street, and we're off. Isadore Stein, Dentist, and they'll come pouring in. There's the Jewish Congregation alone'll keep me. Zelek, no offence, but I could do as good as that.' He referred to Zelek's dentures, which had always given a bit of trouble.

Moshe spoke from the judgement seat, where he sat hunched over his tobacco tin, picking the stub end of a cigarette from his yellow ivory holder with a pin: 'A kvestion, Isadore.'

Isadore was all attention.

'Vy five hundred pounds?'

Isadore nodded patiently. 'To buy the surgery and the equipment, and have a nice waiting room, you know.'

Ian stood up with his suitcase. 'I'm going now.'

No one heard him.

Moshe said, 'Ve havenae got five hundred pounds.'

'That's what I'm saying,' said Isadore, 'it's a pity.'

'But,' said Moshe, 've'll pay by de veek.'

'A nedan, on credit?'

Ian said, 'I hope it works out. Give my love to Lala and Queenie.' (Lala was at work, Queenie at school.)

Realising at last that her son was saying goodbye, Rivka got up and embraced him.

'Oh Shlomo, you'll write, every veek, and you'll get vell.'

She made to kiss him but he moved his head. 'Not on the lips.' She hugged him.

The others began to say their goodbyes, too.

'All the best, Ian,' said Isadore. 'The very best of . . . health now.'

'Thanks.'

Zelek wasn't saying goodbye. 'I'll be up to see you.'

'Right.'

'Soon.'

'Right.'

Sarah said, 'Goodbye, Ian.'

'Goodbye, Sarah. All the best.'

'Yes. And you.'

'Ay.'

Moshe got up from the table and clasped him. He could not say anything.

'Goodbye, Pa,' said Ian. 'I'll write.'

He went out to the lobby with his case.

They all sat down again at the table.

'Poor Ian,' said Isadore.

'He's got a chance,' said the medical Zelek, who had read about it.

'Ay . . . !' agreed Isadore, willing the optimism.

There was a silence. Zelek broke it.

'How much did you say you've got to put down?'

'I didn't,' said Isadore. 'I've got a hundred, but if I put it down, what'll we live on? It'll take a few months, you know, a year maybe.'

Zelek spoke rapidly. 'I'll pay you two pounds a week for

five years. I'll pay her, Sarah, and that's your house-keeping.'

Rivka chimed in with a new thought. 'Vy can't Zelek be a dentist, instead of a student?'

'Because I want to be a doctor, I know nothing about dentistry.'

Isadore sighed a big sigh. 'Well, if you don't have five hundred –' He resigned himself to losing his love.

Ian listened to the conference from the lobby. Sarah was appealing to Moshe and Moshe was saying, '*Ich hob nisht! Ich hob nisht!*' Sarah appealed to Zelek, and Zelek's offer stood at two pounds a week. Isadore said no, he wasn't *meshuggie*. No nedan, no marriage.

'It's a pity,' said Moshe.

'Sarah's a good girl,' said Rivka.

'A dentist's a good business,' said Isadore.

'If you vould be a dentist,' said Rivka, 'you need a good vife, like Sarah.'

There was a sudden silence. Ian had buttoned his coat and put his hat on. Moshe came out to the lobby.

'Have you got your tsitsis?'

'Yes.'

'And your tephillim?'

'Yes.'

'And your tallis?'

'Yes.'

'You'll find a shool?'

'Pa, there's no shool for a hundred miles.'

Another hug, and Ian opened the front door and left.

Ian spent most of the train journey looking at his own reflection in the window. Sometimes he looked beyond, at the blue water of the Forth or the rolling hills of Fife. He coughed a lot.

The village in Banff was far, far away from the front line. It lay at the edge of a wooded slope and Mr Muir's chemist's shop, with the baker's and the general store next door, served a wide and sparse hinterland.

The shop was built of grey stone and its window was an ordinary house window looking out over the village street. Ian lived in the flat above it. He had a living-room and a bedroom. The kitchen was down the wooden stairs and served as the back shop; it had a pleasant medicated smell. A stout old body, Mrs MacIntyre from across the way, came in for an hour each evening and did his cooking and laundry and cleaning.

The shop was open in the mornings to take in prescriptions and give out medicines. The rest of the time was Ian's own. In an emergency, of course, he could be knocked up by anyone. Old Mr Muir doddered in once or twice a week to check the prescriptions but he was well pleased with his new assistant and had faith in him. Ian was not supposed to have the key of the poisons cupboard but this was a matter of a wink and an understanding.

He slept a great deal, because of the change of air and his own weakness. To stop himself brooding – and he was aware of the dangers of this – he travelled into Banff every so often to borrow books from the library, and bought more books, till his living-room spilled over with them.

One big change that he noticed here, taking an hour or so of his first day trying to identify it, was the silence. There were no clocks ticking in this house; and he kept it that way.

One evening he was sitting by the fire, reading *Mr Polly* by H. G. Wells, when he heard the sounds of preparation in the kitchen below. It was supper time. He got up and put another log on the fire. Even this effort brought on a small fit of coughing. He sat down again.

Footsteps on the stairs outside. A knock on the door.

'Come in, Mrs MacIntyre.'

The door opened and it wasn't Mrs MacIntyre. It was a freckled girl of about seventeen, in Mrs MacIntyre's apron, and carrying a steaming tray. She came to the table and put the tray down and set out the supper.

Ian didn't hide his surprise. 'Where's Mrs MacIntyre?'

'She had to go and look after her mother, so she asked if I would see to you tonight.'

There was a plate of fish and potatoes, a teapot, milk, sugar, bread, butter, scones, oatcakes and honey.

Ian inspected it, then the lass with the soft, northern voice.

'What's your name?'

'Greta Buchan.'

'Buchan. You're not Mrs MacIntyre's daughter?'

'No. I'm her niece, she's my auntie. There's trout for you, is that all right?'

'Ay,' said Ian.

'Only she said you were particular.'

'With some things.'

'No meat.'

'No.'

'Well, that's fish.'

'Fine.'

'No lard.'

'No. What's the trout been fried in?'

'Butter.' A defiant note, as if asking him to question it.

He didn't. 'Fine. Thank you very much. I haven't even seen you in the shop.'

'No. Well . . .' She went to the door. 'I'll wait downstairs till you finish. Then I'll wash up.'

'Is that what your auntie said?'

'Yes.'

Ian sat himself at the table. Greta didn't go, she stayed to watch him.

Ian, for something to say, to reach through to her, asked, 'Do you read?'

'Not much.'

'I've got a lot of books here.'

'So I see.'

'You're welcome to try some.'

She was silent, waiting till he took up his knife and fork. Then she said, 'Why don't you eat meat?'

132

Ian put his knife and fork down. A far-reaching question, he would have to answer it. 'I'm a Jew,' he said. 'We have laws about what we eat.'

'I heard you were. I heard that Jews drink babies' blood.'

Ian's mouth went dry. He looked down at his thin hands, which were trembling.

'No,' he said. 'I've never drunk babies' blood. Never.'

Greta stood in the doorway. 'I wouldn't be friends with a Jew.' She shut the door after her.

Ian sat letting his food get cold.

12

When he went to bed that night in the cold wooden bedroom with the cream-painted ceiling, Ian felt a mixture of rage and despair at the waste of him. He tried to make himself cry, but could not. He cuddled the wrapped-up stone hot-water bottle, and pleaded with God: to make him whole; to give him love. Tiredness overtook him and he fell asleep and woke up sweating with fever.

The spring sunshine made the woods a place of wonder for Ian. He went for slow walks and gazed at the vistas of green and brown with the hills beyond, and thought that eternity was now. He didn't recognise all the birds in the trees but he tried to memorise the birdsong and listened for the pattern of notes day by day. He marvelled at the banks of colour the flowers made, and then at the individuality of each one. And he coughed.

One evening after a paroxysm which left him out of breath and kneeling on the ground, he heard the crackle of twigs. He looked up and saw Greta walking along the track. She passed him, giving him a glance.

He got up. 'Hello.'

Greta stopped. Then turned. 'Hello.'

Again the defiance. Ian felt the challenge.

'I was just having a walk,' he said.

'Well, I'm going home.' But she stayed where she was and made no move to turn on her way again.

'Where d'you live?'

'Bonnyburn.' As if to say, what's he going to make of that?

Ian said, 'I like the trees you have here.'

She looked up at them, then back at him.

Ian added, 'And the flowers.'

'They're daffodils.'

'Do you know the poem about daffodils?'

'No.'

Ian decided not to recite it. It was the wrong sort of poem.

'Or the one about trees?'

'No,' said Greta, her feet planted apart, her head to one side, her skirt swinging just a little. She was staying to talk.

Ian recited, 'Round the corner, behind the tree. Say that.'

'Round the corner, behind the tree.'

'The sergeant-major, he said to me.'

Greta repeated that line too.

Ian decided not to go on with it.

'Said what?' asked Greta.

'You're very pretty.'

She stood looking at him and he knew she had never been told so before.

'You're as pretty as daffodils.'

She kept very still, looking straight at him.

'Pretty as . . . a poem.'

And so they looked at each other, without moving. At last Ian said, 'Safe journey.'

'Why shouldn't it be safe?'

'You know the story of Little Red Riding Hood?'

'Yes, I do.'

Another long silence while they stared at each other from a safe distance.

'*Au revoir*,' said Ian.

'What does that mean?'

'It means, till we meet again.'

Greta said, 'I'm coming to make your tea tomorrow.'

'*Au revoir* then.' Calm words to cover the tingling all through his body.

'*Au revoir* then.' But she stood there.

He inquired with his eyes. She inquired back at him.

He turned and walked along the path for a little, then stopped and looked back. She stayed where she was. He turned again, slowly, and walked on. When he turned again she had gone.

He took a deep breath, coughed on it, and walked home.

In the morning Ian got up at his usual time, took off his striped flannel pyjamas and shivered into his woolly vest and long-johns, his *ghatkies*. He put his coat over his shoulders and went down to boil the kettle. He came up, poured the hot water into the basin and modified it with cold from the ewer. He sat on the edge of his unmade bed to shave.

He dried his face, pulled on his trousers, smelled his shirt, then put it on. Then he brought his yamulkeh from the top drawer of the chest of drawers, with his prayer-book and the red-velvet bag that held his tallis and tephillim and tsitsis.

He put the yamulkeh on the back of his head, and said the blessing for putting on the tallis, half in earnest, half ironically. What had God done for him so far? The Jews had made a covenant with the Almighty, but a bargain had to be kept by both sides.

'*Boruch atoh adounoy* . . .' he intoned. God had commanded him to wrap himself in a fringed garment.

He put his tallis round his shoulders, and proceeded with the prayers and the complicated sequence of putting on tephillim, on the arm, the head, and the hand.

He continued with the morning service while he put his shoes on, and wandered round the room, looking out of the window down the village street, and hiding to one side when anyone passed and looked up.

The ritual took half an hour if he rattled through it. It was mostly psalms, and the Sh'ma Yisroel, and more praises. There was very little meaning in the way he said it but the repetition, when it was done, made him feel good, in communion with the Great Being and with other

Jews, and he rewarded himself with a breakfast of bread and butter and marmalade and good brown tea.

That evening, Greta brought his supper of boiled eggs and toast and the scones and oatcakes and jam to round it off with. They said little, and she waited downstairs while he ate. Then he took his seat by the fire and pretended to read a book till she came to clear away.

The sound of ascending steps, a knock on the door.

'Come in.'

She came in, shut the door behind her, leaned against it.

'Have you finished your tea?'

'Yes, thank you.'

'Were the eggs right?'

'Very good eggs.'

She came to the table, picking up the tray from against the wall where she had left it. She started to put the dishes on the tray.

'I've got a message for you. Could you make Mrs Gregor's pills not so bitter?'

'Did Mrs Gregor tell you to say that?'

'Yes, she did so.'

'I can't do it,' said Ian the lawful pharmacist. 'I only make up what the doctor writes in his prescription.'

'Oh,' said Greta, 'because when old Mr Muir makes up her pills, he puts sugar in.'

'Well, I could,' said Ian, considering it, 'but I won't. Mr Muir can do what he wants. He's the master, I'm not. I'd get into trouble.'

'Oh,' said Greta. She bent low over the table and looked round at him. 'Do you put poison in?'

'No,' said Ian firmly.

'Oh. Do you have a cure for warts?' She continued loading the tray.

'Yes. Who's got a wart?'

'Me,' said Greta.

Ian was very interested indeed. 'Where?' he asked.

'On my hand.'

'Show me.'

'No.'

'I can't cure it if I don't see where it is.'

'I'm shy.'

'Come here,' said Ian. 'Leave your tray.'

She straightened up and went to him. He took her hand, cool and rough-skinned. He felt it, stroked it. 'Where? I don't see a wart.'

'There. You've passed it.'

He peered at her hand. 'That's a very wee wart. D'you think it'll go away if I stroke it?'

Greta answered in a small voice, 'I don't know . . .'

'I can hardly see it,' said Ian, 'it's so wee.'

'I don't like it.'

Ian said, 'There's a far bigger one.'

'Where?'

'There.' He pointed to her nipple under her blouse.

She looked down. 'That's not a wart.'

He found the other and stroked them both and they didn't go away, and he said he'd have to look for more. She was eager to be searched, for she hated warts, and they went through to the bedroom for a check-over. And she said she didn't mind if she checked him for warts, too, and it was easier to do in the bed, and then she wanted to kiss him.

He said not to kiss him on the mouth because she might get his cough, but she didn't care and lay on him and kissed him and kissed him and thrust at him with her body; and he took the mastery and reached the paradise he'd dreamed of, which was wildly beyond his dreams.

They slept together all night, making love half asleep, half awake. Ian woke with the dawn chorus, and slipped out of bed and put on his woollies, gazing at her red hair on the pillow, her mouth open in sleep. He went down for hot water with the image of her still present in his mind.

He came up with the kettle, and shaved. He could see in the mirror that she was awake and watching him.

'You'd better get up. What'll Mr Muir say?'

Greta pulled the blankets up to her chin. 'He's that blind he wouldn't see me.'

'Come on up.' He dried his face and turned to her.

'Turn away.'

'No.'

'I'll not get up then.'

He gazed down at the vision, grey blanket, white pillow, freckled nose, grey eyes, curly red hair. He took a corner of the blanket and whisked it off. She screamed and snatched it back to cover the fuller vision.

'What's the matter? Last night –'

'That was different, it was dark. Turn away.'

Obediently he turned.

'And that mirror.'

He sighed and turned the mirror to the wall. He opened his drawer to find a clean pair of socks, and looked down at the red velvet tallis bag and the prayer book. He turned to her again.

She clutched the blanket to her. 'No!' she said. 'I'll wait till you go out the room.'

'You'll have a long wait.' He put his yamulkeh on, took out the tallis and tephillim, and said the first blessing. *'Boruch atoh adounoy elouhainu melech ho'oulom . . .'*

She watched with fascination as he put on his tallis, and then his tephillim.

He turned to face her as he continued the morning prayers, lifted her blouse and knickers from the floor and gave them to her, whipped off the blankets good and proper where she couldn't get them back, and watched unashamedly as she scrambled into her clothes. Blessed was the Lord his God, King of the Universe, who formed man in wisdom, and created in him many orifices and vessels. Fair was fair.

13

'. . . They say that people with TB have extra desires. It's true and I'm very ill. It's making me exhausted and I'm not getting the sleep I should be getting.'

The letter had just arrived, addressed to Zelek, and he was reading it to himself. It had interrupted another Kaydan conference. The parlour was full. Isadore sat with Sarah now at his side. Moshe presided at the head of the table, with Rivka beside him. Lala sat opposite her sister Sarah, and Sarah's opposite indeed she was, dark and slim and bright and lovely at eighteen. The dumpling at the foot of the table was Queenie, because that's what Sarah had called her; Zelek had mentioned that dumplings don't have pigtails, but Queenie had them, hanging down her back.

'Nu?' asked Isadore.

Zelek folded up the letter. 'He isn't well.'

'Can I see?' Sarah put her hand out for the letter.

'No, there are – personal things.'

Lala said, 'Can I?'

'No, Lala.'

'Does he send his love?' Queenie had found the important question.

Zelek unfolded the letter again and read the end: 'Love to Ma and Pa, and Sarah and Lala and Queenie. Your loving brother, Ian.'

'He's no' earning nutting.' Moshe brought the conference back to the point.

'I thought he was?' said Isadore.

'Vell . . .' said Moshe, and shrugged to indicate the finite term of Ian's earning capacity. 'Consumption . . .'

'So,' Isadore sighed, 'we've gone to the end of the road. We've kept right on to the end, and this is it.'

Zelek put the letter in his pocket. 'A hundred and fifty, and two pounds a week for three years.'

'Four years,' cut in Isadore with his finger raised.

'In four years,' – Moshe's eyes were at their most hooded – 'Lala vill need, Kveenie vill need.'

Isadore was frankly incredulous. 'Queenie?'

'Maybe,' said Rivka bravely. 'Who knows?'

'I thought,' said Isadore, 'that Queenie was staying at home.'

Queenie echoed, 'Maybe, who knows?' She was a good echo.

Zelek's eyes were on Isadore. 'And we can't pawn Ian's future. He can't raise money.'

Isadore came back with, 'But Lala's working now.'

'She needs it!' said Moshe. 'I said.'

'Well,' huffed Isadore in resignation, 'we'll say goodbye then. I need a practice, I'm no use without one.' He made a last appeal. 'Zelek –'

'I've got fees to pay. And stock to buy. I don't know where I can raise a hundred and fifty.'

'You can pay off when you qualify. That's only five years away, Zelek.'

'He'll pay de hundred and fifty in five years.'

'Aw, now –' To Isadore this was going into the realms of the preposterous.

Sarah said, 'Please?'

But Zelek was firm. 'That's the limit, Isadore.'

'Well, it's off then. We've got to face facts.'

'Hundred and sixty,' said Moshe.

They all looked at him. Queenie breathed, 'Hurray!'

Isadore said nothing, then he nodded. 'And two pounds a week for three and a half years.'

They looked at each other. Zelek scribbled figures on the writing pad in front of him. They watched.

'Forty months,' said Zelek.

Sarah looked at her beloved. 'Isadore?'

Isadore said, 'No.'

'Finish. That's that.'

'It's a dentist you're getting. A new set for you,' – he nodded to Rivka – 'for the girls when their time comes. A dentist in the family.'

'A quack,' said Zelek.

'Now, Zelek –!'

'Quack, quack. It's off.'

'Three and a half years.'

'Forty-one months.'

'All right.'

A silence in the room. A gasp for air from all of them. Then it was handshakes and hugs and mazeltovs. Rivka hugged Sarah and went straight to the JNF box and brought it round, shaking it for all to contribute.

'Coom, put something in de *pushkie*.'

And amid the hugging, the men dipped into their pockets for pennies and put them into the blue box.

The wedding was arranged for September. Zelek started his medical training, and the week before the wedding he went on a sales trip up the east coast, and made a detour to meet Ian.

They had lunch together above the chemist's shop, served by Mrs MacIntyre. Zelek asked all the searching questions about the stages of Ian's illness, and remarked on how well he looked. Ian answered that he had been given six months to live and he had already had five of them. He'd always been good at counting.

Zelek pressed him to come home for the wedding but Ian did not feel up to it. But he walked Zelek to the station; Zelek was going to do Elgin that afternoon, and Forres and Nairn next morning and Inverness in the afternoon. And swot on the train.

'All this country could be opened up. I mean, chemist's

shops – I could do . . . sponges, perfumes, what an opening.'

'How's medicine?'

'Interesting. Anatomy this year – I'll have to stick at it. God knows how we're going to live.'

'Does he?'

'Who?'

'God.'

Zelek turned to look again at his brother. 'You are coughing less.'

Ian obliged him with a paroxysm that left him limp on the ground. Zelek sat beside him.

'I'm so tired.'

'Well, all these shiksies . . .'

Ian said nothing. There had only been the one; many, many times, it was true.

Zelek asked, 'Have you any money?'

'Nuh,' said Ian.

'None at all?'

'About two quid.'

'Can I have it? For Sarah.'

Ian looked up. 'A hundred and sixty quid for Sarah to marry, and nothin' to send me to a sanatorium!'

Zelek bit on a stem of grass. He chewed and spat. 'Ian, we're up to our ears . . .'

'I'm six feet deep!' Ian was very bitter; Zelek felt it and was uncomfortable.

Ian asked, 'Does anyone miss me?'

'I do.'

'But not Ma.'

'She does.'

'She always loved you best!'

Zelek admitted it. 'Ay, she did.'

Ian cradled his head in his arms on the warm turf at the side of the track. Zelek looked at his brother in compassion.

'There's a doctor in Edinburgh with an X-ray machine. He's worth a try. Come home for the wedding.'

Ian lay as he was. Zelek chewed again.

'Did you read the *Jewish Chronicle*?'

'Here? No.'

'There's a Jew that's got the Victoria Cross.'

That brought Ian's head up. 'What?'

'His name's Jack White. Comes from Manchester. He swam a river under fire to save his officer. Jack White, v.c.'

'A Jewish v.c.?'

'And he's a cousin of ours.'

'Get away – what d'you mean?'

'His mother's father, and Ma's Auntie, Bobbie Bashkie, were cousins.'

Zelek looked at his watch and had to step out for his train. Ian kept alongside, and said that maybe he would try to come after all.

The wedding was solemnised in the shool, and afterwards at the Kaydan house in Summerhall Square. They used the parlour, the lobby and the kitchen, and of course the bathroom. Rivka had filled the house with potted plants. Jostling Jews and Jewesses in their best crowded from room to room, and children scooted all over the place, even into the bedrooms where the coats lay piled on the beds and women checked their faces in the mirrors to see if they were still as beautiful as people said.

The presents were displayed in Sarah's room, and drew expressions of wonder, even as they were sized up for worth and usefulness, and 'Who was it from?' and 'It wasn't as good as the one I gave!'

Queenie went the rounds with a tray of cheesecake, and Lala with little glasses of wine. The glasses had been borrowed from the shool.

'Lovely cheesecake? Oy . . .'

'More wine?'

'I'm Minnie,' said an angular, bespectacled, hedgehog-haired lady wearing floral droops. 'Minnie Fink – don't you remember? My father's brother married –' She calculated. '– Jack White's mother's sister!'

And Isadore, the bridegroom, was incredulous. 'Jack White?' There was a chorus of 'Yankel Veiss!' (Everybody knew his real name.)

Isadore confided, 'My grandfather and his grandmother's cousin, were brother and sister.'

Everyone present, it turned out, was related in some way to the Jewish hero. Ian listened to it as if from a great distance, leaning against the kitchen doorpost. He had come home to die, and no wedding could take his mind off that.

The parlour was Rivka and Moshe's court. Moshe was his shy, proud self; Rivka was unashamedly enjoying it, because it was her daughter's *shidduch*.

Sarah was in white. She bent to kiss her mother's brow. 'Are you all right?'

'I'm verra vell. Coom.' She drew Sarah down and kissed her on the face.

Queenie came in with a new tray of cheesecake, and still there were takers. Lala put her empty tray down. Her eye caught Zelek, standing in a corner with a well-built dark-eyed girl. Lala flashed her mother a look. Rivka was eyeing Miss Dark-eyes with deep suspicion, hostility even.

Lala crossed over to her mother and sat down on the arm of the chair. 'Zelek's got a girl.'

'So?' Rivka feigned indifference.

'She seems nice.'

Rivka pretended to look at the girl for the first time, where she was deep in conversation with Zelek.

'Who is she? Vot's her name? Find out.'

Zelek was asking her name at that very moment.

'Mary.'

'Mary? It's a lovely name, but –'

Miriam.'

'Ah.'

And Mary, from the Hebrew 'Miriam', went on to explain that her mother's mother's mother, and Jack White's mother's mother's father, were twins.

Zelek could hardly believe it. 'Then you and I are related,' he said. 'We're cousins!'

Isadore stood on a chair in the middle of the room. He tapped his wine-glass and cleared his throat.

'Eh, friends, friends –' He waited for silence, and had to wait some minutes for them all to realise that it was speech-time. They pressed in from the lobby and giggled at the door and apologised and settled into silence.

'Relatives, *machotonim*,' said Isadore.

They cheered and clapped.

'It gives me great pleasure on this happy occasion to say, on – eh, for myself and my – my wife Sarah –'

Laughs all round and applause. Ian sat slumped in a chair.

'Just to say I would like to thank Sarah's parents, Ma and Pa Kaydan, whose guests we are –'

Clapping by those with enough elbow-room. Zelek didn't have enough, but he slipped his arm conveniently round Mary's shoulder.

' . . . for making it possible for us all to be here and cele-brate this *mitzvah*. They've been so kind.'

Moshe nodded from side to side in embarrassment that this truth should be mentioned in public.

'And my parents, I'd like to thank them, and all the people who gave us lovely presents and we hope to see you in a couple of weeks in our new house, and I hope that now there's a Jewish dentist in Edinburgh, though I'm not sup-posed to advertise, well I won't but you know what I mean.'

They did know, and laughed and applauded.

Rivka's mind was elsewhere. She stared in alarm and dismay at her son's arm round the shoulder of Dark-eyes.

In the evening, when the guests had departed, and the bridal pair had been waved goodbye (the honeymoon was to be in a Jewish boarding-house in Ayr), the Kaydans sat among the debris.

Moshe was at the table smoking his Turkish tobacco, and feeling the day's events weigh heavily now. Zelek was also at the table doing his sums. Ian sat in a chair by the wall, stifling a cough. Sitting on the floor with her legs asprawl, and rocking slightly, Queenie concentrated on Lala, who was making a gesture of clearing bottles and glasses.

'You're drunk!' said Lala to Queenie, who broke into a fit of giggles.

Zelek said, 'Do you know what my weekly repayments are going to be?'

'Repayments on what?' asked Ian.

'I went to Hughie Mackay.'

'Who's he?'

'He's a money-lender! I took out ninety quid. Two per cent a month. That's half a per cent a week. Nine bob a week. A week! Interest!'

Moshe said, 'I took fifty pounds.'

'You what!'

'Ve had tae have.'

'That's another five bob. Ye gods!'

There was a pause, then Moshe cautioned, 'Shah!' as Rivka came in with a tray.

'Kveenie, get oop. Coom put de cups on.' She bustled in among them. 'So, Zelek, how vos Mary Rabinovits?' She smiled lovingly at her son.

Zelek, encouraged, said, 'She's nice.'

Rivka's smile had an icy edge. 'Good.'

Zelek didn't notice the ice, his thoughts on his earlier meeting. 'Very nice,' he expanded.

'Rabinovits?' Moshe had caught the name.

'She works in Boardman's drapery shop. A very, very nice girl.'

Ian looked up. 'With money?'

'I didn't ask.'

'Vot money?' said Moshe. 'Rabinovits, he's got no

money! He's got a barrow mit vegetables. You find somevon else, Zelek.'

Rivka was honey-sweet. 'Vy?'

Moshe exploded. 'Vy, vy, vy! Look vy!' And he lifted Zelek's notepad and brandished it and threw it violently down. 'Oy . . . Oy veh . . .' He collapsed in woe in his chair with his head in his hand, his elbow on the table. 'How ve going to pay? How ve going to live?'

Ian put his question. 'Can anyone lend me ten bob, I'll go and see the X-ray man . . . ?'

There was a silence in the room. They looked at one another.

Lala quietly said, 'I've got ten bob.'

Zelek collected his notepad and brooded over it. Rivka put a hand on his shoulder. She had decided to appear generous, because a girl dependent on a vegetable-barrow was no danger to the Kaydans at this time. 'If Zelek is in love vit a girl . . . den if she has no money . . . so?' She kissed him on the top of his head.

14

Next day the rain came, ending the golden September which seemed always to be Edinburgh's. Ian felt the chill as he walked up Hope Park Terrace and rounded the corner to wait at the car-stop. He turned his collar up and pulled his cap down and stepped back under the canopy of the Salisbury Kinema-house, stifling thought because it was unthinkable. The approaching metallic whirr took his attention from the still photographs in the display cabinet, and he held up his hand and got on. The car gripped the cable again and juddered away. It was full on both sides, nobody upstairs on a day like this; old men and women with carbuncles, women in veils with shopping baskets, Do Not Spit. Many, many poor spitters like himself.

Along South Bridge with its haberdashery shops, past the sooty grey stone of the University, then on to North Bridge.

The driver got down at the Post Office to help the pointsman shoulder the car round into Princes Street. This was for the rich. Horse-cabs, motor-cabs, a cavalcade of khaki buses filled with soldiers, Jenners with the awnings down. He got off at Castle Street, crossed and went up the hill and over.

He found Dr Tain's name on one of the brass plates, climbed the steps to the front door and pulled the bell. Clip-clop heels and a maid in black and starched cap opened to him. No, he didn't have an appointment.

He sat by the gas-fire in the oak-panelled room, lost for a few seconds in the beauty of the blue and red flickering warmth. There were photographs on the walls of battle-ships and sailing ships, and His Majesty of course, in Admiral's uniform.

Dr Tain opened the door.

'What is it?' A harsh, brusque voice from a stocky, balding man in a dark suit and shining shoes.

'Could I have a consultation please?'

'Who sent you?'

'Nobody.'

'What's wrong with you?'

'I've got T.B.'

Dr Tain examined him as if he had X-ray eyes. 'Come away in then.'

He followed the doctor along the polished wooden corridor and into the back room, panelled too, with a red patterned rug on the floor, and a desk, a couch with a white screen, and a sink. In the middle of the room was the X-ray machine, a tall contraption on iron girders, cream-painted.

'Sit here.'

Ian sat on the leather chair by the desk. He gave his name and address and occupation and his T.B. history. He stripped to the waist behind the screen and came out again. Tain felt him, tapped him, listened to him, with grunts of recognition and 'Uhuh.'

Then Ian stood against the cold screen of the X-ray, holding his arms out of the way. There was a buzz of electricity but he felt nothing. Tain donned goggles and peered at the screen.

'I see. Yes, I see. Can you cough?'

'Yes.'

'Cough then!'

Ian obliged.

'Is that it?'

'Yes, it's bad sometimes.'

'Have you not been in a sanatorium?'

'No, just in the country. Banff.'

'Are ye tired?'

'Yes.'

'But not as tired as ye've been?'

'Well –'

'Ye've got scarring on both lungs. Ye've had tuberculosis as a baby probably, and it's come back but ye're lucky. If ye give it half a chance, ye'll be over it.'

The magic words, the reality of the dream!

'What?'

'It's beginning to calcify.'

'What does that mean?'

'It means a spontaneous remission, it's healing.'

He had been given six months to live! He said so to Dr Tain.

'Who gave you six months?'

'A doctor, Dr Gibb.'

'Was he a radiographer? Did he use X-rays?'

'No.'

'Was he a chest specialist?'

'A general specialist.'

'Aha.'

There lay the explanation, tied up in a parcel by Dr Tain. He switched off the machine and the buzzing stopped.

'I'm telling ye. It's not all that uncommon. Rest, fresh air, good food, and come back in two months.'

He looked Ian in the face. Ian's jaw hung open in disbelieving exultation.

He went back to Banff for two months and came home for his check-up. He was almost clear. Another three months would do it. Greta had long since gone to England, to a munitions factory, and Morag and Annie didn't last so long; they lacked the charm that Greta had, and the warmth and the romance. Morag giggled at him, Annie yawned. He used them only for necessity.

Then home again to Mr Kyle's shop and evening classes and a step nearer the war: food rationing meant a little more in Edinburgh than it had done in the countryside.

There were the newspapers every day and rumours at every *shmuous* with a friend; and sorrows for those killed as the Western Front took its toll.

Zelek married Mary in the Dalry shool, and there were celebrations afterwards at the home of the bride's parents in Dalry Road. After sharing the glass of wine with his bride, Zelek smashed it against the wall, an older form of sealing the bond than the more genteel one of wrapping the glass up and crushing it underfoot. Ian was there to join in the shouts of 'Mazeltov!'

Next day, Kyle asked him how the wedding had gone. Ian was making pills, rolling the paste on the pill-board.

'In my small experience of weddings,' said Ian, 'I'd say it was a good one. I've got a bit of a hangover.'

'And the bride?'

'Oh, nice. I like Mary. Nice girl.'

'What's her father?'

'He's got a horse and a veg. cart. He sells the dung back to the veg. people.' He fitted the roll of paste into the prescribed groove and cut off the excess ends. 'So the wedding was higher up the social scale than Sarah's. By a split hair, I won't say whose.'

He pressed down with the divider, and cut the roll into separate pellets.

'No money,' said Kyle.

'Nuh.'

Ian rolled the pellets under the round roller and popped the finished pills into a pill-box.

'Is Zelek going to be a married student, then?'

'Oh ay. Zelek's got brains. He'll pass all his exams.'

'But what's he going to do when he qualifies? I mean, a practice costs money.'

Ian put the lid on the pill-box, and bent down to write out the label. 'He'll be all right. He's got me for a muggins brother. I'll be qualified. I'll buy him a practice.'

'It's going to be a long haul,' said Kyle.

'Ay. For all of us. You know what Zelek's packed his

152

honeymoon suitcase with? Amber beads. He'll sell 'em. They'll pay the hotel bill, and the train.'

And that turned out to be the case. Zelek saturated the south of England with amber, and drank champagne every night with a flushed as well as a blushing Mary.

When the honeymoon week was over, they came third-class back to Edinburgh, and next day came to pay their respects to the Kaydan parents. Ian was there with the rest of the family in the kitchen. There were hugs, and expressions of joy and thankfulness, and stares from Queenie, who wondered what they had been doing.

Mary remembered every detail of the hotel and the staff and the people they had met; and the flowers Zelek had bought her, and the dress, and the theatres he had taken her to. Zelek recounted the sales he had made and the money he had turned over.

'Can I ask, please,' said Rivka, 'if you've got some left? Pa's vorn out and ve have de end of a loaf! Since dis von's back' – a nod of the head to Ian – 'dere isnae enough food in de Co-op for him.'

Mary turned to Ian. 'You're still earning?'

'Yes,' said Ian. 'We're paying Isadore.' He decided not to mention the money-lenders.

'Zelek,' said his mother, 'can you give me two shillings to buy something for supper?'

It was not only the usual kind of request that had gone round the Kaydan family ever since the children had started earning, it was a device to include the new daughter in the family.

The new daughter had prepared herself. 'Now listen to me, Mrs Kaydan –'

'Vos Missus Kaydan? You are Missus Kaydan!'

Zelek sorted it out. 'You call your mother Mother, this is Ma. An' Pa.' He was glad of the diversion, and looked it.

'Ma –'

'Good!'

'And Pa.' Moshe nodded his acceptance.

153

Mary went on quietly but clearly, 'Zelek and I have set up home, in two rooms, all right, but it isn't a home yet, and that's what I'm going to do for Zelek, make a home.'

Rivka's mouth set in a straight line. She put her hands on her hips.

'It's a woman's life,' Mary explained to them all, her eyes wide open, 'a woman's right. Now Zelek is a student, and he is working very, very hard, and he's got no time to do any extras. And whatever little he earns –'

Zelek looked uncomfortable.

'– I know how liberal he is with whatever he's got, but what he earns is his, and mine, and for the future. And if we're to remain on good terms –'

They gaped at her. Zelek was looking out of the window.

'– which, please God, we will, I'm sure we will,' she assured them with her hand on her heart, 'then that's how it's to be. And I'm having no weekly hand-over, no back-handers, nothing for Palestine, or your cousin back in *der Heim*. And Ian's a grown man, and Mr –' She corrected herself, '– Pa, will have to make do. And that's how it's going to be.' She ended with a sweet smile of friendship, which was as far as it went – certainly not as far as love.

She sensed the dramatic effect of what she had said, and feeling the strain of it, she got up with dignity and walked out of the room.

Zelek hovered, distracted. 'Ma, just give it time. We'll be all right.'

He came to give his mother a hug, but she stood stiffly, and he had to make do with kissing her brow.

'Zelek?' called Mary from the lobby. He went out. The Kaydans heard the front door open and shut.

'Oy . . .' said Moshe. 'Oy veh!' And he covered his face with both hands.

Rivka sank into the chair beside him. She put her arm round his shoulder. He was too busy rocking in his sorrow to notice that her eyes were wet.

'Ve can't even pay de interest. Isadore – he'll go to law!

Oy veh!' Moshe clutched his forehead to still the beating of the drums there.

Ian said to Lala, 'You aren't thinking of getting married?'

Lala shook her head.

'Queenie?'

'Nobody's asked me.'

'Soon, soon,' said Rivka automatically. She turned to Ian. Her voice was wooden. 'You'll have to marry a rich girl.'

'That's right,' said Queenie.

Rivka hugged Moshe to her. 'Who's de new President of de Shool's brodder? He's got a furniture shop. And a daughter.'

Moshe looked up. 'Ay, he's got a daughter.'

'So? Ian vill be qualified soon. He needs a vife.'

'Alright. I speak to Levets.'

Ian whistled. 'And I'm not given the choice, like Zelek!'

'Choice?' shouted Moshe, 'Vot choice?'

Levets's daughter turned out to be unavailable to Ian. 'It's no use coming around here, Shlomo Kaydan,' said Mrs Levets, who remembered him too well from his boyhood. Ian in turn made himself unavailable to the baker's daughter from Sunderland; couldn't stand the wealthy auctioneer's daughter's breath; quite liked the daughter of the Lieutenant who came back after the war, but he proved to be unemployable – he should have stayed in the army.

He meantime relieved himself every Saturday night with a girl down Leith Street, at a cost of one shilling, in a doorway, and sometimes another one after that.

A victory parade was passing Kyle's shop with a crash of drums and the pipe band playing 'Cock of the North', as Ian came back from his graduation ceremony. He watched it as he had watched many such parades, then came in waving his red cardboard cylinder. He went through to the back shop and planked the roll down on Kyle's desk.

'Got it!'

He took the end off the roll and brought out the parchment inside. He unrolled it and read: 'Pharmaceutical Society of Great Britain. This is to certify that Ian Solomon Kaydan is admitted this day as a member of the Pharmaceutical Society.' He rolled up the parchment again, put it in the cylinder and tapped the lid on. 'Me – an M.P.S.!'

Kyle said 'Congratulations, Ian,' and held out his hand. Ian shook it warmly and with gratitude. Then Kyle indicated the presence of someone else in the back shop. Harry Cochrane stepped into view from the fireside.

'Congratulations, Ian.'

'Harry!' He was overwhelmed with delight to see his old friend again. 'It's good to see you, Harry . . .'

Harry shook hands with his left hand; he had a loose sleeve on the right. The shock of the wound hit Ian. 'What – ?'

'Last year,' said Harry, 'St Quentin. I'm all right. It's good to see you.'

'What a noise!' said Kyle, as the big drum of the band passed the shop.

Harry nodded at Ian's scroll. 'You've won a great victory, Ian.' And he meant it.

'You've won it, you mean.'

'Oh, now,' said Kyle, 'the country needs pharmacists, and you've been through the mill, Ian.'

Harry grinned at him. 'And you're in the money now.' A sad grin. 'Who wants a one-armed apprentice?'

Ian took him out of the shop to a tea-room and they talked and talked, and resumed their friendship again, but Ian went home sick at heart.

Lala had always been very close to Ian and now she was happy to let herself be used as his sounding-board.

'I'm tired of it,' he said one day when they were alone in the parlour.

156

She viewed him with compassion. 'I'm sorry for you.'

'Money, money, money. Every step up, the load's doubled. I'm a qualified chemist and I owe every penny. And the other thing's worse. You know there's a new rule in Edinburgh?'

'What about?'

'Women. If she's Jewish, and ugly, and got more than tuppence – introduce her to Ian Kaydan.' He stared out of the window, twenty-four years old.

Lala went to the heart of the matter. 'Do you want to get out of it?'

Ian was surprised at the directness of the question, the easiness of it. There could only be one answer: 'Ay.'

'Up to the north again?'

'Why do you say that?'

'Wasn't there a girl?'

'Ay, there was. A shiksie.' He smiled happily to confess his guilt, ruefully because it was over. Maybe Greta would go back, now the war was over. 'I was thinking of writing the old man, to see if he still has the shop.'

'Is there a living there? I thought it was a wee place?'

'It is. There isn't much of a living.'

'And a shiksie – you don't want to get tangled up.'

'No – no . . .' A shiksie that no one knew about was one thing, and delicious; to settle with her was a lunacy that had never crossed his mind.

'And you'd have to come home every time Ma and Pa shouted for you.'

'That's true.'

'Well, then.' That was that avenue explored.

'Well, what?'

'Are you going to look for other jobs? Your *Pharmaceutical Journal*'s full of them.'

'I know.' Ian had been looking for weeks, since long before he qualified.

Brother and sister looked each other in the eyes.

*

Rivka, dressed for summer shopping, stalked up and down in the kitchen carrying her basket with her. Queenie was bent over the sink peering down to the street below.

'He's coming!'

'Nae gelt in de hoose! How can I gae tae de store? He's coming, I vish he'd coom! Vill I give him tsorris! An hour I've been here!'

Almost her claws were out in exasperation. The front door, banged.

'Moshe! Dere's nae dinner! For vy, because you left me nae gelt!'

Moshe came in, still with his hat on, as excited as he ever got.

'Dere's a job for Ian. Boots de Chemists, in deir big shop in Princes Street. You ken how much – ? Five pounds a veek! Ve'll be all right! Is Lala in?'

He took off his hat, leaving his yamulkeh on underneath.

'In the bedroom,' Queenie informed him.

'Tell her to go to de shop, tell Ian to coom. And dere's a new butcher coming.'

'Vot butcher?' asked Rivka, slightly mollified.

'A kosher butcher.' Of course a kosher butcher, vos she meshuggie?

'Vit daughters?'

'I believe so.' He shouted, 'Lala!'

Lala was entering the kitchen, the shout was superfluous.

'Pa?'

'Tell Ian to coom hame.'

'There's a letter for you.'

She opened her bag and brought out an envelope.

'Vot?'

'A letter.'

'Who from?'

'Ian.'

Rivka said, 'Ian? Vot you mean? Vy did you no' give it to me?'

'It's addressed to Pa.'

Queenie said, 'You never told me – !'

'No, it's for Pa.'

Moshe took it, turned it over.

'You ken vot's in it.'

'Yes, I do.'

'Vot's in it?' asked Rivka impatiently.

Moshe opened it in silence. Queenie's eyes were on stalks.

Moshe read: 'Dear Pa and Ma and family, By the time you read this, I will be on the train to London –'

'London!' cried Rivka.

'On my way to Tilbury.' Moshe looked up. Tilbury! 'I have a passage booked on the P. and O. ship *Lavinia*. It sails on Friday for the east. I am going to Rangoon, in Burma. I have a post as British Resident Chemist not far from there. I will keep writing. Your loving son, Ian.'

Moshe was an old man; it took him a long time to raise his head from Ian's letter, to look at Rivka. The bitterness of life etched her face. She picked up the poker and poked the dead ashes of the fire and beat the hob.

But the world does not end when it seems like ending. The Kaydans would not starve to death, and only death is irreversible.

On the s.s. *Lavinia*, Ian found a new world to talk to and to look at: it took him nearly the whole voyage to believe that he had broken out.

15

A summer's day in Fife. A horse comes jogging along the coast road, pulling a trap full of trunks and hat-boxes and people. The driver sits up front with a bemused expression on his face; he has never carried such a load nor has he heard such talk. Behind him in the trap are the Kaydan women, and the new generation.

There is Rivka with her grandson David on her knee. He is three, the son of her own son, Zelek. Zelek's wife Mary is there, clutching the baby, little Shirley. And Lala is there, dark and beautiful and pregnant, for she is married now, too. And Queenie, not so lovely and not likely to be pregnant, twenty years old and never been kissed except as a forfeit at parties. They are all in summer dresses, and holding on to their hats and coats and scarves in case it turns cold, or wet.

The driver, in a collarless flannel shirt and peaked cap, listens and drives on. He is a professional.

They jog on with the sea behind them. It is 1923. The sorrows of the past are forgotten. When Solomon departed to the far-flung Empire, and Mary put the bar up, Moshe had had to face the facts. He called Isadore to the house and explained them, with many a shrug, and much hand-wringing and smiles and fits of sobbing: there was no way he could fulfil the dowry promises in the immediate future. Next year, please God.

Isadore, despite his pleasant and soft exterior, was no fool. He knew he could not get blood from a stone and he knew a stone when he saw one. Tight-lipped, he asked

Moshe to sign a statement of the amount owing, which Moshe readily did. Then with no more than that to his name, he reneged on his own money-lender, sent back his surgery equipment and reception room furniture to the hire-purchase firm, sold off the wedding-presents and the remaining furniture and took ship to Canada. With him went his wife Sarah (*nee* Kaydan). Isadore had an aunt in Winnipeg, and to her they went. Isadore gave up the idea of dentistry and took up the timber business, then farming, then mining. After that letters didn't come very often and it was difficult to know exactly what Isadore was doing, because Sarah said she didn't see him from one month to another. Then the letters stopped.

Zelek gave up his medical career when Ian left home: the war was truly over, so there was no more conscription, and besides, there was the whole of Scotland to be opened up with the new products that were flooding the market, and there were American firms demanding 'specialty' salesmen. Zelek was a 'specialty' salesman and he prospered. On his rounds, a lucky break at Ayr races ('Nothing venture, nothing gain,' said Zelek) brought him a treble: one hundred and forty pounds! Even Mary agreed that the money-lenders could now be paid off.

Moshe did not do so badly either, with his clocks and mending and picture-frames and chairs that had an antique look about them. Lala brought a weekly wage home and – what a *simcha*! – fell in love with the nicest fellow, Jack Lipsey, one of the Dundee Lipseys, whose mother had been born not ten miles from Rivka in Lithuania. So they had the happiest wedding, just after *Chanukah*, the winter festival of light, and now Lala was seven months pregnant.

The horse and trap with the lucky Kaydans rounded the brow of a hill. The whole of Fife is little hills, with white rocks pushing through the rich green grass.

'Have you got de return tickets?' asked Rivka.

'Yes,' said Lala, 'in my bag.'

They had caught the train at Edinburgh (Waverley)

with barely half an hour to spare, had loaded the trunk into the guard's van, and kept the cases and hat-boxes for their own compartment. The train had puffed across the Forth Bridge with the lovely blue sea far below, and the Bridge had not given way under them. Then round by Inverkeithing to Aberdour, and shouting along the platform for the train to wait till all the luggage had been unloaded. Then the puff-puff went away, all gone, bye-bye puff-puff, and they found the man with the horse and cart.

The horse plodded up a hillock and at the top they were blinded by the brilliance of the sun on the sea. Queenie inhaled deeply. 'Smell the sea!' she said.

Rivka asked David if he was all right but the little boy was too entranced by the ride in the cart to give any answer. Rivka bent round to inspect him. 'He's all right.'

Mary sang a lullaby to her baby, 'Aylie-lully-bye-bye . . .' and Queenie asked whether they would get there soon.

'Soon,' said Mary, and she answered Queenie by leaning over to David and speaking to him. 'Where are we going? We're going on our –' She supplied the answer, '*Holidays!* To the – ?' And again she made the recitation for all of them: '*Country!* And the – ? *Seaside!* Look at him, wee face. It's going to be – ? *Lovely!* In another – ? *House!* With a – ? *Garden!*'

Lala shifted her weight and eased her back.

'All right?' asked Rivka.

'I'm all right.'

They were between trees now. The driver flicked one of the reins and the horse left the road and plodded more softly now along a track. They craned their necks around. Mary caught the change in mood.

'Now you're not to expect a palace. Zelek and I have done what we can, but –'

'We know,' said Lala. Only too well they knew. Mary had told them often enough.

'It'll be all right,' said Rivka with conviction.

'It'll be *very nice*,' commanded Mary.

This silenced them all, then Queenie voiced a doubt.

'Does the driver know where it is?'

'Of course he knows.' Mary eyed the man in front. She prodded him. 'Do you know where you're taking us?' Her voice had the clear ring she adopted when addressing a Goy of the servant class, and she presumed that most of them belonged to it.

The driver understood what she was saying and replied in his own tongue, which was thickest Fife, 'Ay, I ken, Missus.' (The Fife language has slurs and glottal stops and everything rises in pitch at the end as if in perpetual surprise.)

The Kaydan ladies eyed each other.

'What?' said Queenie.

Mary said, 'What did he say?'

Rivka told them. 'He kens de vay.'

Lala shifted again.

'Do you want to sit here?' offered Queenie.

'No . . .'

'Not comfortable,' observed Rivka who had been right through it six times with several other bad starts. She tapped the driver's back.

'Slow!'

'Let's get there,' said Lala. 'Quick!'

'Not too quick,' said Mary. 'Take it slow, driver.'

The driver raised his weather-beaten face to heaven and rolled his eyes to a circling gull. He pulled up.

The Kaydans were surprised.

'He's stopped,' said Rivka.

'Why have you stopped?' demanded Mary with authority. She was having no nonsense; after all, she was paying the fare.

The driver pointed with his head. They looked. Set back from the lane was a small farm cottage standing on its own. It had a door with a window on each side of it, and another window above it, under the eaves of the slate roof.

Mary's hand went to her bosom to still its palpitation. 'Is this it?'

'Ay,' said the driver. They understood him.

'It's verra nice,' said Rivka loyally.

'Yes, it is nice.' Lala was more sure. She liked the look of it.

'Lovely,' echoed Queenie.

'That's what Zelek picked.' Mary was hedging her bets.

The driver dismounted and undid the back gate of the trap so that they could step down. 'Woa, wumman!' he said, probably to the horse to keep it still while they got off. He took little David and lifted him down.

'Careful!' exclaimed Mary.

'Careful!' warned Rivka.

'Let me,' said Mary.

'I'll go,' said Rivka, overruling her daughter-in-law. She put her hand on the rail to steady herself, and was handed down safely by the driver.

'Steady now,' he said, but with the glottal stop and the rise at the end they didn't understand him.

Rivka turned and took a hat-box. 'Bring de basket.'

Mary came down next, with the baby. She hesitated half-way and tried the other foot on the step.

'Ye're a' richt, missus, come on now, come on!' coaxed the driver.

Mary reached the ground. 'There we are. Now –' Without looking at the driver she made for the house with an air of expectation.

Lala came down easily by herself, bringing a basket. That left Queenie, who did a series of steps on the top level, not knowing how to come down. The driver looked up at her. 'Ay, weel, missus.' He understood the problem. Queenie got down one step, turned herself on it, went up again, came down, reached the second step and so down to the ground. She grabbed two hat-boxes and ran for the cottage.

The driver leant against the trap. Then slowly he turned to size up the large trunk that was left.

Meanwhile Mary had opened the front door and was peering through the hall. There were steep steps going up to the upstairs room. To the left was a door, to the right was a door, and straight ahead at the end of the little hall, the open door showed stone flags and a kitchen sink.

They crowded in behind Mary and stood on the bare boards.

'Now let me,' said Mary, 'it's my house, we'll see who's having which room.'

Mary chose to open the door on the right, at the foot of the stairs. It was a small bedroom with a double bed and a chest of drawers and no room for anything else. They pushed in and surveyed it.

'One double bed,' said Mary, considering it. She sniffed. 'It isn't damp, is it?'

They all sniffed.

'No,' said Lala.

'No!' scoffed Rivka.

Queenie continued to sniff, and looked to Mary for the final judgement.

'No,' said Mary with decision, 'very nice.'

'Whose room?' asked Lala.

'Wait,' said Mary, and led the way to the room opposite.

This was the parlour, with a cane table and chairs, and a worn rug in front of the fireplace. The driver now caught up with the exploration and stood in the doorway with the trunk on his shoulder. They inspected the parlour.

'Very nice,' said Mary.

'No beds,' said Rivka with a puzzled shrug and an arm-gesture that showed she was expecting a bed in every room.

Mary explained that it was the parlour, which Rivka had already understood and appreciated, but her gestures still expected a bed.

Mary planted a kiss on the baby's cheek by way of ending the discussion.

And Queenie said, '*Very* nice. Bright!'

Mary was calculating ahead, from the outside appearance of the cottage, where the other beds might be. 'Uhuh,' she said, and led the way out.

She went through to the kitchen at the back of the house. It was a bare room with a range, a table and chairs and a dresser, and a back door. They went round it, running fingers along ledges to inspect for dust. The driver got fed up and dropped the trunk down to stand on its end on the stone floor. He leaned on it.

Mary said dubiously, 'Very nice.'

Rivka said, 'It's all right,' with a shrug and a nod.

Queenie caught the tone. 'We'll make do,' she added.

'And this?' asked Mary. She led through to a little room off the kitchen. It had a pram and cot as well as a bed.

'A pram. Whose pram? *Your* pram!' she told the baby. She sniffed the pram closely. 'Uhuh.'

'So dis is your room,' said Rivka. It was a premature guess.

Mary said, 'Wait, there's still a room upstairs. Let's see. We can move the cot if we want. Queenie, stay with the babbily.' She handed the baby over to Queenie and went out, smiling sweetly to the driver as she passed him.

She went upstairs and David toddled after. Rivka, Lala and Queenie with the baby watched her ascent.

'She'll take the best room,' said Lala.

'Where'll I go?' asked Queenie. They looked at her.

Upstairs in the room under the eaves, with the sunlight streaming in, Mary looked at the double bed.

'Yes,' she said. 'Is this Mummy's room?'

'Yes,' said David.

Mary sat on the bed. It sagged and creaked. Mary moved her bottom over it, considering. 'Uhuh,' she said. 'We'll tell the driver to bring up the hat-box and the cases. Come here.' David went to her obediently. She took out her handkerchief, licked a corner, and wiped David's cheek with it. He hated that.

Down in the kitchen they were still counting the beds.

'Dere's von bedroom not here!'

Lala said, 'The house isn't big enough. We need four beds, she knew that.'

'Zelek chose it,' said Rivka defensively.

'Trust him.'

Queenie was counting with her eyes, 'One, two, three bedrooms.' The baby girned in her arms.

'Listen,' said Rivka, 'ven you vos babies, ve had two rooms for all of us.' She took the baby from Queenie and put it down in the pram.

Lala said, 'We're not babies.'

'All right, but ve're lucky.' Rivka shushed her grand-daughter in the pram, and rocked.

'She wants her bottle.'

Queenie shouted, 'I've got no bed! No bed!'

The driver took his cap off. 'Eh, Missus.'

'Vot?'

The man pointed with the back of his hand. 'S'a bed.'

'What?' said Lala.

'S'a bed'n the wa',' said the driver.

They looked at him.

'What's he say?'

'He wants paid,' Lala, guessed.

'Naw, 's a bed 'n th' wa',' said the driver.

He left the trunk and went over to the wall. He pulled a lever that stuck out there and the wall hinged outwards and downwards and became a bed. The driver lowered it carefully to the floor.

They looked at it, then at each other. They burst out laughing and slapped their thighs and held each other by the shoulders.

The driver was satisfied; he raised the bed again and pushed it flat against the wall. The lever clicked and held it in place.

'Y'a' richt then?'

'What?' said Queenie through her laughter, 'What's he say?'

Rivka understood. 'Ve're a' richt.' She had caught the inflexion and recognised it. 'Dey speak here in Fife like dey spoke in *der Heim*, in Lituania.' She enunciated clearly to the driver, 'Ay, man, ve're a' richt.'

Mary came down the stairs with David. She sang in a chanting refrain, 'I've got my room then, I've got my room. It's a very nice room.'

Rivka and Lala and Queenie met her in the hall.

'It's a lovely house, Mary,' said Lala.

'Beautiful.' Rivka made a wide sweep with her hands.

'We'll have a grand month.'

'Yes, we will.' And the way Mary said it, there would be no arguing. 'Ma, you have the nice front room now, it's bright. And Lala take the room off the kitchen. And Queenie – ?'

'The kitchen,' said Queenie.

'Not the kitchen.'

'It's got a bed in it.'

'A bed?'

'I'll show you.' Queenie made proudly for the kitchen.

'Eh, missus,' said the driver, 'can ah hae ma fare?' This being an actual question, his normal rising cadence rose to a high squeak at the end.

'What did he say?'

'He vonts his money.'

'Oh, yes,' said Mary as if she had forgotten. She opened her handbag and took out her purse and opened that. She brought out a half-crown. 'There. And there's threepence for yourself,' she said grandly.

The driver put his cap on. 'A' richt, missus.' He nodded and went. It was a tip, and anyway he'd had an interesting drive.

There was a resounding crash from the kitchen. They all froze. Mary's hand went to her heart.

Queenie said, 'The bed!'

'Where's David?'

They crowded through to the kitchen. The bed had hinged down. There was no sign of David.

'David?' called Lala.

Mary panicked. 'David!' She crouched her body, ready to spring or cower. The cupboard door beneath the dresser opened and the little boy poked his head out.

'He-llo,' he sang.

They unpacked everything but the trunk, while Lala lit the fire from the kindling in the fireside box. Then came the trunk. Mary opened it and handed out the sheets to be aired. They had been packed three hours ago but Mary insisted. 'You never know,' she said with a flip of the hand and a turn of the head. 'It's how I like it.' So Rivka lowered the pulley and she and Queenie hung the sheets as Mary handed them out.

'Just for an hour or two, then we'll all be safe.'

Rivka heaved on the pulley rope. Queenie came to help her and they hoisted the sheets to the ceiling and tied off.

'We can air the blankets outside,' said Mary. 'We'll get them off the beds and hang them up.' She knelt again at the trunk. David peered over the edge. 'Now what have we got?' asked Mary.

'Pots!' shouted her son.

The trunk was full of pots and pans and crockery and cutlery, all packed separately.

'One for meat,' said Mary, handing out a pot to Lala, who handed it to Rivka, who put it on the dresser.

'And one for milk,' said Mary.

Being orthodox Jews (and being Jewish meant being orthodox) they were forbidden to mingle meat dishes with milk or fish dishes. So to prevent any possibility of contamination, and thus any possible breach of any part of a letter of the law, they had two sets of everything, and two sets of towels and cloths for washing and drying them. The utensils provided by the owner of the cottage had to be put away because they might have been used at some time in their existence for cooking pigs, or by someone who had cooked pigs elsewhere, or any part of pigs, or had touched pigs, or had touched someone else who had touched or cooked or eaten anything that had had any connection with pigs.

Mary explained this to her son while the unpacking and stowing away continued. 'You know that, don't you?'

'Yes.'

'Do you?'

'Of course he does!' said Mary.

'Good,' said the wise Rivka.

Lala sat wearily by the fire. 'I could do with a cup of tea. Queenie, put the kettle on.'

'Right.'

Queenie took the kettle from the hob and went to the sink with it. She hovered there. The sink had no tap.

Mary said, 'And put some water on for the potatoes.'

Rivka handed her the cooking pot. Queenie stood at the sink with the kettle and the pot.

'Meat-plate,' said Mary, unwrapping the plate from its newspapers. 'And a meat-plate.'

'There's no tap,' said Queenie, not believing her own eyes.

They came to the sink.

'No tap . . .' said Mary wonderingly.

Rivka started to laugh. They were puzzled and Rivka held her sides at them and dismissed them with a hand-flop.

'It's like back in *der Heim* – you never knew, you vere born here, de lot of you. Coom – outside –' She led the way and they followed her out, blinking in the sun.

'Nu.' Rivka pointed to the pump, and they went to it and stood looking at it guardedly. Mary took the pot from Queenie.

Rivka demonstrated with a gesture. 'De handle, oop and doon! In *der Heim*, de voter vos vell voter. Nu?'

Mary rattled the handle. They watched for signs of water.

'*Los mir,*' said Rivka. She worked the handle with a proper spirit, for the first time since she was a girl, and though that was forty years ago, it seemed like yesterday. The water gushed into Mary's pot and splashed over.

'Kveenie?'

Queenie approached the pump, and so did a hen. Queenie backed away.

'It von't touch you.'

Queenie circled the yard and came back to the pump, without the hen. They watched the gushing water: one stroke of the handle filled the kettle. Queenie put the lid on, then, her own pent-up excitement released by the flow and the sound of the water, she asked, 'Where's the thingmy?'

They looked round the yard.

'I need to go,' said Queenie.

They went back to the kitchen, where the kettle was deposited on the fire, then Queenie and Lala made another tour of the house. There was no closet.

They went out of the front door and looked up and down the road, they walked round the house and over the fields, wandering, looking.

'There must *be* a place,' said Lala, 'we can't just –'

'Well, I don't know,' said Queenie, preparing to use the long grass.

There was a tumbledown hut in front of them, with its door hanging off. It had a large open pit behind it.

'There it is,' said Lala.

They studied it. They went to it. Lala sniffed the air. That was it all right. Queenie went inside and came out again hurriedly.

'It's just a chute! Down there!'

They peered over the edge of the pit at many months' usage of the privy. A pig stared back up at them. No, it wasn't a kosher closet.

'Oh, Lala . . .'

'Go on, try it.'

Queenie was desperate. She made to go back in, and the door fell over on one hinge. 'Don't leave me! You go first.'

Lala went in and raised her skirts and lowered her

knickers. 'It's like Ma says, what they used to have when she was a girl,' she shouted, and peed down the chute.

As she waited, Queenie grew alarmed. 'Are you all right?'

Lala was fine. 'Yes,' she shouted, imitating her mother, 'it's verra nice!'

Mary was wheeling the pram by the front of the cottage and singing a lullaby to the tune of the song in the morning service, 'La lully-lully by-by, Lully-lully by . . .'

The pram had its sun-canopy up. Rivka came walking to Mary with a posy a bluebells and buttercups. She looked into the pram at the baby.

'Vell, babbily?'

And Mary translated for the baby's benefit, 'Well, baby?' Together the two women sang the lullaby as they walked along back to the cottage.

'Where's David?' asked Mary.

Rivka spotted him by the coal-heap in the yard. He was intent, with his back to them.

'David!'

He looked round: his face and hands were black from the coal.

Mary rushed to him and spanked his bottom and dragged him shrieking and weeping by one arm to the pump. She pulled his clothes off and held him under with one hand while she pumped with the other. The little boy howled and Mary relented.

She kept pumping the cool water over his head, and trying to still him with her mother-love. 'And some day,' she comforted, 'some day – listen, listen. Listen! Some day you'll marry a nice Jewish girl.'

She took him in to the fire and dried him and dressed him in clean clothes and kissed him.

16

Friday night came. The four Kaydan women sat in a row on the grass outside the cottage door, looking down the road in silence. David was on the look-out further along the road.

The shadows of the evening sun were long. Almost they might have been back in *der Heim*. Inside the cottage all was clean. In the kitchen they had set the wooden table with a white tablecloth and two brass candlesticks, and eight place settings *fleischekky*, for meat. And now they were waiting.

Rivka looked at the dipping sun, then down the road again. 'So vere are dey? It'll soon be Shabbas.' She got herself to her feet and went inside. She went to the range in the kitchen where the fowl was boiling in a big pot, with another pot beside it boiling the potatoes. She poked at the fowl with a fork.

Queenie followed her in.

'It's ready,' said Rivka. 'Vere's de *lockshen* for de soup?'

'Here.' Queenie brought it from the dresser.

Mary came in, sniffed the cooking smells, went to the draining board by the sink, lifted a teacloth from the ashet there. Underneath the cloth, arranged in concentric circles on the big plate, were balls of cold boiled *gefilte* fish. Mary admired them. But it wasn't enough, she needed confirmation from the others. 'There. Gefilte fish, for tomorrow.'

'That's nice, Mary,' said Queenie. She had said so before but that was what one always had to say when Mary displayed a plate of gefilte fish.

'Now, Ma,' said Mary, satisfied, 'what can I use for the – ?' She waved a hand.

'Salad,' obliged Queenie.

Outside in the road with David, Lala called, 'There he is!' and the little boy jumped up and down with excitement. Lala called loudly so that the others could hear inside the house, 'He's here!'

They heard, looked up, and bustled out to meet the visitor.

The horse and trap came into view. There was the driver up front, and behind him on the trap seat sat Moshe, clutching a battered suitcase to him, wearing a shiny dark-blue serge suit and a bowler hat jammed well down on his head.

The women crowded out of the front door.

'Pa!'

'Moshe!'

'*There* he is!'

'At last, we thought you'd missed the train.' And Mary turned to David, her son. 'There's who – ? Grandpa!'

The driver had reined in and jumped down. He undid the back gate of the trap and Moshe turned and came down, lugging his suitcase and an attaché case with him. He had a grin of achievement on his face.

'How much?'

'Half a crown.'

'Here.'

He completed the transaction, with no tip. The driver mounted, turned the horse, and drove off again philosophically.

Moshe turned to the bosoms of his family. 'Rivka . . . Lala . . . Kveenie . . .' And to Mary, 'Good evening. And David –' He held out his hand to his grandson. '*Vos machs du?*'

David was afraid and shy.

'Say *vos machs du!*' said Rivka.

Lala bent down and whispered to the clinging boy, 'It means, how are you keeping?'

'Fine,' said David.

'Good, David,' said his mother.

Rivka linked arms with her husband. 'Coom. And see de

174

hoose.' Their eyes met. It was a communication between them that spanned the years and said more than words.

'It's nice?' he asked formally.

Mary was a little shocked. 'It's *lovely*.'

At the cottage door Moshe paused and looked at the doorpost.

'What's wrong?' asked Mary with a catch of her breath.

'No mezzuzzah?' Moshe was puzzled that they had not put one up on the doorpost of the house.

'Pa!' protested Lala, 'It's not our house! We can't put mezzuzzim up!'

But Moshe stayed at the door with his suitcase in one hand and his attaché case in the other.

'Coom and vosh!' commanded Rivka. 'Coom!' Was this the time to exasperate her?

Moshe shrugged, which meant that things were not quite right, and if things weren't right . . . But Rivka took his hat off, and pulled his yamulkeh from his jacket pocket and plonked it on his head.

'*Nu shein!*' She propelled him into the house.

The teapot was still on the hob, so Moshe was poured a cup of dark brown tea with two heaped spoonfuls of sugar. He supped it loudly and contentedly.

'Good?'

'Good. I have a mezzuzzah –'

'Never mind mezzuzzah. How vos business?'

'All right.'

'Show me,' said Rivka.

Moshe lifted his attaché case on to his knee. 'David? Coom.'

His grandson went cautiously to him, afraid of the wrinkles and the stubbly grey beard. Moshe took his keys from his pocket and unlocked the case and raised the lid. The case was packed with crumpled newspaper, and inside each piece of paper was a watch, or a clock.

David's eyes opened wide as each one was unwrapped. Moshe came at last to a pocket watch, put the others back carefully and shut the case. He wound up the watch, listened to it, held it to David's ear. The boy listened attentively. Then Moshe pressed the pin beside the winder. The watch chimed the time, eight, then another ting-ting meaning a quarter past. David's face filled with wonder.

Moshe said, 'It's nearly Shabbas.'

He was nailing up the mezzuzzah he had brought, using a stone as a hammer, when the rumbling of the trap signalled its rearrival. In it were Zelek and Jack, Lala's husband. He was a gentle, pleasant man, about the same age as Zelek, thirty-two. The driver looked pleased to have completed his delivery as he pulled up.

'Hoi!' shouted Zelek.

The women were standing at the table in the kitchen with their hands stretched towards the two lit candles when they heard the shout. They looked up and Mary sang, 'They're here, they're here!'

Zelek and Jack got down with their cases, no fumbling or turning on the step for them. Down they leapt and met the women rushing from the house.

'So you found it?' said Rivka.

'About time too,' said Queenie. 'You're late!'

'Jack!' said Lala, and Jack put down his case and they hugged and kissed like two lovers.

'Hello,' said Jack and they kissed again.

David ran out. 'Daddy!'

Zelek caught him and lifted him high in the air and cuddled him.

So they went in, and admired, and joked, and washed their hands and dried them, and put their yamulkehs on and sat round the Shabbas table that had the clean white cloth and the candles, in front of the kitchen fire: the men had come home. David sat on his father's knee; the baby was asleep in the pram in the little room off the kitchen.

'Nu?' said Rivka. 'De stars are out.' Which meant that it was evening, the eve of the Sabbath, *Erev Shabbas*.

Moshe nodded, and opened his little wooden-bound prayer book, the one he'd brought from *der Heim* when he was a boy and running for his life. He started the sanctification, the Kiddush, in his own tuneless rumble.

'Excuse me –' said Jack.

Moshe stopped in surprise.

Jack gave a little shrug and a nod and said, 'I know you're head of the family, and it's Kiddush, but I could maybe sing it – ?'

'Go on, Pa,' Lala urged, 'let him, Jack's got a good voice.'

'Of course,' said Moshe, 'of course.' He passed the book over to Jack.

Jack cleared his throat and sang in a rich baritone, '*Va'y'hi erev, va'y'hi vouker, youm hashishi.*'

Then he turned to the wide-eyed little boy and explained. 'In six days, God finished all the heavens, and the earth, and everything in it. And on the seventh day, God rested. Listen –' And he sang again the Kiddush. And all the Kaydans sat in their places round the table and were at home, at peace.

After the Kiddush, the wine and the bread, the soup was served, then more soup; then the plates were cleared away by Queenie and Rivka, though Mary begged the men to have more soup. They said no, and Mary handed her plate up to Queenie. 'That was very nice, Ma,' she complimented the cook, in a voice of slight surprise. 'And it's time *you* were in bed,' she told her son.

'Leave him,' said the indulgent Zelek, 'it's shabbas.'

'De hen's falling to pieces.' Rivka was prodding it at the range, but she spoke with pride. That was how they liked it. 'And here's de salad.' She brought the mixture of sparkling green and red piled high in a chamber-pot.

David's eyes nearly popped out of his head. Rivka caught the criticism and explained that there was nothing else big enough, so she had washed it and it was all right. But he did not eat his salad.

They ate, and then had strawberries, and then lemon tea

(no milk after the fowl!), and cleared away, and said the grace after meals. David was put to bed, and the others went through to the parlour, where there were candles on the mantelpiece.

They sprawled about in the wicker chairs.

'I'm going to see a fountain pen man on Monday,' said Zelek.

'Monday!' said his mother Rivka, in protest that his holiday should be so short.

'Ma, he's offering me an agency. Wyvern pens. I could make a fortune in Dundee alone. I'll be back on Tuesday.'

'So you say,' gestured Mary, who'd heard it before.

'I'll try,' Zelek amended.

Jack asked him whether he had never regretted giving up medicine, and Zelek thought out loud of the times when he did imagine himself as a doctor. But money was money, and this was his cottage for the whole month. And Mary smiled her satisfaction.

'You inherited your business,' Zelek remarked to Jack.

Jack was pious. 'Not yet.'

'You will. What's Pa got – ? A case full of watches.'

'I like votches,' said Moshe.

Rivka said, 'It doesnae matter vot you inherit, it's vot you like.' And she meant it. She should know. She'd been through all those years of poverty to arrive here tonight. 'Look,' she said with a proud gesture, 'de family all gathered for Shabbas.'

Queenie remembered Sarah and Ian, who weren't with them.

'She's halfway round de vorld. Vit her baby, *lieber Gott*, and Isadore, *lieber Gott*, ve spread all over.'

'When'll we see them?' asked Queenie.

There was a silence. Moshe filled it. 'Ve go to Canada.'

'Haw-haw,' said Queenie, meaning that it was nothing to joke about.

They began to talk about Ian, half-way round the world

in the other direction. They had not heard from him either for a month or two.

Moshe wasn't worried. 'Dat von, he'll be all right.' And he fumbled in his pocket and brought out his cigarette papers and his packet of tobacco.

'Vot are you doing!' demanded Rivka.

Moshe remembered, 'It's Shabbas!' and he blushed deep red as he put them away, very annoyed with himself.

Zelek eyed the near-sin. 'Jack,' he said, 'are you coming for a walk?'

'Eh?' said Jack. Then he caught Zelek's meaning. 'Oh ay,' he said and got up to go out with his brother-in-law.

'Now – !' said Mary.

'No smoking on Shabbas.' Rivka brought the thought out into the open.

'They'll just get bad-tempered,' said Lala.

'No.' Moshe contradicted her, his temper beginning to show already.

'It's true,' said Rivka, 'but you cannae smoke.'

Lala made a suggestion. 'Why can't we all go out?'

But Queenie was afraid of the hens. 'Not just the hens,' she protested.

'Come on then.' Zelek led the way, at least to the door. Mary found an excuse. 'What about the kinder?' Children, her children, couldn't be left in a strange house in a strange country. Moshe offered to stay.

Jack helped Lala out of her chair. 'Stars, moon . . .' he promised her and she knew what he meant. 'Beasties,' added Queenie.

There was a honking of a car's horn from outside. They stood still; Mary's hand went of course to her heart.

'Who's dat?' exclaimed Moshe, his eyes small and burning.

'A motor car,' said Zelek. That much was obvious.

'What's the lights?'

'Its headlights.'

The honking came again, and again.

Moshe was afraid. 'Soldiers?'

179

'No, Pa!' shouted Zelek as he went out. They all followed him out into the moonlit road. In front of the cottage was an open tourer with its headlamps on. The driver wore a cap pulled down over his eyes, and he kept one hand on the horn till the whole family was there, then he stopped.

Zelek was the spokesman. 'What do you want?'

'Is this the Kaydan household?' An Oxford drawl.

The Kaydans looked at each other.

'Yes, it is,' said Zelek.

The driver stood up and held out his hand. '*Sholoum aleichem!*' he said without the drawl, just plain Yiddish.

They stared at him. He took his cap off. 'Well?'

Then they knew it was Ian, *their* Ian, their brother, their son, their Shlomo, and they shouted and shrieked with delight. And they laughed and wept and dragged Ian and Solomon and Shlomo down from his car – his car? Vot a car! – and they clapped him on the back and kissed him and turned him round.

'Oy,' was all that Ian could say, and 'Oy – wait.' He shushed them into silence. 'So I've missed Kiddush, so it's Shabbas, so it's a sin to drive on Shabbas, but I'm here!'

They pulled him into the house, begging him to tell, but first he must eat, now tell them . . .

He was sat down and given the pickings of the fowl, and the soup was heated up and he knew it was no good protesting that he'd had a bite in Edinburgh but he protested just the same and forced down a delicious spoonful or two. And bread and they'd eaten all the strawberries but there was an orange and *kichlach*, little cakes with his lemon tea, as he recounted the adventures of his homecoming and the nonsense people he'd met – ve're does he get it from? – and how they had missed him!

'Vy didn't you write?'

'I had summer leave so – Rangoon is a downpour and hot, I was going to Kashmir, up in the north, or China, or over to Canada to see Sarah, and they said, you're due home leave, so I said to myself, will I climb Mount Everest or come home, so I came home.'

'On a boat?'

'I swam some of the way.'

'Och, go on!'

Ian turned from Queenie to Lala, and patted her pregnant bulge. 'And when's that coming?'

'September.'

'Is it a boy, or a girl?'

'A boy!' said Jack.

Lala thought it was a boy.

'Anyting,' said Rivka.

And Ian met Jack for the first time. 'How are you, Jack?'

'I'm all right, Ian.'

'You've got a furniture shop in Dundee.'

'My father has.'

'Sounds all right. I haven't had the pleasure of shopping there.'

'I hope you will.'

'Come to Rangoon and buy some teak trees, they make the best furniture, and see the elephants.'

Mary tossed her head round. 'Elephants!' How could they believe that?

'Oh ay,' said Ian, 'I've seen things that would make *you* blush, Mary,' remembering her of old.

'Go on,' said Mary, turning away to hide her shock in a display of sportiness. But Ian didn't. Instead he bent low to dear Lala. 'Is Jack looking after you?'

'Yes, Ian, he is.' Her hair was ruffled in affection.

Then Zelek demanded to see Ian's snapshots, and out came the bulging wallet and one print was slid out and slapped on the table.

'My wives,' said Ian.

They peered and ogled at a panoramic photo of three long rows of dusky women with Ian undeniably in the middle, in a heroic pose with a smirk on his face.

'Yer vot?' asked Moshe, staring at it.

'The British resident staff are allowed forty wives. I couldn't get a snap with all the children, the camera wasn't big enough.'

The kid-on exploded in 'och-away' and 'shut-up' but still they weren't quite sure, and Ian relished every doubting face of his family. 'And this was my chief wife!' He flourished another photograph.

They craned to see and snatch, and dissolved in laughter at the photo of a cow. Rivka got hold of it and her eyes crinkled up tight shut in laughter.

Mary said he was daft.

'Here,' said Ian, 'you've got a son and daughter that I've never seen!'

'I'll get him!' Zelek leapt up and to the door.

'No!' cried Mary.

Ian said, 'I'll creep in,' and went out and up the narrow stairs with Zelek.

'He can recite,' said Zelek the proud father, and Ian was impressed.

The family followed them up. They pushed open the bedroom door with a creak; Zelek fondled his son's hair, then his ears and the little boy awoke, girning. Zelek took him up and when David saw the audience he knew it was something special. Zelek stood him in his cot, clinging on to the bars, and there he recited the party piece that his father had taught him, the music-hall saga of Nellie, that Zelek and Ian had adored when Billy Bennett came to the Edinburgh Empire.

The little boy in pyjamas pushed his piping voice from the deepest to the highest register:

> Years have rolled on since that happened,
> Time healed the widow's pain;
> One day she met a diver,
> And the widow married again.
>
> Nell was a diver's daughter,
> He dived in the sea, under ships,

He walked on the bed of the ocean
And trod on the fish, and the chips.

The Kaydans were in fits. The little boy said it through
to the end and was hugged, and whirled round by his new
Uncle Ian, and put back to bed and tucked up, and left to
sleep.

They went down to the parlour. Tea was brought, (more
lemon tea) and over it they talked and talked about Ian's
adventures, and about old times.

A bed was made up for Ian by pushing the two cane
armchairs together, with cushions and blankets. He assured
them he would be fine: after a camp-bed in the monsoon,
it was paradise, or so he said.

After they had left him, he undressed slowly in the candlelight. There was a tap at the door and Jack looked in.

'Hello.'

'Hello, Jack.'

'Lala's just settling.'

'Sit down.'

'She's a bit tricky just now – her body.'

'How?'

'Aw . . . you know.' Jack sat on an upright chair by the
window. Ian offered his cigarette case.

'It's Shabbas.'

Ian remembered: four years was not so long since his
last Shabbas. But Jack took a cigarette, and Ian took one.
They lit up from the candle.

'How is Lala keeping?'

'She's all right . . .'

'Did her cough clear up?'

'Oh ay . . .'

Ian confessed that he was very fond of his sister Lala – in
fact, fondest.

'I know,' said Jack, 'she talks a lot about you.'

Ian speculated on the baby; it seemed strange that Lala,

his little sister, should be having a baby. And Zelek's two! 'Nell was a sailor's daughter.' Ian chortled. The little boy hadn't understood a word of what he was saying.

'Mary didn't like it,' observed Jack.

'What d'you make of her?'

Jack shrugged; he understood that she was part of the family. Ian accepted that, too. So Mary was all right.

Ian thought of the last four years and could see no change in his parents, not a bit. They had come through the pit, walked through the valley of the shadow, and now look at them! At this joy: a summer holiday, with children – golden summer, unthought of! It was nice, nice.

Zelek lay awake beside Mary, his wife. He rolled over on to her. Oh Zelek, what about the kinder ... ?

In the parlour below, Jack and Ian looked up at the ceiling, from whence came rhythmical, springy creaks.

In the room opposite the parlour, Moshe rolled over and put his arm round Rivka, his wife.

'Oy,' said Rivka.

'Coom,' said Moshe.

And they celebrated the Almighty's goodness.

Queenie snored in her wall-bed in the kitchen. Jack tiptoed past, carrying his jacket and his shoes. He gently opened the door of the little room off the kitchen. Lala started up in the bed. He shushed her and undressed and crept in beside her and they snuggled together. . . .

Ian, alone on his two arm-chairs, day-dreaming of elephants and ships and love, leaned up and blew out the candle.

17

The next day was Shabbas. The men held a shortened service, there being only four of them instead of the ten necessary for a full service. The women had banked up the kitchen range the night before, and Lala rescued it in the early hours of the morning, so they had plenty of tea to drink with their delicious cold gefilte fish.

In the afternoon they walked round the cottage, and talked, and slept till it was time for the evening service. Then milk broth with vegetables, and boiled eggs and pickled herring on black bread thick with farm butter (Moshe had inspected it and passed it as Kosher). Then cards round the kitchen table, and the cottage was filled with the aroma of Turkish tobacco and the sound of laughter.

Sunday was perfect: bright sun, blue sky. They went to and fro between the cottage and Ian's car, loading it up for the picnic. Ian stood in the dickey seat.

'Yes, there's room.'

'Here's towels and jerseys,' said Rivka. 'Have you got a jacket?'

'Yes, Ma.' He called to Zelek in the hall, 'Bring it out!'

Zelek and Jack wheeled the pram out and hoisted it to Ian in the dickey.

'One, two, hup!'

'You'll need a rope.'

Mary came out with the baby and uttered her usual, 'Be careful!'

Lala and Moshe came out carrying the hamper between them.

'Dis can go in de back too.'

'Round here, Pa.'

But Moshe was not to be told by any child of his. '*Dis* vay! *Los mir!*' He would do it himself. He took the hamper and carried it to the dickey. Then he stopped and looked along the road.

A man on horseback was riding slowly along to the cottage, followed by two children, a boy and a girl. They were both about twelve.

Moshe spoke quietly. 'De laird.'

They stopped what they were doing and waited, a little fearfully, because Rivka had told them what men on horses did to Jews when she was a girl.

The laird inspected them as he passed. The children gave them a glance.

'Good morning,' said the laird.

The Kaydans returned the greeting, then Moshe spoke alone.

'Good morning . . . sir.'

The riding-party continued on its way without looking back.

'They weren't Cossacks,' said Ian.

'*Shveig!*' said his mother.

At the privy in the field, the door was pushed open and David slid out and ran away. Then Queenie came out, looking for him. She was nearly in tears.

'David!' she scolded and ran after him, all the way to the road where Ian and Zelek were roping the pram and hamper on to the dickey.

'What's the matter?'

Queenie had caught up with David and held him tightly by the hand. The little boy seemed unconcerned.

'Vot's wrong?'

Queenie sniffed. David had dropped her beads down the chute. She said so.

'Your blue beads?' asked Mary, panicking. The little boy confirmed it. 'Her blue beads,' he piped.

So there were apologies (but not from David) and explanations and offers of replacement and acceptances. Ian swung the starting handle and the car coughed and purred and spluttered.

They all climbed on board, with elbows in eyes and arms round necks and thighs on knees. Ian couldn't find the gear lever and when he did there were such loud grindings that they shrieked and wanted to get off. But Ian had enough glee left to try again and the car juddered forward and stopped. Ian got out, swung the handle, leapt in; ground the gears once, with a groan, twice, with another groan, and then into gear and away with cheering till the wind knocked the breath from their lungs.

The sea was gentle, with little waves breaking on the sunny beach. A few other families were scattered over the empty sands. David, in white cotton shorts and a big floppy sun hat, dug a channel near the waves with his spade. It was a new game, better than the old one of making sand-castles in the red tin bucket. He tramped down the castles and emptied the bucket and used it to fill the channel with the sea.

Up on the dry sand, the Kaydans had dug a sand-hole; the men had dug it while the women watched and waited. Seats were shaped in the corners of the hole and the women descended and tried them out for size and safety. There were shrieks and protestations but they fitted. Tests were made to see if the children were within sight and sound; they were. The baby was put to sleep in the pram with its sun-canopy up, resting at an angle in the sand. Zelek and Moshe took off their jackets and collars and ties. Moshe even took off his yamulkeh. Everyone took off their shoes and stockings.

Mary and Rivka had their knitting, so they could talk to each other and at each other at the same time.

'Since I was there,' Mary was saying, 'I thought I'd walk along. It was blowy but nice, the kinder were wrapped up in the pram. So I walked along Princes Street, and who should I bump into but Babsy Cohen with her two in the pram. So we looked at each other, and down Hanover Street comes Esther, Esther Jacobs with her two. You knew she – ?'

'Yes,' said Rivka. Everybody knew the secret about Esther Jacobs, whatever it was.

'So what were we all doing in Princes Street?' Mary asked her own question for herself to answer. 'I said, *I've* been buying toffee apples, for the kinder. It was true.' Her eyes opened in innocence. What did they think she was doing? 'And Babsy said, that's what I've been doing, and Esther said, that's what I've been doing – it was true! Laugh? We stood there –' Mary dissolved into laughter as she had then, at the recollection of it and of the laughter of the others.

Rivka joined her, but the men didn't catch the infection. The baby in the pram babbled away.

'Listen,' said the grandmother Rivka. 'Listen to Shirley.'

'She's happy,' said Moshe.

Queenie was not in the sand-hole. She sat at a respectable distance away on the sand, trying to change discreetly into a black bathing-costume. With a towel draped around her she had managed to take off her knickers and wriggle into the bottom half of the bathing-suit. The top half was somehow trickier. Her pink camisole was dangling below the towel for anyone to see who wanted to look.

She risked an extra wriggle and got the camisole down one arm and off. The towel slipped off the other shoulder and a melon breast fell out of the other side of the camisole.

Ian saw. He pointed dramatically. 'Aha!' he exclaimed, but no one else looked, not even the Goyim.

In the sand-hole Zelek asked Mary if she would come for a swim. Mary declined. Zelek showed her Queenie, now costumed and running down to the sea.

'It's too cold,' said Mary.

In the shallows, warm and rippling, Jack and Lala had their clothes hitched well up and were blissfully paddling, happy, wandering about together, pointing out the small silver fish darting under their toes, and the blue shells. They stood up, face to face, Lala's bulging tummy touching Jack's belly. They leaned towards each other and managed to kiss.

On the firm tidal sand, Ian had rolled up his trousers to run in and out of the water. He danced and pranced with great high steps, and David, whooping with laughter, tried to catch him.

They watched Ian from the sand-hole.

'Dat von,' said Rivka, 'he should be married.' She turned to Moshe, 'Vy don't you dance in de sand?'

'You tink I cannae dance?'

'You havenae since ve vere married.'

They watched Ian waltz around David. His movements were angular, rhythmical, blissful.

'Go on,' urged Rivka. But Moshe made his hand gesture of dismissal so far as he was concerned.

Zelek appeared over the rim of the sand-hole carrying a large paper. In the paper were ice-cream sliders, one for each, cool and dripping in the sun.

'Ice-cream!' he shouted, 'Ice-cream!'

After the ice-cream, and after the hamper had been opened, and sampled, and emptied, Lala lay asleep on a towel laid on the sand. David slept in the shade of a towel draped over two sticks.

In the shallows, Moshe Kaydan and Rivka Kaydan his wife were paddling. They held hands. So Rivka looked at Moshe, and he knew his wife was looking at him.

'Nu?' he asked.

It was a small word to cover the span of his life, of the hard days in *der Heim*, and the harder days and broken bodies and broken hearts in this new homeland, and to encompass God. God was there all right, in the little word, as in everything – the warm sand and the sea and the happiness of children. To enjoy, that was in the word too, and Rivka didn't often hear it from him. But she understood it all from the beginning to the end, and gave her answer to his question with a nod of her head.

They went on paddling.

In the woods behind the beach there was a park, and in the park stood a fine Adam mansion. Outside the front door, on the gravel driveway, on a bench in the sun, sat the laird. He was reading *The Scotsman*.

The two children came out from the house with their air-guns. The laird asked what they were going after.

'Pigeons,' they said.

'Good shooting.'

He resumed his paper, and the children went off down the drive with their guns over their shoulders.

It got hot in the afternoon, the dry scorching heat that comes no more than once a year, if that, on the east coast of Scotland.

Mary was still knitting in the sand-hole. Queenie was nearby, drying herself after her third swim (well, nearly swimming), but with her costume all on.

'You should go in,' she told Mary.

Mary gave a big shoulder-shrug of lassitude under the sun. 'It's too hot,' she complained.

'Hot?' said Ian, who had taken a place in the sand-hole. 'This is temperate. I was in the tropics, you know. Temperature a hundred, and rain – ! When you put a milk bottle out it fills in five minutes.'

They thought about it.

Jack asked what they did for chemists when Ian was on leave.

'Witch doctors,' said Ian, of course.

'Go on!' said Mary, and Zelek had to tell her not to be silly.

Ian nearly split himself laughing, and had to keep it low so as not to wake little David. He explained, 'There's a duty chemist. I did it last year.'

Mary asked him what he did with himself if it was so hot and so wet.

'The Burmese are ingenious people,' began Ian.

'What do you mean?' Mary asked, and Zelek had to make Ian shut up because he knew the sort of thing Ian had in mind, and he could not visualise what the reaction would be if he tried to tell Mary.

Ian knew he must shut up.

Jack asked him if he was going back to Burma.

'The pay's good,' said Ian. 'Nice people. I'm well treated there. Looked up to, for the first time in my life.' Ian had been conscious of that, but had never got accustomed to it so that it was always a delight.

'He's going back,' surmised Jack.

Mary pointed out that there were no Jewish girls in Burma, but Ian corrected her: 'You'd be surprised what they have in Rangoon.'

'You're a *lignor*,' Mary told him.

'No, I'm not,' said Ian, 'I could marry there.'

This was news to Zelek, and he was impressed.

'But,' Ian continued, 'the old folks are here. And you. And your children.' Ian liked children, he was part child himself still, and Zelek's children were special. A new vista lay before him; he shrugged off his dilemma; he just didn't know. He passed the question to Zelek.

'What's your future?'

'Wealthy, I hope, Ian. I'm a good salesman.'

Mary spoke up from counting her row. 'He is!'

'Set up my own business, sole agency.'

Jack said it would need capital. Zelek knew.

'Where you going to get capital from? You should have stuck to medicine.'

Mary told them that Zelek was already making more money than he would have done as a young doctor.

Jack knew a little about capital. 'My father brought the money with him from *der Heim*. Otherwise I'd be nowhere. I know you're ambitious, Zelek.'

'What are we talking about?' asked Zelek. 'My capital's around me, my wife, two kids! And here we are by the sea, sun shining! What future are we planning? Let me tell you folks, life can't be better than this.' He meant it.

Mary asked him, 'Why are you going away tomorrow then?'

Zelek held the thought, had a momentary glimpse of the contradiction and the madness in it, then the big grin took hold of his face. 'Business,' he said. That was even better than wife, kids, sea and sun, although he didn't say so.

When the beach had long shadows, when the tide was in, they packed up and took everything to the car, away up on the road above the beach.

Ian sat at the driving-wheel with David beside him. Lala and Mary with baby Shirley sat in the back seat. The car glided along silently, with all the other Kaydans behind it, shoving. It had somehow failed to start. But they managed to get home and parked the car off the road, had supper and went happily to bed.

Monday was a grey day. Zelek put on his business suit, a brown pin-stripe, with a white shirt and stiff collar and floral brown silk tie. He breakfasted on porridge and the last egg and bread and butter and marmalade and tea; then took his attaché case, checked and rechecked, and went out to the roadway with Mary and David. They were going with him in Ian's car as far as the station. He would catch the train to Glasgow, and they would drive on towards St Andrews, for the market and the Abbey with the dungeon, and the sands.

Across the road from the cottage, the car stood where they had pushed it at the end of last night's journey home. The bonnet was up on both sides; Moshe was looking at the engine one way, Ian the other.

'Of course I'll fix it.'

'*Los mir.*'

'Listen, Pa, you're a watch-mender. This is a bit bigger.'

'You dinnae ken.'

'I'm a chemist, a scientist. I have a trained mind.'

Rivka came out of the cottage with a pitcher and a basket. She called, 'Kveenie?'

Queenie heard the call from the pump where she was giving her face a dab of water. She dried her face on the towel hanging over her back.

'What?'

'I've got something for you!'

Queenie walked round the house to the front.

'Here,' said her mother. 'Go to de farm.' And as Queenie's face filled with fear, she added, 'De hens von't bite.' She handed over the pitcher and basket.

Queenie asked what they were for. Milk and eggs. Eggs?! They assured her that the hens were more scared of her than she was of the hens.

'Lala,' called Queenie, 'chum me to the farm?'

'No!' shouted Lala from the chute.

Queenie hovered.

'Gey!' commanded her mother. 'It's time you vent on your own!'

Queenie turned and went, swinging the pitcher and basket to show the world she went with a light heart. The flies buzzed under her feet in the long grass as she passed.

At the car, Ian was tinkering with spanners, loosening, tightening.

'It's this, you see. Needs adjusting.'

Moshe looked witheringly.

'Look!' said Ian.

'*Los mir.*'

'No, I'm doing it.'

Little David toddled over.

'How does a car go, Uncle Ian?'

Ian answered from the depths of the bonnet. 'When you sit inside, you push it with your knees.'

'Will I push it?'

'Please do.'

He looked up, laid his spanners down and came to lift the wee boy into the driving seat.

Moshe took the chance to fish inside the engine for what he had seen. He pulled out the fan-belt and waved it in Ian's face.

'*Tsebrochen*,' he said. It was broken. 'And you dinnae ken de electricity.'

Zelek came to see. 'Ian, surely . . .' He was vexed. 'I'll have to run for it!'

Mary had another solution. 'Stay, don't go.'

'I've got to see the man. I'll be back tomorrow.'

Mary demanded to know how he was going to get to the station. Zelek would run, only a mile. He asked her to take care while he was away, kissed her brow, kissed David.

'Look after Mummy!'

'What?'

Mary explained the joke, 'He means, we'll look after each other.'

Zelek banged his attaché case on the nose of the car. 'Good luck!'

'And you! Sorry about the car.'

Zelek waved and sprinted down the road.

Queenie approached the hen-house with her basket and pitcher. She had asked the farmer's wife for eggs, and the good lady had directed her to the source. She stood now on the cinder path between the nettles, with thistledown beginning to blow. The wire-mesh around the hen-run looked forbidding. She laid the pitcher down.

'Mrs Brown, she called, 'do I just go in?'

There was no answer from the farmer's wife. Queenie went to the door of the hen-run. There was a cluck. She opened the door and went in. She stepped to the hen-house, went round it till she found the low door. She opened it. Squawks and feathers. Hens came running out, almost falling on their beaks.

It was dark and smelly inside. Queenie told herself just to go on, never mind, find the eggs, other people did. She waved her arm to clear the hens from her eyes, bent low over the nesting boxes and was amazed to find the warm eggs, so round and smooth among the litter.

She searched around for all there were, and came out. Easy. She shut the hen-house door. Exhilarated and triumphant, she made for the wire door of the run.

The cock raised its comb and crowed at her. She froze with fear. The cock took a strutting step towards her; she backed. The cock flapped its wings of power. Queenie found her back against the wire; she eased sideways and as the cock took a peck at the ground, she got to the door and through it, grabbed the pitcher and ran. The cock gave a great cockadoodledoo-o-o. Queenie crashed through the undergrowth.

It started to rain. Ian put the car hood up, then continued to poke at the engine with wet hair and clothes.

The other Kaydans, in waterproofs and hats, sat huddled in the open doorway of the cottage. David had a blue oil-skin hat and coat, and wee wellies, and he paddled about happily in the rain. The pram had its hood up, and under it, baby Shirley gurgled away to anyone or no one.

Ian straightened up, let down the bonnet and screwed it in place. He wiped the wet from his hair and deposited the spanners and screwdriver and pliers inside the car. He crossed to the others. He looked up at the heavens.

'There you are, folks. If the motor car was working, we'd be in St Andrews by now, in the rain. We're lucky.'

Queenie appeared along the road, hair dripping down her face and neck, blouse soaking, bulges rippling with every step.

They watched her approach.

'You're soaked.'

'You should have taken a coat!'

Queenie sulked. 'I got the milk and eggs!'

'No trouble,' said Rivka.

Queenie answered them with great dignity. 'I was chased by the cock,' she said. She made her way through them in the doorway and went inside. The Kaydans burst into laughter.

So they accepted the rain and went for a picnic in the woods. In waterproofs and hats and wellington boots they were fine. Ian pushed the pram. Jack and Moshe carried the covered baskets.

Mary inhaled deeply. 'Smell the smells!'

Rivka observed that the rain was going off.

Moshe had his bearings better than any of them. 'Up dere is de laird's hoose. A big von.'

'Rich people.'

'Very rich,' said Moshe. 'I go tomorrow.'

Jack asked what for.

'He'll hae clocks and votches.' The questions people asked when they should know already . . . !

'Big clocks,' Queenie amplified.

Moshe smiled at her simplicity. 'Von or two.'

Ian crowed like a cock and Queenie jumped, then walked on. 'Shut up!' she said.

They passed along the path in the woods and did not see the laird's children watching them. The boy and the girl crouched behind the rhododendrons. What were these disgusting people doing? On their private grounds, too. Poachers obviously. They had to be dealt with, but how? The boy and the girl argued with passion, the girl prevailed, and both darted back along their own secret path towards the big house.

The sun broke through. The Kaydans found a glade and chose their positions and put their waterproofs down for sitting on. The tablecloth was brought out and spread. Then they changed positions according to Mary's ideas and laid out the picnic. Tomato sandwiches, bananas, cheese sandwiches.

196

'And what's this?' Mary felt in the bundle. 'It's Grandma's – ? Cake! Oh, it's light.' She turned in pleased surprise to the others.

'Here's the eggs,' said Queenie with special emphasis, as if she had laid them herself – well, she had almost. 'Will I shell them?'

'Spread de cups,' commanded Rivka and there was no room for argument in her voice. 'And don't spill de milk,' she besought.

Before the repast, Ian and Jack had gone behind some trees with David. They stood in a row and admired the three arches of pee and were content. They folded away their peeshkies and did up their buttons. Ian did up David's; the little boy was busy asking about how the old folks talked. He thought they 'spoke funny' and Ian and Jack agreed.

'They say "Vot",' said David.

'Vot?' said Jack.

'And "de",' said David. 'Vot ees de matter?'

Ian explained as they strolled back to the party. 'They have their own language, their own way of talking. They're not like us. Do you know how they say yes?'

David was listening intently. Ian demonstrated how Grandpa and Grandma said yes, by putting a thumb to the nose, and spreading out the fingers and wiggling them. He got David to practise a little, so that the grandparents would be really pleased. Jack watched dubiously but didn't interfere.

At the picnic-place, they were waiting to begin; some had even begun.

'Where's Jack?'

'Where's David?'

The trio appeared from the trees.

'Dere. Nu, sit down, enjoysach.' Rivka looked at her grandson and was filled with joy at the beauty of him. 'Look at him . . . oy!' The little syllable surpassed whole sentences and summed up human inability to express delight in mere words. 'Are you ready for your picnic?' she asked him.

David put his thumb to his nose, spread out his fingers and wiggled them at his Grandma.

Mary was scandalised. 'A boy doesn't do that to his Grandma!' And Rivka was upset. 'Vot have I done?' (With both hands on her chest.)

Moshe tried to smooth it over, whatever it was. 'Coom,' he said to the wee boy, 'do you vont an egg?'

And David put a thumb to his nose and spread out his fingers, and to the littlest finger he attached his other thumb and spread out the fingers of his other hand, too, and wiggled every one of them at his Grandpa.

'David!' shouted Lala.

Queenie just squealed.

Mary waved her hands around her head. 'I don't know what –' she began in distress.

Ian and Jack roared with laughter.

In the trees the laird's children were stalking the trespassers, their air-rifles at the ready. The sound of helpless laughter only tightened their lips. They edged round to see.

The Kaydans, every one, were rolling with laughter on the ground, even Mary, and Rivka and Moshe; Ian was quite doubled up.

The laird's children rose into view and aimed their guns. The girl shouted, 'Get off our land!' She fired. And the boy fired.

The laughter turned to screams. Lala doubled up; old Moshe's hand jerked in the air. The laird's children took fright and ran away.

The laird was standing on the gravel outside his massive front door with one foot up on the garden seat, drinking sherry, when the children rounded the house with their guns at the trail, in the safe position. They passed him on their way into the house. He called out to them that the gong had just gone: it was time for lunch.

His daughter told him that they had shot some poachers, which the laird thought was a jolly good idea; he continued to sip his sherry. Then, because they seemed to be staying with him instead of going in for lunch, he asked them where the shooting had occurred. The boy answered that it had been in the pond wood, whereupon his father asked whether he had bagged any. The boy said yes, and mentioned that they had screamed. The laird laughed at that: it was an amusing picture, the two children shooting with air-guns at rascally poachers!

He asked what they had been poaching. The girl didn't know, neither did the boy. The boy added that the people had been picnicking; the girl thought that they were probably tinkers. The children went on into the house.

Then the laird called his daughter back, she being the older of the two, and the leader. He asked how many people there had been. A dozen or so, she thought. A little man with a beard. And a pram. Awful.

The laird recognised from this description the holiday people in his grieve-cottage. He asked the girl positively, had she actually hit 'em? But she didn't know, and anyway, it was only with air-guns. She disappeared into the house. The laird pondered for a moment, and downed the rest of his sherry.

Lala had been hit in the thigh; Moshe had his knuckles grazed. The idyll and the beauty had turned to ugly terror. Jack clutched Lala and walked with her, supported her through the forest. The others looked out for more attackers, but there were none. They got to the cottage, where Lala's labour pains started. Ian ran all the way to the village.

Later on in the afternoon, the laird was walking his horse through the woods and came upon the picnic spot. The cloth had been abandoned there with the picnic. The milk pitcher lay overturned. Flies and ants were thick on the sandwiches, biscuits, cake and fruit.

The laird stopped his horse and observed. Litter. He walked his horse on.

He took a side path and came to the roadway above the cottage and trotted round and down. The cottage door was open. The laird pulled up. There was no sound.

He called, 'Hello?'

No one answered him. The afternoon was silent.

'Anyone there?'

The laird looked along the road and spurred his horse into a trot. He was disturbed.

Ian had failed to find a doctor, or a motor car. He hired the horse and trap and the driver obliged by whipping the horse into a near gallop. When they reached the stricken family Lala was lifted into the trap, the Kaydans hastily threw their possessions into the trunk and cases and set off at once for the station.

The driver led the horse on foot. Rivka knelt on the trap beside Lala, soothing her, cradling her head. Moshe walked beside the trap carrying bundles, things wrapped in towels. Behind came Jack and Ian carrying the heavy trunk between them, and Ian cursing his own car that he'd have to come back for. Mary carried baby Shirley in her arms and David trailed behind her with Queenie, who was carrying two hat-boxes.

The laird took a short cut and came down to the road near the village. The driver saw him ahead, and said so. This time they all understood what the man was saying, despite his accent.

And Moshe spoke, and his word was law. 'Don't say notting!'

Ian hissed that it had been 'his bloody kids', but Rivka said, 'Do vot Pa says!' She was remembering.

Moshe added the further command – for there had always been a rule in cases like this – 'Don't make trouble!' It would be foolish for the lower classes to challenge the doings of the upper classes, doubly and trebly so and more if you were the Jewish lower classes.

Lala moaned in pain.

Jack nearly cried. 'Lala, dear . . .'

They came abreast of the laird on his horse. They kept their eyes down. The laird gently eased his horse along and kept pace with them. His manner was charming as he asked what had happened.

Rivka answered that her daughter had had an accident, and that she was miscarrying. When she had finished, she added, 'Sir.'

Moshe spoke to the laird. 'Ve're gaun hame.' That was all he said.

The laird stopped his horse. The Kaydans walked on, and as Ian passed the man on horseback, he gave him a mock salute.

They straggled on along the road to – where? Memel? Babylon?

18

Lala lost her child. Her cough came back that she had had as a baby; maybe it would have come back anyway, but the following year she took a long time dying. Lovely Lala. Jack took to drink as the only solace; became, shamefully, a *shiker*. It was a good job that he had a furniture shop in the family.

The Kaydans mourned grievously, none more so than Ian. He did not go back to Burma; instead he got a job with Fain the chemist in Glasgow, and rented a flat there for during the week, coming home at weekends. He was good at buying, so Mr Fain retired and Ian moved into the little office behind the shop as manager.

Moshe bought and sold, bought and sold, kept himself alive. He picked up a piano for nothing because it was being thrown out, and Zelek and Ian and he heaved it up the stairs to the front room. It never was tuned but Ian bought a vamping chart and banged away on it.

'*In your dear little Alice blue gown –*' he sang to his own playing. He was thirty-eight now, his hair beginning to recede at the temples. Queenie sat at the window looking down into the square. At thirty-four, with a bulging body and heavy face, she was as Jewish as a bowl of gefilte fish. On her lap was a copy of the *Woman's Pictorial*, open at a picture page. Oh, Queenie loved looking at the pictures in it! She loved the gramophone, too, the solid mahogany box on legs that Moshe had picked up, not for nothing mind you – for two pounds with a packet of needles.

'Where are they?' asked Queenie over Ian's singing, still gazing down at the street.

Rivka came in, in her apron, shuffling in her slippers. She had passed her sixty-fifth birthday, her hair was steel grey, tight still in a bun behind her head. Deep lines marked her face, from those days. . . . They were past now, she was all right.

'I've put de kichlach in de oven. Vere are de kinder?' She stood at the window, looking down.

'They'll have gone into the sweetie shop for *chazzerai*.' Queenie knew well how tempting were the sweetie-shop's rubbishy delights.

'Shlomo,' – his mother stopped his playing by a hand on his shoulder – 'give me a *phoont*.'

'What for?'

The money wasn't for her, it was for his brother Zelek. Ian swung round on the piano stool, but Rivka pleaded.

'He needs. I vouldnae ask if he didnae need it. And I know you've got.' That was true: Ian was the provider – a good son, and clever, a good living he made, even in these hard times. She would put the pound in an envelope and give it to the children and they would take it home, not knowing anything about it. So Zelek wouldn't be ashamed, he'd have something in his pocket.

Ian took out his wallet and extracted a large white five-pound note. Rivka took it.

'That's a fiver!'

'Kveenie, an envelope.'

Queenie went to the sideboard drawer and opened it to find an envelope. She was to put the fiver in, and write 'with love'. She knew all that, why tell her?

Rivka told her. 'Mister Zelek Kaydan. Private.'

The doorbell jangled and died away. The children! Queenie said not to open the door till she had found an envelope amongst the crumpled mess of doilies and candle-ends in the drawer, but Ian and Rivka took no notice and went out to the hall.

Rivka shouted for Moshe to come from the kitchen. Then

she opened the front door. David and Shirley stood there side by side. He was thirteen now, not adolescent yet, dressed in a blue blazer and shorts and blue school cap, a Heriot boy; Shirley was ten, in maroon blazer and skirt and grey hat; Gillespies had claimed her. Their faces were polished, their hair was combed.

Rivka gathered them in her arms and kissed them, 'Oy . . .' and they returned the affection politely. They were in between kissing stages.

'Hello,' said Ian.

Shirley lept into his arms and hugged him. Uncle Ian was different; him she could love.

David, to disengage from his Grandma's embracing, asked where Grandpa was. And Moshe came out from the kitchen in his waistcoat and slippers. He was smaller than he used to be, even smaller, from stooping. Sixty-six years of age.

He gave the greeting, as always: 'Nu, David, *vos machs du*?'

And David held out his hand to be shaken, and replied that he was fine, thanks, and how was Grandpa? Moshe smiled, and shrugged, and also put it into words: 'Not too bad. '

Shirley greeted her grandfather from Ian's arms, and he smiled his greeting back to her and shook her hand.

'What a weight,' said Ian. Shirley slid to the floor. Queenie appeared at the door of the parlour.

'Well, big children?'

'Hello, Auntie Queenie.'

Moshe said 'Coom,' and waved them to the kitchen.

Rivka told him, 'Don't say coom! I'll say coom. In five minutes.' She turned to the children. 'You've got tae vait, can you smell it?'

They sniffed, and guessed, and they were right. Kichlach, those little cakes that were half-way to biscuits.

'And?' said Rivka. They guessed that, too. Teglach. Though not from the smell. Rivka always had teglach for them that you couldn't buy in the sweetie-shop because they were little biscuits dripping with soft toffee and rolled in coconut. Rivka shooed them into the parlour to go and play till she called them.

Shirley went straight to the piano and banged the keys by the handful. 'Play, Uncle Ian!'

He would play anything she wanted him to play. She chose the tune he had played when she was there last, because he played it best, and it was his favourite, too: 'When I Grow Too Old To Dream'. Ian blew a raspberry at her, and broke into his latest piece.

'*In your dear little Alice blue gown –*' He ta-ra'd the words that followed.

'What's an Alice blue gown?'

'Ask your Auntie.'

Queenie rolled her eyes a little and then she found it. She pointed to a thread on the embroidery of the table-covering. That was Alice-blue. At the piano, Ian took Shirley's finger and tapped out the melody of the Alice-blue gown.

Queenie plumped herself down beside David on the sofa. 'Well, have you got over your barmitzvah?'

It was four weeks ago now. David answered politely 'Och, ay.'

'And have any more presents come in?' She always asked that, too. He recited the number of pens and wallets he'd had from distant aunties in Leeds, and great-uncles in Dundee. All the duplicates – three wallets, two watches, three pens, and two copies of *Ivanhoe*. Queenie put her hand to her mouth. She had given him one of them. David realised his blunder and assured her that he was going to change the other copy, not hers. He hadn't actually read it yet. 'Have you?' he asked her conversationally.

'What?' said Queenie, 'No, I don't think I have.'

'Play properly,' Shirley told Ian, which meant the song he played best. She knew the words too. So Ian vamped a little and they both sang.

'When I grow too old to dream
I'll have you to remember;
When I grow too old to dream,
Your love will stay in my heart.'

Over the singing, Queenie asked how much money David
had received in the end. Sixteen pounds, he told her. That
was a lot of money, a fortune. Had he spent it yet? No, he'd
given it to his Dad. Queenie thought that was very wise, so
that his Dad could put it in the bank for him.

David was too wise to agree or disagree. He wrinkled up
his nose in a smile. 'Eventually,' he said.

Rivka could hear the piano and Ian and Shirley singing
their duet from the kitchen. They were happy, so she was
happy. She opened the oven and took out the tray of cakes.
'*Tsubrennte?*' Of course they weren't. She carried the tray
to the table, already set with floral cups and saucers and
scones and butter and the painted plate with teglach. She
emptied the hot cakes on to her wire grid and put the tray
in the sink.

Moshe stood at the dresser, engrossed with his hand-
scales and gold-testing box. He had bought some gold-
rimmed spectacles and was scraping off the surface with his
pocket-knife. The knife-blade was worn down to almost
nothing by years of repeated sharpening.

'Shlomo gave me five pounds,' Rivka told him.

'For Zelek?'

'In an envelope, don't ask.' She eyed the brown paper
parcel on the dresser: a brisket and a vorsht that Ian
had brought from the kosher butcher in the Gorbals.
She'd give that to the kinder, too. Moshe caught her looking.

'You don't need,' she said, 'you got bread and herring.
So, is it gold?' (to change the subject).

Moshe took a drop of nitric acid from his bottle with the
glass rod fixed to the stopper. He touched the scraped surface with it, and together they watched. The metal turned

green. It wasn't gold. Moshe put the stopper back in the bottle and washed the drop of acid off at the sink.

'De voman I bought it from –'

'How much?'

Moshe shrugged. 'A few shtiber. I told her it vosnae gold. But I t'ought, maybe.' He crunkled the wire frame in his fist and put it in his attaché case. Maybe somebody else would take a chance on it. The woman who had sold it to him had told him he ought to be retired. He related this to Rivka and laughed and dismissed the idea with a wave of his hand. Him retired?

Rivka thought the woman was entitled to her point of view.

But it was stupid. How could he retire?

In the parlour, the talk had got round to barmitzvahs in general. Ian remembered Zelek's, in 1904.

'It was the social event of the Edinburgh season.'

The children jeered.

Ian went on, 'All the Jews in Edinburgh were there.'

'In this house?' asked David.

'No, in Crosscauseway. We had two rooms for all of us, Ma and Pa and six kids, no light, no water.'

It was too much for Queenie. She tried to shush him.

Ian remembered with a mixture of pride and shame. 'A slum.' He said the word with his voice and his shoulders and his face at an angle.

Queenie wouldn't have it. Shirley asked how old she was then.

'Oh, I don't remember your Dad's barmitzvah.' How could she? She was new-born. Ian cradled his arms and pretended to have the baby Queenie there. The children jeered again.

Ian told them that when he was eight his father had broken his eardrum by hitting him. 'I had a great big bandage round ma heid,' he said, exaggerating the slum accent, 'and Lala was there, and Sarah . . . Anyway, we were all in the old shool in Richmond Street, waiting for your Dad to sing.' As David had sung last month. As all Jewish boys had sung for three thousand years. But when Zelek had opened his mouth he only croaked.

'Why? Why?' David and Shirley demanded to know.

'We couldn't afford to have him taught, he was taught by your Grandpa – have you ever heard *him* sing?'

They hadn't. David had sat beside him often enough in the shool and had heard him pray, in a funny way. He'd often thought about this, and wondered why his Grandpa, who was an authority on all things religious, should pray differently from the way he, David, had been taught at the Cheder, his Hebrew evening classes.

'Your grandpa's tone-deaf,' said Ian.

Queenie got up and wound the handle of the gramophone; she wasn't.

David and Shirley were curious about Auntie Lala, and why she had died. Their Mummy would only tell them that Lala was ill and didn't get better.

Ian bore only a little grudge against the laird. He was a realist. Lala had died because she had a bad beginning: slum-kids don't get a good start in life. Her lungs gave out and her heart gave out. 'You're all right,' he told Shirley; and David was all right, they didn't know the half of it.

Queenie set the gramophone needle on the record, and dance music filled the parlour. *'Have you ever seen a dream walking? Well, I have. Have you ever seen a dream talking? Well, I have.'* Queenie danced up and down, and round the table with the handsomest partner she could day-dream of – a bit like Melvyn Douglas – and her arms clutched the air as she ta-ra'ed to the record.

David pursued the subject of the effect of slum-upbringing on adult health. He tried to be offhand when he mentioned his own father.

'Aw, your Dad's all right, he's through it, and me and Queenie.' He slapped Queenie's rump as she was passing. 'Eh, hen?' Queenie yelped.

Ian got up and picked the needle off the groove. Queenie got angry but Ian calmed her. He put the needle into the blank grooves at the end of the record, and shouted into the fabric covering the speaker, 'HOI!' He lifted the needle and replayed it, and back came his shout, muffled but true: 'Hoi!'

The children were delighted. They crowded to the gramophone as Ian started the needle again on the blank. He chanted into the speaker: '*I went doon the Coongate, Tae buy a penny drum.*' It was the forbidden song. David and Shirley had been told very strictly by their Mummy that on no account were they to sing it: if they did they might turn into a fly.

They joined Uncle Ian in the chant:

> 'I knocked at the door but
> Nobody come.
> I knocked at the window
> And brokc a pane of glass –'

Rivka was at the door. 'Kinder,' she called, 'de kichlach. Tea, teglach, bread, butter, jam –'

But they went on chanting:

> Doon came a wee man
> Sliding on his ask
> No questions,
> Tell no lies,
> Shut yer mouth and
> Don't catch flies –'

and they dissolved into shrieks of laughter. Queenie's voice was heard above this: she thought it was terrible for Ian to teach them that awful song.

Ian took the needle up and started the gramophone again. Moshe joined Rivka at the parlour door. All listened intently to the muffled recording of the song and the shrieks. Even Queenie smirked. Rivka tut-tutted and Moshe nodded in time to the chant. It didn't matter one way or the other to him. The invention he knew about; its use by his children and grandchildren was good.

At tea, Queenie asked Ian, 'Why don't you take me to Glasgow?' She had asked this before, many times. Ian had a flat, why couldn't Queenie be his housekeeper? It would save him the wages he was paying out to a *goiety*, a non-Jewish, working-class, dim-witted cleaning woman – well, she cooked too, but not like Queenie would cook.

Ian didn't answer her this time. He hardly answered her any time she asked him about coming to Glasgow because it was self-evident that he was a grown man and should be free to have his own household, no matter how tiny. But Queenie suspected the worst: that he preferred pork sausages and such-like chazzerai to good home-kosher food, and that his Glasgow flat was a den of sin. Pork and bacon and lard . . . Ugh!

But this tea-time it was different.

'I've had an invitation,' said Queenie to the Kaydans. 'The Levenes. The *wedding*, Ian. Next month in Glasgow, the Levene wedding!' How could anybody not know that? She betted even the children's mummy and daddy knew that. Her brother knew the Levenes, everybody knew the Levenes. 'So get yourself an invitation, Ian, I'll get one for you and we'll both go, eh?' And he'd maybe find himself someone, a nice Yiddishy girl, and she'd find someone herself. Hope sprang eternal in Queenie's breast – both of her breasts.

19

Ian sat in the third-class compartment, a smoker of course, thoughts far away from the speeding yellow gorse on the railway embankment and the rhythm of the train wheels.

The ash fell from his cigarette and he took it from his mouth and stubbed it out in the metal ashtray, then dusted his waistcoat with a flick of his hand. The man opposite wore a bowler hat and eyed Ian balefully.

'Sorry,' said Ian, 'did I – ?' He didn't know what he'd done, if anything.

The man said, 'D'ya see that fella Hitler?'

Ian caught his breath. He prepared himself.

'In Germany,' said the man. 'Chancellor. The heid one. like the Kaiser.'

'What about him?' Ian played the man along.

'Good man. We could dae wi' him here. Get the unemployment down. Get roads built, there's nae unemployment in Germany. That's what we need. And nae Jews.'

The panic stirred and fell away in Ian's frame.

'The Jews are the trouble,' said the man, eye to eye with Ian. 'They're the cause of a' the unemployment.'

'How's that?'

'Eh?' said the man. 'Because they're stinking rich.'

'All of them?' asked Ian, knowing better.

'The Jews,' said the man. 'You ken that. Here, in Britain.' He tapped Ian on the knee. 'You ken what Hitler's done? There's nae Jews in Germany noo. They've a' left.'

Ian knew that they hadn't. Letters had been coming; the new wave of refugees had started, even to Scotland.

Central Station, Glasgow, had a grimy feeling. Ian shouldered his way through the crowds outside the barrier, having given up the return half of his ticket to the wee collector. Then his searching eyes lit up.

She stood against a hoarding for Haig's, her blonde hair down to her shoulder. She saw Ian and made her way to him. They kissed lightly on the lips.

She linked her arm through his and they walked together to the taxi-stance.

Ian rented a flat in Pollockshields, two up. It had a living-room-kitchen, two wee bedrooms, a parlour and a bathroom, all leading off the hall. He had had it painted, with linoleum right through, and a rug for the kitchen hearth, and one for beside his bed.

When he came in with Marjory they had a clinch in the hall because they hadn't seen each other all weekend. Then Marjory broke the embrace and came through to the kitchen.

'Give me a chance,' said Ian.

But the flat was chilly and Marjory said so. Ian switched on the little electric fire, then put a match to the kindling in the grate.

Marjory took up a note on the table. It read:

Dear Mr Kaydan,

There's soup on the stove just light the gas and maybe stir it. Put the oven on first there's a shepherd's pie in it give it half an hour. And a jam tart in the press for with your tea.

Yrs truly,

Mrs MGuire.'

She put the note down, and opened the oven door to see. The shepherd's pie was there all right. Ian looked too.

'D'you fancy that?'

'Uhuh. Do you?'

He did. He handed her the matchbox. Their eyes met and they smiled, because love was funny.

Marjory struck a match and lit the oven. 'Plouff!' She shut the oven door. She blew out the match and this also seemed amusing, though neither of them could have explained why.

'How's Edinburgh?'

'Windy.'

'How's the family?' Ian had told her who was who.

'Poor but honest,' he said, after the song. They were close now, and lips were enticing.

'How was the train?'

Ian remembered the Hitler man, and the train's dirtiness.

Marjory asked if she should set the table and Ian said it would indeed be a useful thing to do. Then they'd have half an hour till the pie would be ready, a cosy half-hour in front of the fire. Marjory dodged away from his hands. 'I'll tell you about *my* weekend.' 'Please do.'

So she set the table and told him the minutiae of her weekend and they settled in front of the blazing fire and made love before supper.

The office in Ian's shop was tiny and crammed from floor to ceiling with files and advertisements and samples and extra stock for the shop. He had a desk there, with ledgers and receipts on spikes and a high-built Remington typewriter that he tapped invoices on with one finger, very fast. The locked poisons cupboard hung on the wall beside his desk. Ian was on the phone, receiver to his ear.

'But we're no exception, turn-over is down –' The man at the other end was surprised. 'No, it's not picking up here, I assure you. Nor in the Gorbals branch, anything but.' Trade was the worst that anyone could remember. 'I'm sorry, Mr Thomson, but I can't force people to buy things they can't afford, your prices are still too high.' Firms were going bankrupt all over the place, and bankrupt stock was cheap and even so there was a lot of it for Ian to buy on behalf of his firm. The man on the phone said he might be going bankrupt too if Ian gave him no order at all.

Marjory came into the office, in her white overall, carrying a prescription. She took her key to the poisons cupboard from the overall pocket, unlocked the cupboard and brought out a bottle.

'I'm very sorry,' Ian was saying, 'I hope you don't, Mr Thomson, it's bad for all of us.'

Marjory waved the bottle at Ian. He nodded and slipped his hand up her skirt.

'I think I might lose my job if I did that,' he replied to Mr Thomson on business matters. Marjory kissed the top of his head and went out.

'Sorry,' said Ian, 'goodbye.' He hung the receiver on its rest, and sighed. It was a difficult year.

They lay on the sofa in the living-room, in the firelight. Ian caressed Marjory's face with his. They were happy.

'I want it to last,' said Ian.

'I've got to go home,' said Marjory.

'I don't mean tonight, I mean –'

They caressed. Marjory wanted to know what he meant: he meant, he wanted it to go on. How, go on? Like this – like lying together in the firelight, like nosing noses, like kissing hands and arms. Marjory maintained that it couldn't go on like this and Ian said it had to.

After a pause Marjory said, 'My mother's been in the shop, you've met her. Why can't I meet yours?'

'Because she lives in Edinburgh.'

'What a long nose you've got.'

Marjory was stroking Ian's nose at the time, but Ian took another meaning from it. A long nose belonged to a Jew. But she hadn't meant that, she had simply remarked what a long nose he had. And there was only one way to make their present happiness last.

Ian had a funny feeling inside him as he said to her, 'Would you marry a Jew?'

Marjory replied, 'It depends which one.' And they caressed each other and were silent. Then Marjory asked, 'Would a Jew get married in church?'

'No, he couldn't do that.' Ian smiled broadly.

'What's the joke?'

Ian tried to imagine telling his parents that he was going to marry a girl who wasn't Jewish; in fact, she was a Christian, and they were going to get married in a church.

'What's wrong with that?'

'The main thing wrong is that my father left Lithuania to save his life, and to keep close to God.' His father had left because he had to keep on speaking terms with God. 'If I went home with that story,' said Ian, 'I'd be saying good-bye. It would break him.' And his mother, he didn't know about his mother, but it would break his father.

Marjory sat up and stared into the fire to think about it.

Ian went on, 'They're fighting in London, in the streets, marching.' Mosley's Blackshirts were in the papers every day, and not just the *Jewish Chronicle*. Down with the Jews! – like Germany, with Hitler and his Brownshirts. 'What I'm saying is, you'd have to turn. You'd have to become Jewish. It's a big thing to take on.' For Ian, it was the essential condition for marriage.

He sat up now, too. She looked round at him, at her man. She told him she was going to have a baby.

Ian found himself drawing back. Staring at her. Realising that she was staring back. Then they were themselves again and made loving love frenziedly.

Lemon tea is very good if you dip the teaspoon first into blackberry jam, then into the glass of tea, then sup it through the spaces in your teeth with a gurgling, squelching noise. Moshe sat at the kitchen table enjoying one of the pleasures of life.

Queenie came in, dressed to mid-calf in a red and black brocade, wearing high-heeled lace-up shoes and a straw hat with cherries pulled low over her black curls.

She stood beside the window. After a bit she said, 'Well?'

Moshe looked up and registered her appearance. 'Who are you going to meet?'

'How should I know who I'll meet?' She was going to a wedding, she could meet anyone. 'Do you like me?'

Moshe shrugged. 'I like you.'

Queenie called 'Ma?' and asked Moshe the time.

He took a silver fob-watch from his waistcoat, and looked through the centre glass, then checked by opening the window and seeing the whole face of the watch. It was ten minutes to five, unmistakably, and he told her so.

Rivka came into the kitchen lugging a suitcase. 'Vot you got in here?'

'Just things,' said Queenie. 'Put it down.'

Rivka left the case on the floor. 'Tings?' It was as if Queenie were going to get married too. Well, one never knew, she was right to pack what she could.

The front door bell clanged and Queenie rushed out to answer it. Moshe and Rivka exchanged a look; it concerned Queenie's appearance, and spoke volumes.

'Vell,' said Rivka, 'she's got to try.'

'Keep trying,' corrected Moshe.

Queenie opened the front door to Ian, who was looking tired but trying to look cheerful.

'Ian! Why are you late?'

'The train,' said Ian. He stretched and took off his hat and hung it on the hall peg, then doffed his coat ritually, one hand then the other hand, then up on the peg. 'Ooooh!' – an exhalation of ease and weariness. 'Stiff,' he explained.

Queenie said 'Well?' and Ian looked at her and took in what she was wearing.

'Very nice,' he said loyally. His sister pirouetted for him, and again, 'Very nice,' he said. As he passed her on his way to the kitchen he squeezed her shoulder.

Rivka on hearing who it was had put the kettle on the fire. She turned and saw him. 'Nu Shlomo?', which was to ask how he was. Then she saw how he was. 'Vot's de matter?'

'Nothing. Why?'

Moshe said, '*Vos machs du?*'

'All right.'

They saw that he was nothing of the kind. He was pale, for one thing. Ian protested that he was fine, at which his mother offered him a little whisky.

'No,' said Ian, 'just a cup of tea.' He sat by the fire in the wooden armchair.

Queenie came in from the hall where she had been admiring herself in the mirror. 'Have you met the Levenes?'

'Who?' asked Moshe. It was a Jewish name, he had to ask.

'The wedding!' Queenie told him angrily.

Ian said, 'I've met the brother.'

'Whose brother?'

'The groom's brother. He's been in the shop, travels for Palmolive.'

Queenie was interested, and made a note. Not consciously, it was the kind of thing she remembered, so that she could identify, and ask, and ask again of other people, and gradually build up a picture of the person and everything he did. 'What's his name?'

'Who?'

'The brother.'

'Benny.'

'Benny Levene . . . Cyril Levene, the one that's getting married's in souvenirs, I hear he's getting quite a lot – you know. . . .' She meant the dowry. He was getting it from old man Stungo because Hetty Stungo, that was Dolly Stungo's cousin, had told her that Cyril Levene was getting enough, by marrying her, to set up.

'Set up as what?' That was Ian's domain and he wanted to know. Queenie didn't know that one. She sat at the table facing Ian in his fireside chair.

'Quite a do, eh? D'you think John Rosen'll be there?'

'I don't know, Queenie.'

But Queenie knew who would definitely be there. Hetty, .

and Batty Cohen, and Totty Lurie. 'My, Ian,' she said, 'you're going to have a time. Listen, I'm taking a few things through –' She pointed with her head at the case. 'I am going to stay, amn't I? A couple of weeks, then I can come back for the rest of the stuff. There's no point taking everything now, I've got, well, enough. And we'll have to see how Ma and Pa do on their own.'

'Fine,' said Moshe; he'd do very well on his own.

Queenie's imagination had it all planned. 'I hear they have whist drives. Fancy me, eh, in Glasgow!'

Ian's mouth was dry. 'Is the tea coming, Ma?'

'In a minute.'

Queenie hovered. 'Is – er – Jacky Cohen still around?' She remembered him fondly. He'd smiled at her; put his arm round her, once.

Ian didn't know if Jacky Cohen was still around.

'Och, you don't know anything! What's wrong with you? Have you got your dinner jacket cleaned?'

He hadn't. He said so. Queenie stared at him.

'Why?'

Rivka caught the mystery, the tension. She turned from the kettle on the fire to look at Ian. Moshe raised his eyes from the teaspoon of jam and tea and also looked at his son.

Ian said to Queenie, 'You can come back with me to Glasgow. And I'll see that you get to the wedding. Don't worry. And you can stay a few days.'

'A few days!'

Ian said nothing more; he longed for the tea to be made.

Rivka spoke quietly, 'Vos ees de tsorris?' It was the Yiddish word for trouble and sorrow that crushed and tore and had to be relieved.

Moshe demanded to know. 'Say!'

'Nothing.'

Queenie spoke the dreadful words: 'You're not going to the wedding.'

'That's right.' Ian took a breath.

The kettle rattled and hissed on the fire. Rivka lifted it

to the side. There was silence in the room. Moshe looked piercingly at his son, then he raised his fist and crashed it down on the table.

'Say!'

The silence took over.

Ian knew there was no way round, and no way out. He said, 'I didn't mean to tell you but . . . I've got a girl.'

Rivka's face was a mask. She'd been ready for anything in this life; she'd had to be to survive. But this was beyond thought, she'd think about it later.

Queenie was so surprised she was stupefied. Moshe looked and looked at Ian's face. Rivka poured the boiling water into the teapot on the hob, put the kettle back on the side of the range, then put the teapot lid on.

'Ma,' said Ian, 'please, Ma –'

Rivka turned back to him. 'Vot's her name?'

'Marjory.'

'Marjory vot?'

'Kerr. She's my dispenser at the shop. We've . . . been . . . friends for over a year.' That was a correct way to put it; it would do for the time being.

Rivka's face was tired, and all the lines were heavy and pulled the flesh down.

Moshe's eyes were hooded, ready to consider, ready to think. When he heard Ian's words, 'She's pregnant,' they became coals of fire.

Queenie just didn't believe him.

But Ian went on as if it were true. 'We've talked about . . . turning . . . I'll go and see the Rov in Glasgow. She could be Jewish.'

Moshe stood. 'In nine monts!' And the volcano in him erupted and he shouted, 'You cannae be Jewish in nine monts!'

He stood in his place in the silence of the room. Ian looked up at him and thought, it's over, it's done, I've said it, they know. Out loud he said, 'Let's allow the thought to settle. I'll have my cup of tea, and then the best thing would be for Queenie and me to go, and I'll see you again next week and we'll talk about it.'

Moshe still stood there. Queenie asked, how could she go?

'The wedding,' said Ian.

Queenie changed her weight from foot to foot; she swayed to the window, then to the fire, as if straining at ropes that were binding her. Then she was sure. 'I'm no' going tae no wedding . . .' She stumbled to the door, not seeing. She turned back to Ian and added, 'Obviously!' She went out, and they heard her bedroom door slam.

Rivka poured milk into a cup on the table, then brought the teapot and poured a good dark cup of tea. She handed it to Ian and replaced the pot on the hob and put its cosy over it.

'Sorry, Pa,' said Ian. 'Sorry, Ma . . .' He sipped his tea but couldn't taste it.

Moshe sat down in his place again. He put his head in his hands and his elbows on the table, and rocked back and forward, back and forward. And he moaned, 'Oy veh . . .'

20

In the little office behind the shop, Ian sat doing his accounts. He punched holes in invoices and filed them and wrote them up in the day-book.

Marjory came in with a notepad and went to the telephone. She consulted the list of local numbers on the wall above Ian's desk, then picked up the receiver.

'Hello, four-three nine-double-two.'

Ian worked on, while Marjory spoke to a Dr Melvin, about a wee girl who had just come into the shop and said her prescription had blown out of her hand in the street when she'd been tying her bootlace. The doctor confirmed that he had written the prescription for the girl's mother and Marjory wrote it down on her pad. She said she would make it up while the wee girl collected another prescription from the doctor's house. She hung the receiver back on the hook.

Ian looked up. Their eyes met, for a moment of tenderness.

'All right?'

She touched his cheek with her finger, and went out.

On Saturday afternoon, Ian caught the train for Edinburgh. There was a different atmosphere in the Kaydan house, the shock was a week old. A businesslike air.

They sat in the kitchen for it. Ian faced Moshe at the table, Rivka was in the chair at the end.

Ian said that Marjory was a very nice person.

'A shiksie,' said Moshe.

'Pa, I'm not a saint. You know that. I never have been.'

'It's a shiksie.'

'Yes a shiksie, yes a shiksie – what do you want me to say!'

Rivka leaned forward. 'You tink she's nice.'

'I do.'

Moshe pursed his lips. 'A bit of fluff.'

That surprised Ian. He asked where Moshe had heard the expression, but Moshe's eyes remained hooded.

'She is not a bit of fluff. I could . . .' Ian searched for the word – 'be . . . with Marjory for the rest of my life.'

'You love her,' said his mother, the realist, the practical one.

'Yes! I love her!' The declaration was made, Ian's cards were on the table. He felt they were sizing up how the game would go. 'Out of . . . deference . . . my respect, my love for you, I kept that life apart but I can't now.' He waited for them to play.

'Shlomo,' asked his mother, 'how old is she?'

'Thirty.'

Rivka shrugged. 'Not a kind.'

'No.' Marjory was not a child.

Moshe's turn. 'How are you sure she's pregnant by you?'

Ian was exasperated, and turned away, and calmed himself. 'Because we've been together for a year.'

'In de von house?'

'No, she stays with her people.'

'So how do you know?'

'Pa, we see each other every day, she comes to my flat three – four times a week.'

'Is dat *genug?*' Was it enough!

'Pa, she's having my child!'

Moshe was silent, then he said quietly, 'Don't shout at me. Dat's de last time.'

Ian commanded himself inwardly to keep his temper. He said evenly, 'I have spoken to her about turning Jewish. I know it takes more than a year, she's got to see all the seasons through, but what are the other possibilities? None!'

Moshe asked, 'Vot ees *dees* possibility? She has de kind, and in a year, in two years, you marry? Is dat de possibility?'

'No, we'll get married now.'

'Vere? Vere vill you get married?'

'In Glasgow.'

Rivka turned to Moshe. 'He means in a church.'

'In a Registry Office!' Ian's temper was rising, his hands doing the big gesture.

'And she agrees?' Rivka was asking in surprise.

'She knows I can't marry in a church.'

'Does she agree?'

Ian controlled himself. 'I hope she will.'

They took the implication, and paused to turn it over in their minds.

'And de kind?' Moshe asked.

It would be their grandchild. Ian told them this.

'I ken . . .' said Moshe. He slowly ran his fingers to and fro across the wood of the table. He was in sorrow. Ian felt it, welling round his father. It was an old sorrow, three thousand years old.

'If it's a boy I'll have him circumcised . . .'

Silence filled the room. Rivka looked from her husband to her son. She reserved her thoughts.

Ian went on. 'Marjory would like to come through next time, and meet you.' He looked straight into his father's eyes: it was the first time at this meeting. Moshe looked straight back, and saw his son, and was shocked to find this other human being, this other chosen man of God. He dropped his gaze, then looked again.

'No,' he said.

And Rivka knew the tone was definite and she rocked with sadness.

Ian, he didn't know what to make of it. 'What are you saying? That I should part from you?'

223

'No. I don't vont to part. You're my son.'

'What are you saying then? That I should get Marjory to get rid of the baby?'

Moshe drew back. 'No!'

His mother threw up her arms. God forbid that any such thing should be done!

'So what else? I can't, just, leave Majory! Can I?'

'Yes,' said Moshe.

Ian was amazed and angry. He got up. He leaned with his hands on the table. 'Pa – Ma – who's the breadwinner of this family? Me! I'm the prop! Times are hard! Are you saying? – you can't just say to me – to leave the mother of my child!'

He walked up and down, three steps across the hearthrug and back, then to the window, to look down at the green grass and the washing. It was no use being angry. 'Pa, next week, let me bring her.'

'No,' said Moshe.

Ian turned to his mother. She was shrunken in to herself; she gave him a shrug, a distant hug of despair.

In the bedroom in Ian's flat, he lay in bed, staring, thinking the game through. Marjory lay beside him.

'There's no question,' said Ian.

'Isn't there?'

He turned to her. 'I love you.'

Yes he did, she knew that. 'I can't turn Jew any more than you can turn Christian.'

Why was that? Neither of them had profound religious beliefs; it was the same God however you worshipped him. They accepted that. In a sense they were of the same religion.

'Come to church then.'

'I couldn't do it.'

'Not for love?'

'That wouldn't be love.'

So they debated, round in circles, till Marjory came back to the beginning.

'It's silly, in these times, for me to be a Jew.'

He accepted the point, but corrected her: 'Jewess.' And the answer to that was a grimace.

'I mean,' said Marjory, 'I'd like to meet your folk.'

'I'd like you to. They're not evil, or wicked.' His love reached out to comfort him. 'But cutting off from them . . . it's a way of life. They can't change.'

'You'd be richer.'

That was so. His family cost him a packet. So they came round to the money question.

'I haven't been doling out all these years like you,' she said. 'D'you know how much I've got in the bank?'

'No.'

'Guess.'

'Tuppence?'

'Two hundred pounds.' She let it sink in, and Glasgow-fied it, 'Did I no' tell you?'

He smiled at her voice sliding up in the middle and down at the end. 'Two hundred . . . ? Oh Jeez!'

She'd been working nine years. He'd been working – what? – twenty years? How much had he got to stake against hers?

'My insurance,' admitted Ian.

'How much is that worth?'

'Well, I wouldn't cash it, it's an enforced saving.'

'How much?'

'About two hundred.'

'Shake, partner.'

And she shook him under the covers and he doubled up laughing but he wasn't ready for more sex yet and he took her hand away; she being reluctant to let go.

'With an insurance policy they'll give you a mortgage. We'll take a shop, plenty shops going. We're rich.'

'Ah, but . . .' Ian had been over this in his own mind. 'Look at all the folk with their own wee business who're going bust. It isn't the time, is it, to start.'

'When is?'

225

That was a point. But here in Glasgow?

'What's wrong with that?'

The thing wrong with Glasgow was that it was the other end of the railway line from his mother and father. Would he pine for them? How could he help it?

She asked, because it was different with her own parents, if it would really break their hearts.

'Oh, ay. I'm not their favourite son, but my father's God won't have it.'

She leaned over on him and rested her head on his chest.

'Folk'll come into the shop, wherever, and they'll have been to Edinburgh, they'll bring hints, messages, and I'll say, I'm cut off from my family. I'm cut off from the Jewish community. That's all my friends in Glasgow.'

Marjory sighed. She said she'd brought a heap of trouble on him but he wouldn't have it. He turned over on his elbows.

'I've got experience, I'm manager of four chemist shops in Glasgow. I could go to Boots, Timothy Whites, the Co-op, the wholesalers, get a top job anywhere in Britain. At least try for a top job. We could emigrate.'

'Eh?' It took her by surprise.

'My father emigrated. Mind you, he was eighteen. I'm . . .'

She knew. 'Thirty-eight.'

'So? I've got a sister in Canada – Sarah.' They had lost touch with her, but he could go and find her. Except that they knew in their hearts that she'd gone down in the Depression, with or without Isadore. Ian remembered something else, that Sarah had been a mean bitch. 'But I know folk from Dundee who've gone to Australia.'

'Jews?'

He couldn't get away from them. 'Ay, Jews.'

'You're a great clan. Must it be Jews?'

'No.'

She kissed him, and climbed on him. 'Can we go to sleep now?'

226

'What?'

She caressed him till he was ready and put him in her. He was content to let himself be used, and afterwards she settled on him and he stroked her hair. She fell asleep, but he was wide awake and unhappy.

They had boiled eggs for breakfast, with tea and toast.

'I'll take the bus,' said Marjory, 'and you take the tram. Or I'll take the tram and you take the bus. If we still can't arrive together.'

'No, we can't.'

The doorbell rang. They looked at each other. Ian got up and went to answer it. Marjory listened to the voices in the hall.

'Are you Mr Kaydan?'

'Yes.'

'Could I have a word with you?'

The caller was a young man with sandy brushed-back hair and brown checked plus-fours.

'What's it about?' asked Ian.

'My sister, she works for you – Marjory.'

'You're Marjory's brother?'

Marjory came through to the hall. 'Andrew, what the hell are you doing here?'

The young man gawped at her, as if she had been an apparition. Ian invited him kindly into the kitchen.

'Well, what are you doing?' Marjory demanded. 'And take your cap off!'

Andrew slid his cap off and stood with it.

'Mother said –'

'I know, I told her I wouldn't be home.'

But Marjory had told her mother she would be at Jenny's. Her mother hadn't believed her, and had sent Andrew to Jenny's and Marjory wasn't there.

'Have a cup of tea,' offered Ian.

'No, I won't have a cup of tea. So –'

How did he know to come to Mr Kaydan's flat?

'A wee burd.' said Andrew.

Marjory explained to Ian that her brother had been reading letters in a handbag in one of her drawers. Was that the wee bird? Andrew just stood there with his cap.

'So you followed the wee burd. And you found me. And aren't you shocked?'

Andrew said, 'Eh, you've to come home.'

'I'm not coming home! I'm going to work!'

'You're coming home. C'mon, get your things.' He took her by the wrist.

'Andrew, take your hand off!'

A threat in her voice that he knew, but he held on. 'Naw. C'mon.'

Marjory blazed. 'D'you want me to clunk you! I'm a big girl! You've had a night or two in your time, haven't you?'

'Aw, now,' said Andrew, because that was different: that was unfair.

'What's the difference?'

'There is a difference.'

'What!'

Andrew dithered.

'Say it!'

'He's –' he pointed at Ian, 'he's –' He almost choked on the word, then ejected it with a screech in his voice, 'he's a Jew!'

Marjory flung her arm up and disengaged from his hand. She nursed her wrist.

Ian had felt the tone of his voice like a sledgehammer on his chest, but he could still speak. 'That's right, I'm a Jew.'

Andrew stood still, with his cap, saying nothing.

'Go away, Andrew!' Marjory told him. 'Go home! We're getting married next month.'

Andrew went cross-eyed trying to focus on her. He took a quick gawp at Ian, but Ian faced him squarely and he couldn't take that. He returned to Marjory.

'Aw c'mon, Marjory. I mean . . . Whad'ya mean? You can't marry him. I'm no' having one of him.'

'Andrew, shut up. It's me that's having him, now you go home, you're insufferable.'

Andrew was in distress, and found it difficult to get words out at all. 'Whad'ya mean, marry?'

'Husband and wife. Me and Ian, Ian and me . . .'

Andrew tried hard to take it in, to understand what she was telling him. 'But you can't have them, Jeez, Marjory – !' He suddenly got it. His eyes dropped to her belly. 'You mean – are you – has he done – ?'

'That's got nothing to do with you. We're getting married.'

Andrew backed away. He turned his cap in his hand. He summoned up all his spittle and ejected it over Ian. He went out of the kitchen, through the hall, and banged the front door so hard that the panes of glass in the kitchen window rattled.

Marjory was distraught. 'Oh God Ian, I'm sorry, he's an idiot. He's just a fool, always has been.' She was wiping off the spit with a dish-towel.

David and Shirley stood near the pathway through the Links at Bruntsfield, watching the people. It was Shabbas and they had nowhere to go. They wore their blue raincoats to guard against the November dampness and the wind that bowed the trees over and bowled the few remaining leaves along the ground.

They watched the tramcars grind and sway along Melville Drive. The number six turned at the foot of Marchmont Road and stopped. It was Shirley who recognised Uncle Ian. Her face lit up and she shrieked and raced along the path to meet him; David trotted after.

Ian caught Shirley and lifted her and she clutched him and pummelled him.

'What are you doing here?'

'I've come to see you.'

'Me?'

'You and David, and your Mummy, and your Dad.'

David asked what for, in a serious way that made Ian laugh. He had come just to see them, did they mind? David and Shirley didn't mind. Mummy and Daddy were in.

'Are you coming up?'

'No,' said Shirley pouting, 'we've been put out.' Mummy had told them to play. None of their friends were there and they couldn't go to the pictures or anywhere. They'd been put out in case they made a noise in the house, because Daddy was ill.

Ian asked as casually as he could what was wrong. David said his Dad had a cough, and Shirley added that he was better today, Mummy said so. David thought that he'd had a fever.

The fears of a lifetime rose in Ian. How long had their Dad been ill? David shrugged, and Shirley thought it had been a day or two.

The three of them walked hand in hand up the Links to Warrender Park Road. It was easy and natural for them; David would never have held his Mum's hand or his Dad's, but with Ian it was a link with another human being.

They stopped at the grass verge and watched him cross the road. He turned and waved; he'd see them before he left. He walked up Spottiswoode Street and turned in at their door. They loved him; all would be well.

Ian climbed up the tenement stairs with the shiny tiles on the walls and good daylight from the wide stair windows. He stopped on the first-floor landing, at the door with the mezzuzzah. He pulled the brass knob and heard the clang of the bell. Before it died away there was a rushing of feet, then a silence.

Mary's voice inside, tense, asking who it was. Then when Ian answered, the key was turned back in the lock, and the door opened a little. Mary's face, haggard, grey, staring at him.

He asked if he could come in – a joke, it was his brother's house. She opened the door, then shut it behind him when he stood in the hall.

'Well?' she was tense and defiant.

'I saw the kids downstairs. They said Zelek was ill.' No joking now; he kept his voice low, to say what had to be said before anything else was broached.

'He is ill. He's over the worst, thank God.'

'What was it?'

Mary, middle-aged, swept a hair from her face and dabbed an eye with the same gesture, and shrugged, because it was beyond her that such an affliction should come upon her husband. 'Some kind of pleurisy, the doctor said. He thought he'd torn his lung but . . . he's sleeping.'

Mary didn't burst into tears at saying the truth out loud, and Ian was glad. She motioned him into the lounge.

It was an over-clean room with a carpet, and polished furniture. Zelek was always the man for doing things properly if they were worth doing at all. So he was a good salesman, so he lived in style. Ian took in the new clock on the mantelpiece and the matching cut-glass vases. The J.N.F. box was shimmering blue and had not a dent in it.

But Ian had been slipping pounds and fivers to his mother to give to Zelek for long enough. They'd been having a rough time, he observed. This to Mary was an understatement. She scanned him, looked out of the window, came back and sat in the lady's armchair before she chewed out her answer.

'Yes.' The word was unnecessary after the sequence of emotions on her face. 'It's the *zorg* (the worry) for Zelek. No work and no money.' The first leading to the second. 'We can't pay the rates . . . They're at him for this' – the chair she sat in – 'and this, and this' – the rest of the room.

Ian nodded in understanding of the never-never principle on which the furniture had been obtained.

'Well,' said Mary, 'you buy in hope!' Didn't everybody, and hadn't Zelek said, if they were going to have a flat, they were going to have a flat? Mary heaved the deepest of sighs, then composed herself. She looked steadily at her brother-in-law. 'And you?' Which was a judgement as well as a question. She'd been told.

'I'm getting married,' said Ian. 'Now don't fly off the handle, Mary. I've wrestled for a long time. I know what it means. But I'm getting on. And I've met someone, nice. Truly.'

'Nice,' repeated Mary, as if it were the least important quality. She summoned all her contempt, and that was a lot when you were speaking to Mary. 'Eh,' she said, 'you *shtik naar! Gorneit!*'

Ian braced himself. He was not either of those, neither a fool nor a good-for-nothing. But Mary had a power in her voice. How she rocked. 'How could you, how could you? *How could you?*'

He stood his ground. 'I didn't think you would take to the idea, Mary. I'd like to go and talk to Zelek.'

'Well, you can't! What can he do? He hasn't got a shiksie into trouble.' She rocked, and spat out, 'I'm sorry for you!' She rocked again, 'And that's true!' She may have been sorry but any sorrow was buried deep below her resentment at his desertion.

Ian heard Zelek coughing in his bedroom. Mary went on, 'And the kinder, they worshipped you. Egh . . . !' It was the sound of dramatised vomit.

Ian said, 'Can I go and see my brother?'

She shrugged. 'Go.' She flicked with her hand in the direction of the bedroom. As Ian went out she added, 'But don't tire him!'

Zelek was propped up on pillows. Between his single bed and Mary's the little table was crowded with medicine bottles, pill-boxes, fruit, fruit drinks in jugs, a basin and cloth for washing down, a thermometer, a clock and a cup and saucer. On the far side of the bed lay his attaché case, and papers and calculations were strewn on the carpet.

The patient was sunken-cheeked. He looked up as Ian came in. 'Hello, Ian!' A warm greeting, in surprise to see his brother.

Ian put on a bright show. 'What's this? What you doing in bed?'

'Pleurisy. I'm over it. I thought I was gone yesterday – pneumonia. But I'm no' deid yet.'

'So I see.'

'I'm alive.'

'Don't tire yourself.'

Who, him? How could he tire himself? What had Mary been telling him? Ian went as far as to say that she was worried.

'She's a worrier. Listen Ian, I can't afford to die, you know that.' It was a way of looking at it. He'd be all right – 'There's an agency, Sheffield cutlery, the whole of Scotland. As soon as I'm on my feet, it's mine. And it's a cert.'

Ian could remember Zelek saying this as a little boy about anything speculative; Zelek was your natural gambler.

'Unemployment or no unemployment, people get married, they need wedding presents, they need cutlery, good stainless steel. There's a fortune.'

'Good, Zelek, that's good talk. But get on your feet. No hurry. You've got to get well.'

Zelek knew it. He changed the subject by taking a long look at his brother. 'And what's this? Are you jumping in?'

'Ay.'

'Is that what she was going on at?'

'No encouragement there!' Ian made a joke of it.

Zelek said, 'You know her, Ian, she's all emotion, not much brain.'

So Ian asked him what he thought about it, and Zelek puffed his cheeks, and asked him to state his case.

Ian said, 'I love her, she's having my child.' He reminded Zelek what Marjory looked like, because Zelek had met her when he was in the shop, and had said how much he'd liked her. That was Ian's case.

Zelek lay in silence for a long time, gathering the words together. 'D'you want the truth?' Ian did, very much.

233

'Tell me something first. She's a chemist, you're a chemist, you sell contraceptives – how the hell did it happen?'

It had happened.

Zelek said, 'A shiksie's one thing. To get her into trouble's another.'

'I said I love her. She loves me.'

'Well, love's another thing. And marriage is still another.'

'Even with a child?' Ian asked.

'You can have it adopted.'

There was a long silence of no communication between them. Ian said, 'Zelek – a Jew and a Goy: I still have some beliefs, and it's all right to me. You've got none at all, you never have believed. What's wrong with a Jew and a Goy?'

'It's nothing to do with belief,' protested Zelek his brother. 'A Jew is a Jew.'

What did it mean? Cotton-wool statement, you couldn't boil that down to anything. People married out.

'Some do,' said Zelek. He looked up at Ian. 'You're taking an awful stony path. Is she happy about it?'

'Yes,' said Ian.

'And her people?'

Ian said that her mother had accepted it. He mentioned the brother who hated it. Was that all Zelek had to say, just a stony path?

Zelek considered. 'It's a hell of a lot in this world.'

Ian reminded him that there was happiness too.

'Oh, well,' said Zelek, thinking of his own mixed fortunes in the land of happiness. He tasted the word. 'Happiness. If it's true, Ian, it's worth hanging on to.' Then he was tired and shut his eyes.

Ian saw, and said that he would go. Zelek flickered an eyelid in acknowledgement. Ian took up the towel and wiped Zelek's brow; then he sat watching.

Zelek's voice was weak. 'I wish you well.'

Ian bent over him. 'Listen Zelek, don't worry. I'll see you right. I've got a quid or two.'

234

Zelek opened his eyes and squinted at Ian. 'You mean, I *can* afford to die?'

Ian couldn't take it as a joke. He felt sick at the thought. 'No. Don't die, Zelek. Don't die.'

Mary opened the door and stood there. 'Now that's enough, Ian.' She came to the bed and plumped Zelek's pillows and tidied the bedclothes. 'D'you want anything? A cup of tea? Will you have your soup now, it's an absolute jelly, I'll heat it up in no time.' Her voice was gentle, encouraging, assuring that all was under control, all would be well.

Zelek said, 'There's one thing.'

'What?' said Mary, 'what?'

'I could do with a cigarette.'

Mary was scandalised. 'No such thing! Ian, don't you dare give him cigarettes, it brings his lungs up.'

Zelek said she'd hidden his Goldflake, and Mary told Ian she'd put them in the bucket. Ian upheld her in this.

'Oh for a smoke!' sighed Zelek.

Ian made the point that at least it was something for him to look forward to, and added, comfortingly, that he was looking not bad. Mary pursed her lips, knowing that Zelek couldn't see her.

'Take care of him,' said Ian.

'I'll tell you,' said Zelck, 'Ian, when you see the kids, send them round for a pink *News*, it'll be out. Here's a penny –'

Ian had a penny, he'd tell them.

'See if my horse came in . . .' Zelek was weak now.

Ian at the door grinned at his brother. 'See you soon, Zelek.'

He went out.

Mary became a temptress. 'Soup?'

Her husband tasted the idea. 'Ay . . . Ay, I'll have a wee drop.'

Mary was overjoyed. She rushed to the door and went out. Zelek, left alone, gave a big sigh. He lifted up his

bony hands and examined them. He dropped them down.
Hope ebbed away from him.

After the funeral they came back to the flat for the first
night of sitting *Shiva*, the ritual of the first seven nights in
a house of mourning. The family sat low, in their oldest,
tattered clothes. That was Mary, on a cushion on the floor,
clutching Shirley and David. She was shattered; after a
lifetime's plumpness she had become gaunt. The children
were afraid: their father was alive yesterday, now the impossible had happened – what were they to do, what was
Mummy to do, brave, brave Mummy?

Rivka and Moshe sat hunched over on the settee, rocking
with grief. His eldest son, her beloved!

Queenie sobbed and sometimes howled into a hankie. At
the back of the room, in the shadow, sat Ian. He knew what
was going to happen.

'*Tzvei* an' *fiertig*,' rocked Moshe, 'dat's all . . . *Tzvei* an'
fiertig . . .'

Queenie spoke: Mrs Lucas had said at the cemetery that
Zelek was in the prime of life.

The door-bell clanged. Mary started from her dream,
her nightmare. 'Is the kettle on?'

Queenie said, 'Yes, yes, everything's ready, Mary.' She
asked Moshe if they would say the evening service first, or
have tea first. Was it time for the prayers? Moshe brought
his watch out from his waistcoat. It was time.

'What?' said Mary.

'They'll say the prayers first, Mary.' Queenie told her.
And David rehearsed the Mourner's Kaddish to himself.

The bell went again. Ian got up to answer it.

'Sit, sit,' Mary told David and Shirley, keep sitting low.

Ian went to the shop early and typed out the letter. He
typed the envelope, put the letter in and sealed it. He heard
the door open and close, and the familiar footsteps.

Marjory came in, wrapped up against the fog.

'Good morning.'

'Good morning.' Greetings between boss and senior assistant. Marjory took off her coat in silence and hung it on the coat-stand.

'Your brother . . . ?' All she knew was that Ian left hurriedly yesterday in response to a trunk-call.

Ian's brother was dead and buried. Jews did it within the day.

'I'm sorry. Was it terrible?'

'Yes,' said Ian. 'This is a letter to his solicitor. He'd cashed his insurance, he's got nothing.'

The letter was about Zelek's debts. Ian had to see them right. Mary had broken down completely. The children were going to Ian's parents and Mary would go back to her father in the meantime but there was no money there either, none.

Marjory stood and looked at him. 'Are you telling me something?'

Ian said, 'Ay . . .'

'You're taking on two orphans?'

'Ay . . .' He was.

'You aren't cutting off from your family.'

Ian said, 'No.'

He got up and reached out for her, to communicate where words failed him. She turned away.

Ian said, 'It's difficult . . .'

Marjory said, 'Very.'

He paced the tiny office, and she noted this. What could he do, he asked. Did he mean about his other child?

Ian stopped pacing. He didn't look at her, nor she at him.

'I'll support it,' he said.

She didn't answer for a while, then, 'Good for you.'

'Unless –'

'What?'

'If you're going to keep it. I mean, there is –' She let him go on. 'There are . . . adoption societies.'

237

Then they looked at each other, stared at each other; the two people saw and recognised and were frightened of each other.

He had said it. He added that it was as hard for him –

'Liar!' The word burned from her lips and seared him. He was angry but he suppressed it. She said, 'I knew. I did! I'll get myself a locum job.' She was suddenly a strange, hard woman with a whip-tongue. 'I'll let you know.' She took her white coat from the stand. She was sorry for his brother's family, sorry for all his family. But it was a mighty convenient excuse. He was a runaway. Out of the wood. And she ejected the dirty word, 'Jew!'

She tried to stop herself crying as she put on her white coat, and buttoned it, and belted it, and opened the office door and went out.

Ian spent much more time at home now, at his parents' home, in Edinburgh. He played the piano a lot, banging away, vamping on the out-of-tune keys for Shirley. But the first time he came home he had the parlour to himself and he played the one about growing too old to dream.

> *So kiss me my dear,*
> *Then let us part,*
> *And when I grow too old to dream*
> *Your kiss will live in my heart.*

He hadn't shaved and hadn't slept much; nor had he changed his shirt, so his collar and cuffs were grubby. If you looked closely you could see this, and that his shoes could do with a clean. He had found Moshe's bottle of whisky and there was an inch left so he drank it.

Was it his fault? Was it God's? How could omnipotent God have a fault? Was it Marjory's?

> *Have you ever seen a dream walking?*
> *Well, I have.*
> *Have you ever seen a dream talking? . . .*

238

He realised that of all things God didn't care, of all omnipotent things, God just didn't care. He was outraged, and leaned forward to rest his forehead against the dull, cool piano where he wept.

21

In the spring Ian, keeping his woes to himself, took a job with Gore and Fletcher Ltd, Manufacturing Chemists, as their General Manager on the retail side. There were eight shops up and down Scotland, with the main one in Frederick Street, Edinburgh, where Sir Walter Scott had come to buy his laudanum for his gall-stone. Ian had a big office with a leather-topped desk on a rich red carpet.

He took a mortgage on a house in Newington, on the south side. It had a garden, back and front. A garden! And an upstairs – a proper house to bring up David and Shirley in, for Mary to recover in, and for Rivka, especially Rivka, to be comforted in. It solved all the problems, because being a *gantser macher* ('a big shot') restored Ian's morale too.

But Rivka didn't go. They say the reason more people die in the winter is that they go to their relatives' funerals, and Piershill Cemetery where the Edinburgh Hebrew Congregation burial ground is, has the cold wind blowing from the east from October till April, so if somebody dies, you go to see him off and you catch your death. So Rivka caught a cold at Zelek's funeral.

There was more to it than that. The life seemed to go out of her on the death of her beloved. She became shrunken and the smile that she put on for the kinder took a lot of strength, you could see. She had been borne up through the terrible years by love and hope, and now the impossible had happened, they were ended. She looked forward all right to the new house and the prospect of comfort at last, but she got a sore chest from coughing and went to bed in the afternoon of the day they moved house. Moshe found her in the evening, just as she'd gone to bed, nothing out of place, still.

Moshe cried and cried, all through the move, for days and days, and now and then for weeks. Was it love? It was a sore loss and it had once been love. He remembered falling in love, kissing her for the first time, with her hair blowing and the laugh on her face but not in her eyes because she shut her eyes when she laughed. He remembered that now. All those years ago how happy they were going to be! They were a proper match, and would lead a simple life in the service of God, planting and reaping the good things that God gave man, especially to His Chosen.

Who would make all the little decisions now, and understand him, his need to do God's commands, who would cook and clean? There was Queenie, of course; that was why you must always keep one of your daughters at home, that was why one of your daughters was always unmarriageable.

So they moved to this house with a garden. Mary said that two *bollidosties* (good housekeepers) in one house was a recipe for *tsorris* (misery), and a bad *tsimmus* (stew), too. They all stuck it for six months, then an auntie of Mary's died, leaving four middle-aged helpless sons, and Mary was offered the job of housekeeper to look after them. She took it on condition, of course, that David and Shirley moved in with her. Ian still paid for clothes, schools, holidays and pocket-money but that was that.

When the war came, Moshe and Ian and Queenie lived on alone in the big house. They had wooden frames made for the windows with black cloth stretched over them for night-time. Moshe dug some of the back garden and grew cabbages and potatoes and beetroots and peas and beans. He knew from his boyhood how to do this.

And in nineteen hundred and forty-three, Queenie Kaydan had her fortieth birthday. She didn't mind at all. She enjoyed the war, because Edinburgh had no blitz, only all-night alerts when the German bombers droned overhead to burn down Glasgow and the shipyards. She shopped and cooked and talked with other Yiddishy housewives, and understood Moshe, and was a real ballibostie. And if she felt something was missing she didn't feel it often.

A few weeks after her birthday, she was walking along the street in her brown coat with the half-belt, dumpy, plump and defiant. She clutched a bulging brown paper parcel, carried her old crocodile-skin handbag by its strap, and her gas mask in its rexine case patted her bum as she walked. There were no railings to the gardens she passed; all had been removed for the war effort, but she eyed the stumps every day. Part of her vision of peace was the return of the garden railings. She came to her own house and turned in where the gate had been. She opened her bag, took out the bunch of keys and unlocked the front door.

Moshe was in the parlour, riffling through his own private drawer in the sideboard: that is, the collection of watches, fob-watches of gold and silver, wrist-watches, insides of watches, mechanisms, empty cases, alarm clocks, travelling clocks and some necklaces and rings. His hair was thin now and pure white, as was the stubble on his beard. He had his yamulkeh on the back of his head as always, and was wearing his shiny blue serge suit, and his waistcoat, and his boots. He was seventy-six years of age.

Queenie called from outside and he picked up a watch and wound it lovingly. She came in and said loudly, 'I've got the shoes.'

'Vot shoes?'

Queenie held up her brown paper parcel and hissed that it was meat for the weekend that she didn't want the daily to know about. Moshe said, 'She's in de kitchen.' As if Mrs MacPhee would know anything about meat for the weekend in the Kaydan house. 'Vot is it?'

'A nice bit of brisket.'

'Vere did you get it?'

So Queenie explained how Ian had given the butcher

two pounds of sugar from the shop because chemist shops had a quota of sugar for making up medicines with, and the butcher had showed his gratitude in the usual way.

'It's no' kosher.'

'It's kosher! It's got the stamp on.' Kosher meat was stamped with a purple stamp, and because Moshe sometimes suspected the origin of the meat that Ian brought into the house for the weekend, Ian took care either to trade with the kosher butcher or to use some purple ink from the office on whatever he could get from the friendly butcher next door to the shop. It was always beef or mutton of course, never pork, God forbid! And fowls weren't rationed at all.

But this time Moshe didn't suspect the meat so much as the business of getting it; that didn't sound kosher at all. Queenie dismissed his objection. 'Listen,' she said, 'Ian'll no' get caught.'

Mrs MacPhee called from the other side of the door in the clear shrill tones of the West Port, 'Is that you, Miss Kaydan?'

'Yes, Mrs MacPhee.' Queenie put the parcel on the sofa and covered it with the *Jewish Echo* as Mrs MacPhee came in, with her apron and old shoes, and her glasses on the end of her little beak nose. She had rickets when she was young and her legs were bowed out, which made her even smaller.

'I just missed you this afternoon.' She had arrived minutes after Queenie had gone out, so the old Mr Kaydan had informed her. And now she'd cleaned upstairs, and the bathroom, and in here.

'So I see,' said Queenie. 'Good.'

'And I'll just scrub the kitchen and get away.'

'Fine.'

Mrs MacPhee wasn't to be dismissed so easily. 'I had a postcard from George.' (Her son.)

'That's nice.' Queenie took a share of Mrs MacPhee's joy.

243

'He's "Somewhere in England",' Mrs MacPhee quoted from her memory of the card which she had read and reread.

'Still?' said Queenie, sitting on the arm of the sofa to mask the parcel.

'And he's fine,' quoted Mrs MacPhee, 'full of beans, he says.'

'I'll be in in a minute, Mrs MacPhee, and we'll have a blether.'

'All right, I'll get on wi' ma floor.' Mrs MacPhee went cheerily out.

'She talks,' said Moshe the long-sufferer.

'I'll give her a minute to fill her bucket,' calculated Queenie, 'then I'll get past her into the pantry.' She uncovered the parcel and felt it through the brown paper. 'I'll do it tomorrow for the weekend.' She looked at Moshe with the watch in his hand and the drawer open. 'Are you going out to do business?'

'No.' Moshe put the watch back in the drawer, shut it and turned the key. 'Tonight it's Yortseit.' He put the key in his pocket.

Yortseit was the anniversary of a death. Whose? There were so many now, but they had to be remembered. Queenie wasn't sure what happened to a dead person if you forgot their anniversary, but you mustn't forget. 'Who for?' she asked.

'Your muzzer.'

Queenie clapped her hand over her mouth.

'Nine years,' said Moshe.

'Ma's Yortseit, I forgot! Well, we've got Yortseit candles in the cupboard.' She always kept a stock of them, they were useful in the Anderson shelter in the back garden because they lasted the night. Not that they'd been in the shelter since the Clydebank raids and that was two years ago, but she still had a fine stock of the candles-in-tumblers.

'Listen, Pa,' she said, 'I was going out tonight, to the Maccabi Hall, but I don't need to. I'll sit with you.'

244

'Vot's in de Maccabi Hall?'

'A dance, you know, some army boys, and air force, and all the usual crowd. I'll see them through the week. They don't need me. When Ian comes in, I've got gefilte fish, and we'll be together.'

'Good,' said her father.

Queenie took up her parcel and went to the door with it. 'I'll tell you,' she said, 'I'll just go for an hour, and make the tea for them, and I'll be back.'

Moshe was not deceived. 'You got a boyfriend?' He had time now for jokes; he knew that his Queenie had no boyfriend, but he was curious to know why she wanted to go out. 'Vy d'you go to a dance?'

'To see the gang, what else? Listen, I'm the only thing that nobody queues up for. I'll be back and I'll sit with you.'

He knew that. She went to the kitchen.

The Yortseit candle was brought out and put on the mantelpiece beside the JNF. box. Moshe lit it in the evening after he had said the evening prayer, and he and Ian remembered Rivka. What a hard life she'd had, how beautiful she once was, what spirit, what fun there was in her, and her earthiness! Moshe cried a little, and Ian cried a little, and then he set up the card-table in front of the fire and they sat playing.

Bezique was the best game for two. They both had their jackets off but Moshe kept his yamulkeh on. Ian's hair had receded; he thought of himself as bald. The lenses were thicker in his glasses. He peered over them as his father won the last trick.

'Yours.'

Moshe laid his hand down and counted, '*Fiertig, huntert fiertig, huntert funftig, huntert sechtig.*'

Ian studied it, then flung down his own double bezique, card by card. '*Keesh'n tochas, keesh'n tochas, keesh'n tochas, keesh'n tochas!*' ('Kiss my arse!') He slapped the rest of his hand down, and clapped his hands high over his head in triumph. 'Who's won?' It was a rhetorical question.

Moshe dismissed him with a gesture. He took out his watch. Queenie was late; what was she doing?

'Enjoying herself.'

'She should be home. Yortseit for her muzzer.'

Ian shrugged; he looked at the candle in the glass. Poor Ma. 'She was an optimist.'

Moshe said nothing.

'You're a pessimist, she was an optimist. She could laugh things off.'

She couldn't laugh death off. 'Oy vai . . .' said Moshe with a deep sigh.

'You've survived without her.'

'I miss her.'

Ian understood that. Moshe looked at his watch again; 'Half past eleven. Go to de Maccabi Hall –'

'Naw!' said Ian. 'Queenie's a big girl, she's all right, she's got her torch.' He gathered in the cards. 'Another game?'

Moshe declined. Ian put the pack down and sprawled back in his chair. 'You know what old Gore told me today? He's nearly your age, you know. When the war's over, he'll retire. His son's in the army, he knows nothing about pharmaceuticals. So he'll be a kind of sleeping chairman, and I'll be the Deputy Chairman and Managing Director. Eight shops. No' bad, eh? And I know where to expand. It's a good time to be in pharmacy.' And David when he came out of the army would go in for research: sulphonamides, a limitless field. He'd do well. And Shirley would marry.

Moshe nodded away by the fire and at midnight he started up and demanded to know where Queenie was. Ian got up and put his tie on, then his jacket, and went out to see.

Moshe put more coal on the fire and kept himself awake by staring at the Yortseit candle and remembering; it was easy to remember now, everything was so clear.

Another half hour passed. He heard the key in the front door, the door opening and shutting, then saw the light being switched on in the hall. Ian came in with his torch and gas mask and coat and Anthony Eden hat. He was alone.

'Nu?'

'She's not there, the dance is over.' He took off his hat and dropped it in his chair.

'Phone de police!'

Ian looked at his own watch. 'Where the hell can she be?'

They both heard the scuffling outside. They shushed each other and listened in alarm. Moshe got up and went out to the hall. Ian said to put the light out before he opened the door.

Moshe used the inner switch, then shuffled along the hall in the dark. He tried to make out the giggles and shushes from outside. He opened the door.

On the doorstep stood Queenie, her arms tightly linked with two G.I.s. She was saying 'How can I get my keys? Oh . . .'

The men unlinked. One said, 'Good evening' and the other said, 'Hello.'

'Pa,' said Queenie on the doorstep, 'this is Wolf, Wolf Kapinsky, and Benny Sharman. They saw me home. Come in!'

Moshe stood aside as she led them in. 'Shut the door,' she told him. Moshe shut it and in the dark Wolf held out his hand. '*Sholoum aleichem!*'

Moshe turned from the door and wonderingly took the outstretched hand and shook it. '*Aleichem sholoum.*' And Harry went through the same greeting. At least they were Yid'n.

'C'mon in,' said Queenie playfully.

Ian had been straining his ears inside the parlour. Now Queenie strolled into the light and they went through the introductions and handshakes again, except that this time Benny said 'Howdy,' and Ian said 'Howdy' back.

Queenie had her explanation ready. 'Pa, the dance finished, and Wolf and Benny said they'd see me home.'

Moshe's face was a mask. 'Ven did de dance finish?'

'Some time ago, sir,' said Benny.

'But they had a car.' Queenie was quite the lady.

'A Jeep,' said Wolf, 'so we drove around.'

Queenie needed no asking. 'We went down to Portobello for a smell of the sea, and then round the King's Park, it was very nice.'

Moshe was sizing up the two men behind his hooded eyes. They knew it. 'Yeah,' Wolf said. And 'Edinburgh's a nice city,' said Benny.

Ian was more sociable. He asked them where they were based, and they told him at Kirkliston, from which all Jewish personnel had been invited to the dance, and where they had met his charming sister.

Ian asked, to cover his surprise, where they were from in America. They were from New York. And Moshe's eyes for the first time gleamed.

'I have two brothers in New York,' he informed them.

'Really?' they murmured politely.

'Kaydan, de same name.'

Ian asked, 'Did you ever meet a Kaydan?'

'No,' said Wolf regretfully, and Benny reminded them that New York was a big place.

'Dey write to me,' said Moshe.

They did write, once a year, in Yiddish. Ian explained how his father and two brothers had left Lithuania together as boys, and how his father had got to Scotland, and they had got to America.

Moshe hadn't seen them for . . . ? He could only shrug. Ian calculated it must be sixty years. Which was a long time.

'Well,' said Benny, 'nice to know you.' He was edging to the door.

Queenie said, 'Let's have a cup of tea.'

'No tea,' said Benny, 'no coffee, Wolf and I have to get back.'

Queenie's face fell, she could not hide it. Ian felt a twinge of pity. 'Come again,' he told them.

Wolf said that was an idea and they made their good-nights and Queenie repeated her thank-yous.

22

In the morning, the sunlight splashed into the parlour. Mrs MacPhee had come early and tidied it, and now she was on her knees scrubbing the tiled floor of the hall.

Moshe was in his uncollared shirt and braces, with his tephillin, those two little black leather boxes, one on his head and the other on his left arm, and his tallis loosely round his shoulders, his inheritance from *der Heim*. He wandered about muttering the morning prayers, nodding and swaying, pausing every so often to finger objects on the mantelpiece, or on the sideboard. God was to be thanked, praised and glorified, and His name was to be blessed, sanctified, praised and thanked . . . and how the sunlight lit up the dancing dust! Blessed was the name of the Lord whose glorious kingdom was for ever and ever. . . .

The doorbell rang. Mrs MacPhee got up from her knees in the hall, wiped her hands dry on her apron, and went to the door.

Moshe heard her shrill, 'That's right,' and heard the front door shutting. He mouthed on to the Sovereign of all worlds, but turned towards the door. Mrs MacPhee came in with a huge bunch of flowers.

'Look at thae,' the wee Scots buddy said.

He motioned with his forefinger for her to lay the flowers on the sideboard, and not to disturb him. She laid them down, saying in a low but insistent voice – low so that his God couldn't hear – 'I'll leave them there. She's no' up yet . . . will I wake her? . . . All right, all right.' She took the hint of his wagging finger and went out and shut the door gently after her.

Moshe resumed his affirmation that God was the Lord in heaven and earth, and in the highest heaven of heavens. In truth He was the first and He was the last, and beside Him there was no God. As he approached the bunch of flowers, his muttering became a silent mouthing, and he picked out the card from the corner of the wrapping paper. He got his spectacles from the mantelpiece, and put them on, still mouthing that the Lord had spoken unto Moses saying. . . . He stopped praying as he read the card.

Queenie arose at Mrs MacPhee's bidding, and came downstairs in her quilted dressing-gown and padded into the parlour and took the bunch of flowers and padded out. By agreement with her praying father, she was invisible. She took the flowers through to the kitchen and spread them out on the table and picked bits off and nipped the stalk-ends and put them all in a great blue and white china vase. When she had finished to her satisfaction, and when Mrs MacPhee had repeated enough exclamations at their beauty, she tidied up the mess and put the card into her dressing-gown pocket for safety.

Moshe finished his prayers and came through to the kitchen. He asked the question as he was crossing the threshold. 'Vot did you do?'

She was outraged. 'We did nothing, Pa! We went for a run! It was very nice.' As her father continued to stare at her, she protested, 'There were two of them, Pa!'

'De flowers,' observed Moshe, 'are only from von!'

'One's a bit kinder than the other. Pa, it was a nice run, that's all!'

Moshe shrugged his non-comprehension, turned and went out. Queenie gazed in wonder at the flowers.

Then she had a cup of tea, and a boiled egg and two apples, dressed, and went out to seek advice.

Ian was always pleased to have social visits to his office, because it showed how well he was doing. He listened to

Queenie. Well, miracles happened every day, why not to her? 'Ask him to supper,' he said.

'You ask him.'

'All right.' He wrote on his notepad. 'I'll drop him a note to the base. When? Some time next week?'

Queenie could hardly wait but Ian advised patience. She asked him if he could procure some more – er – shoes. Ian thought, and that decided the date: next Wednesday.

'You don't want both of them, do you?'

'No, I'll stick with the flowers,' said Queenie. She was becoming succinct.

'Right,' said Ian.

'Ian,' said his sister with a pang and an awful realism, 'you don't think he's having me on?'

Wolf accepted the invitation, and came on Wednesday, with more flowers. They had vegetable soup, followed by roast lamb and tsimmus, followed by apple tart, followed by lemon tea and sponge-cake. And afterwards they sat by the fire in the parlour, all of them, and Ian produced a bottle of Scotch.

Wolf told them that he was an accountant, working for his uncle who was an accountant, at least he had worked for his uncle before working for the army. Queenie filled in – because she'd heard it all already – that the accountant's uncle was Wolf's mother's brother. Wolf added that his mother's family came from Chicago really. His father was dead, *alevasholoum*. They sympathised and hoped, too, that his father's soul would rest in peace.

Queenie reminded Wolf to tell them that his sister was in Boston. Halfway through the recitation of the Boston branch of the family, Moshe interrupted to inquire if Wolf had had a barmitzvah. Wolf reassured the old man on this point, chanting the date and the location of the shool.

Queenie, her gaze fixed on Wolf, summed it up. 'He's kosher.'

'I am. Who could have said I'd be drinking Scotch in Scotland, sitting beside your lovely daughter?'

'Och, go on,' said Queenie beside him on the sofa.

Ian asked him to help himself to more of the whisky, and Wolf couldn't see why not, so he did help himself. Queenie pressed him to a fresh pot of tea but he declined that.

Queenie then made the extraordinary pronouncement that it was past her father's bedtime. Ian took the cue and looked at his wrist-watch and said that Queenie was right, and that he'd had a long day too and it was time to turn in. Moshe took out his watch and looked at it, but said nothing. Ian got up and shook hands with Wolf and excused himself and said goodnight.

Wolf drank his whisky. He had some more. He leaned back in his corner of the sofa, Queenie slumped back in hers. Moshe sat on in his armchair beside the fire.

Wolf started on jokes from New York and army jokes, and Queenie laughed merrily. The old man nodded away.

So Wolf asked Queenie if she knew the rules of baseball. She said no but she'd like to hear them.

At midnight, Ian padded downstairs in his pyjamas. He listened at the parlour door. He called 'Pa?' He listened again, and called, 'Pa?'

The door opened. Moshe came out, very worn and tired, his eyes blinking under their hoods. Ian pulled the door shut after him.

'Pa, go to bed! Now go to bed!'

Moshe said, 'No.' Not loudly, but definitely.

Ian, exasperated, said, 'She's forty!'

'I ken,' said Moshe, and turned back into the room. He found Wolf with his arms round Queenie, and kissing her. They drew apart to their own corners of the sofa as he plodded his way back to his armchair and sat staring under his hoods at them.

'Time for me to go,' said Wolf.

'Must you?' asked Queenie, with anguish in her voice.

'Yeah, ma'am.' He got up, straightened himself, got his jacket and put it on. 'Good-night, sir.'

Moshe got up and shook hands. 'Good-night, good-night.'

'Good-night, Queenie.'

She clasped his hand with both of hers. 'Good-night, Wolf.'

She and Moshe saw Wolf out. Moshe shut the front door and bolted it. He told Queenie to go to bed. She stalked upstairs and he followed.

Queenie lay awake in her bed for hours. Sometimes she sobbed, sometimes she pummelled the bed with her fists.

Wolf sent more flowers. So there were more outings, more home visits. Then Queenie dropped in at Ian's shop again where she could have a private talk.

'But you see him,' said Ian, 'you go dancing.'

'It's not the same, Ian. We're not kids! We're not going to canoodle in an open jeep! That house is my home. I want to invite Wolf in and talk to him, and be with him.' She paused to let Ian take whatever meaning he liked, then came to the point: 'Talk to Pa.'

'I've talked to him.' Her Pa was guarding her honour, and he wouldn't be talked out of it.

'Och . . . !' snorted Queenie. 'We sit there, we have tea, he has whisky . . . we talk about everything under the sun except the one thing. And Pa sits by the fire and he sits. So Wolf gets up, good-night, good-night, and I see him out.'

'And?' her brother asked.

'What do you mean?' Queenie was blushing.

'A bit of hunkel-shmunkel?'

So at least Pa left them alone on the doorstep. It was something. What exactly it was, Queenie refused to tell, but Pa came out damn quick with his call of 'Kveenie, Kveenie' and that was that. She opened a box of samples on Ian's desk. Lipsticks. She tried one.

Ian was sorry about Pa's interference. So was Queenie. Ian offered her, in addition to free lipsticks, a box of sample

254

perfumes. He read out the label on one: 'Sweet pea.' That was her, that was Queenie. Ian asked if she wanted anything else. She asked what was there – powder, mascara?

'I was thinking of – Queenie, you do know about things, don't you?'

'What things?'

'To be careful.'

Queenie was outraged. Wolf wasn't like that!

'Like what?'

'Well, he isn't a wolf, is he? I mean –' She asked if she could have the lipstick, and when Ian nodded, she dropped it into her handbag. Then she looked at him pleadingly. 'Ian –'

'I know.'

'You don't.'

'You like Wolf.'

Yes, she did, there was no denying it. With a lump in her throat she said, 'I just think of him.' Wolf was her first love. She got up to go.

'Queenie,' said Ian, 'I've got to do my London trip next week, do my buying.'

'Lucky you! Wi' your London lady-friends!' Ian grinned. He had one or two there.

'Men,' said Queenie, 'you can do what you want.'

Ian looked up at her. 'I'll be away for three days. Can you not get Wolf to wangle a forty-eight hours? With me away you'll have more peace, Pa can't be with you all the time, everywhere.'

Moshe was told after the event. That is, Ian went off to London, Wolf came to supper, stayed on, and Queenie announced that he'd be staying the night, and that Ian knew about it.

So they all went to bed.

Queenie spent a long time in the bath, and a long time at her dressing-table mirror. She took off her dressing-gown at last and noted that she'd slimmed a little, yes she had,

255

surely a little. She pulled back the covers and got into bed and sat with her head against the wooden head-board, waiting; composed, beautiful.

In the still of the night, a bedroom door opened slowly. Wolf poked his head out. Then he emerged with Ian's dressing-gown over his pyjamas. He waited, with the utmost caution; he walked noiselessly along the upper corridor; he stopped outside Queenie's room, noting the light underneath the door, and the fact that the door wasn't properly shut. He pushed, and there was Queenie sitting up in bed. He went in and shut the door ever so gently.

He looked at Queenie and she was a vision, a prize, a plunder. Her dark hair lay in curls around her face; her eyes shone in the light of the bedside lamp, sending to him a questioning expectancy; and for the rest of her, in a pink nightie, those dimpling shoulders, and the shadow cast deeply sideways by the lamp into her heavenly chasm. . . . He went to the bed and sat there.

She put her hand out to take his hands. He leant forward to kiss her. And she stopped him by a gesture. Wolf knew, without looking round, that the door was opening.

Moshe came in, in his long white nightshirt, and no yamulkeh.

He said, 'Vos ees dos?'

Wolf said, 'I'm saying good-night, Mr Kaydan.'

'Good-night,' said Moshe, standing just inside the door, 'good-night.'

Wolf got up. 'Good-night, Queenie.'

'Good-night, Wolf.'

He went out past the old man. Then Moshe went out, shutting the door after him. Queenie waited for a little; then as she was getting out of bed she heard the key being turned in the lock. She ran to the door and turned the handle and tugged. Pa had locked her in. She sank her head against the door and was filled with unutterable woe.

Moshe said his prayers in the morning, no differently from

any other morning of his life, with his tephillim and his tallis. (Except on Shabbas, of course, when one doesn't put on tephillim; but this was an ordinary weekday). He muttered and bowed around the parlour, and heard Mrs Mac-Phee scrubbing away in the hall outside. He knew that the kitchen door was open so that Wolf and Queenie having breakfast at the kitchen table were in full view.

Wolf drank down his tea, which was preferable to Kaydan-made coffee.

'More tea?' Queenie seemed far away, distant.

'No, I gotta go.' He got up and reached for his jacket. He looked along the hall. Mrs MacPhee was on her knees there and in the open doorway of the parlour the old man was swaying and muttering and mouthing and nodding. Wolf put his jacket on.

'Say goodbye to your Pa for me, I'll not disturb him. Maybe it's praying that makes him so smart.'

Queenie asked him, 'When'll I see you again?'

Wolf didn't answer for a bit and her heart grew ice-cold.

Then, 'Queenie, that's up to you,' he said.

'How?' Her voice, attempting to be even, came out as a tragic Edinburgh squeak.

Wolf shrugged his answer. It was the only answer a man could possibly give.

So Queenie got up. She looked along the hall. Then she walked to the kitchen door and shut it and turned around to face her beloved. She leaned back against the door and her eyes were full of love.

In the hall, Mrs MacPhee turned to the shut kitchen door; she knelt up. She turned to old Mr Kaydan. He had stopped praying; he was watching the shut kitchen door. He took his watch from his waistcoat pocket under his tallis. He looked at it, he looked at the door; he waited.

Mrs MacPhee watched the door. It didn't open, there was no sound from the other side – or was there?

Moshe checked his watch; he put it away; he advanced

257

down the hallway; at the door he halted. He cupped his ear to listen. Then he opened the door.

Queenie sat at the table with a glazed-over look on her face. Wolf was dishevelled.

Moshe looked from one to the other.

And when Ian came back from London by the day train, stretching himself and climbing out at Waverley Station, and going up the stairs to Princes Street into the evening sunlight and taking a number three tram to Newington and walking along swinging his weekend case against his gas mask till he came to his own front garden and front door, just as he was sorting out his keys to open the door, Mrs MacPhee opened it for him. She'd heard him and had come flying along the hall.

'Mr Kaydan! There's news! There's news!'

'What?' asked Ian in some surprise.

Moshe came out from the parlour. 'Shlomo, dere's news!'

'What?' repeated Ian.

'Vile you vere in London –'

Mrs MacPhee couldn't wait, she butted in, 'You'll never guess, about Miss Kaydan –'

Queenie appeared at the top of the stairs. She said, 'Ian.' That was all. She descended, dressed as he'd seen her day in, day out, but he could see that her soul was transfigured. As she came down the stairs she uttered a kind of chant.

'Oh – ho – ho!'

Ian stood bemused.

Moshe was explaining, 'She had her friend Volf –'

'He was staying here,' put in Mrs MacPhee.

'Ah – ha – ha!' chanted Queenie.

She came to the foot of the stairs, then to Ian, and slapped him on the shoulders and retired along the hall. She was dancing a primal dance of triumph.

'In de spare room,' said Moshe, very pleased with himself, 'and in de morning –'

'They were having breakfast and I was doing the hall –'

Queenie advanced down the hall again. 'Yah – hah –
ai – yai – yai!'

'And dey shut de door, and ven I opened it –'

'You ken what he said to your father?'

Queenie, with arms whirling and fingers snapping,
revolved among them. 'Wolf – has – asked – me – to – marry
– him!' She squealed and squealed and squealed her joy,
and stamped and laughed and kissed Ian.

23

David got leave for Queenie's wedding, in fact he was a pole-holder, one of the four who held up the canopy in the Kaydans' parlour. The other three were a cousin and two nephews on Rivka's side that nobody saw from one year to another except at weddings and funerals and barmitz-vahs.

Shirley was nursing in London and couldn't get off, she said, so it was a long way and if she could go to a dance that night who was asking? Anyway the Kaydan house was crowded from kitchen to parlour. Rabbi Dr Daiches offici-ated, with the chazan, Mr Ordman, and the beadle, Mr Rubinstein, with his red cheeks and sideways glittering eyes and his feet at the correct angle.

Queenie was in white. Somewhere she had got the cou-pons and what was wrong with white if she wanted white? She stood under the canopy and took the wineglass and sipped; then it was taken and given to Wolf, very smart in his uniform by her side. He sipped and sipped again and finished it to murmurs of approval from the guests. Rubin-stein took the glass, wrapped it in a napkin and put it on the floor. Wolf stamped on it with his heel and that was that.

The room rang with mazeltovs and vibrated with hand-shaking, and the suction of kisses. Benny was the best man and there was a sprinkling of uniforms of all the services. David was in battledress with the RAOC flash on his shoulder and a corporal's stripes on his arm. His mother, Mary, had settled in an armchair, well attended with delicacies.

Mrs MacPhee hovered in the doorway waiting to see if the drinks tray needed renewing.

And the chatter – 'Isn't she nice?'

'Isn't he handsome?'

'Hasn't she landed lucky?'

'Well, she's a good baker.'

'Her sponge-cake –'

'You see, it all comes to those who wait.'

Mary was chatting to Mrs Isaacs. 'My –' she lowered her voice, 'late husband, Zelek, was Queenie's brother. And I have two children, they're not children now. Shirley's a nurse. My Shirley. She's twenty. She asked to get off but – you know.' Mary excused her daughter with a nod and a shrug. 'And I have a son, David, he's here. He's very clever. David?'

David drifted towards his mother in her armchair.

'Come and meet Mrs Isaacs.'

So David was polite and smiled and couldn't quite remember going to Mrs Isaacs for tea when he was three.

Queenie was talking to a wee bald man, Mr Simon. 'Cyril, that's awful nice of you to say so. It's been worth waiting for. And thanks for the lovely pillowcases.' He had done his pleasant duty, had complimented the bride, had kissed her, had wished her well, and now he retired to make way for others, and to resume his war talk in the corner with Captain Cree of the Home Guard.

Mary's cousin Hannah was there of course. She was a spinster, a little older than Mary, slightly deaf, slightly stupid, fairly fierce and determined, with a bony face and a plump midriff. She had cornered Ian. She spoke in her loud unselfconscious way.

'Well, that's her out of the way.'

'That's true, Hannah,' said Ian, 'but I'll miss her.'

'And I'll bet you'll miss her,' said Hannah. 'Who's going to do for you?' It was a question that had intrigued her ever since she had received the wedding invitation.

Ian told her, 'Mrs MacPhee.'

'Eh?' said Hannah. 'I mean, when are you going to get off, Ian? Get a wife to do for you now Queenie's gone? You're still a bachelor.'

'Not *a* bachelor, Hannah.'

'What?' She was astounded.

'Edinburgh's most *eligible* bachelor,' he kidded her.

She studied his face, then got it and guffawed. 'Go on!'

'Make me an offer,' said Ian.

She dug him in the ribs and nearly upset his wineglass.

Moshe spoke to his grandson David. 'You got anodder stripe.'

'Yes, Grandpa.'

'Corporal.'

'That's right.'

'Vot do you do?'

'I'm an inspector, of nuts and bolts.'

'Vy are you no' a general?'

'Soon!'

It was a dry humour they had both shared and enjoyed ever since David had grown up and Moshe grown old.

Kid-ons, giggles, enquiries about relatives, cuddles in the safety of the crowd, flattery, a little business; then it was shushing-time for the wedding-cake: a little, wartime, round cake, iced, and what can you do with dried eggs? It was very nice, anyway. Queenie and Wolf held hands and together they cut. There were gasps and cheers and clapping from the guests. Benny found himself next to Moshe. 'Are you a happy man, Mr Kaydan?' It was rhetorical, but Moshe smiled and nodded and wiped his tears and said, 'Yes . . .'

Mary got David to bring her share of the wedding-cake. Together they munched. Mary knew what he was thinking. She was good at that.

'It's all right, David.' She munched and scanned the crowd to imbibe the atmosphere of it. 'You can say what you like, think what you like, I don't care what you do, or where you go, as long as you marry a nice Yiddishy girl.' He didn't reply and she didn't expect him to, because there was no reply to that.

Queenie was arm-in-arm with Wolf, two radiant people, she forty, he thirty-eight, at the start of a new life, alcoholic maybe, but upright, in charge of themselves and their destiny. Queenie was saying to a pair of jokers in the company, very seriously so that the joke ended, 'We've decided not to have children. We're getting on.'

When the war ended, Edinburgh Jewry was as shaken and shattered as everyone else by the concentration camps. They identified with those skeletal humans in the gas chambers; believer and unbeliever, all had the thought that if they had known they would have fought the war even harder. Chosen for extermination, for genocide! It made the victory a personal thing, the survival of each one of them.

They read the news from Palestine: Irgun and the Stern gang against the British; and this was a time when Britain was broke, the land of austerity.

Young Gore stayed on in the army so the old man remained in his business but left Ian alone as general manager. Ian did well for his boss in the circumstances, and now and then old Gore responded to a little prompting and raised Ian's salary.

It was an art on its own to keep stocks up. Ian toiled long hours in his office, spoke on the telephone to distant places on tip-offs from other places, with his feet up on the desk. 'It's a lovely voice,' he kidded, 'must be a lovely person. What about all these crates of Max Factor?' He heard out the usual protestation. 'Even you? Could you dig into it for five dozen? Four dozen? All right.'

The office door had opened. It was young Gore, thirty years old, well tailored, with an impatient way of moving, having completed his service in the Black Watch. He had account books under his arm, and shut the door behind him.

Ian took his feet down from the desk and continued his conversation on the phone. 'I know you'll do your best. I hope to be seeing you. Yes, I hope so, too. Goodbye.' He hung up and got to his feet. 'Mr Gore, good morning.'

Gore said, 'Morning, Kaydan.'

'Have a seat.'

Gore sat in the chair in front of the desk, and laid his books down.

Ian said, 'I didn't know you were coming. If you'd given me a ring –'

'Sit down,' said the ex-Major.

Ian remained standing. Already there was the tension between them of soldier and civilian. Gore studied the books.

Ian asked him if he was pleased with the profit for the previous year, as the books had just been audited.

'It's all right,' said the younger man.

'Fourteen per cent up.'

Gore said, 'Sit down.'

Ian stayed on his feet. It was his office. Gore looked up at him and said, 'Sit down, Kaydan.'

Ian sat dutifully.

Gore jabbed a finger at a typed memo. 'What's this request for expenses?'

Ian's heart gave an extra-loud beat but he replied smoothly enough, 'I'm going to London on Monday. On a buying trip.'

'You've been doing two London trips a year. You've already been twice this year, why a third?'

Ian explained, because everything was reasonable: 'There are two main reasons for that. Last year we took over two more shops. And things are still very short. The increased turnover I gave you was in sundries, and they're hard to come by.' He gave Gore a smile. 'I seem to have a knack of finding them.'

Gore's eyes stared into Ian's with no expression. 'Can't you use your knack on the telephone, or by letter?'

'No.' It was the only answer to that question.

Gore said, 'Can I have the details of the last expenses?'

Now Ian was a man in authority. He was good at his job because of his authority. Old man Gore had never questioned his expenses. He started to say so. 'Your father —'

'My father has been retired for three weeks,' said the son. 'I am the proprietor of this firm. I am not demanding anything unreasonable.'

Ian considered. 'I have ten shops to buy for.'

Gore said he was aware of that.

'Before I go to London,' said Ian, in a reasonable manner, in answer to the proprietor's reasonable question, 'I make up a list of firms I'm going to visit, and people who I hope will supply me. I estimate how long I'll have to be in London, and I draw a lump sum. I won't come home with much change, I assure you.'

'You mean you don't have the details?'

'Not exactly,' said Ian. 'I can give you a rough breakdown.'

Gore pursed his lips. 'All right,' he said.

'I'll send it over.'

'Tell me now.'

This was surely not reasonable. Ian kept his temper. 'There's the railway ticket, hotel bill, food.'

Gore waited but Ian had stopped. 'That can't add up!' he exclaimed, looking at the request for expenses.

'Small gifts,' added Ian.

'Bribes?'

Ian got a little angry. 'No, Mr Gore, it's more like a wink and a kid-on. It's a game, it eases the way.'

Gore's eyes never left him. 'Like what?'

'Like a pair of nylons. A small bouquet. A lunch. A show.'

'What show?'

'The Victoria Palace!' Ian shouted.

Gore told him to control himself. 'It still doesn't add up.'

'Are you saying I'm dipping my fingers in the till?'

'Are you?'

There was a silence in the office. Ian felt the injustice, and sensed Gore's hatred, and returned it. But he asked a perfectly civil question. 'Who do I do it all for?' And he supplied the answer, 'You!' Gore hadn't understood this.

But Gore said, 'Yes. Let me have the details of these last trips. And the two the year before. What's in these drawers?'

'They're my desk drawers.'

'Yes, your desk drawers.'

What regiment had the man been in? The s.s.? Ian told him what was in his desk drawers: 'Staff files. Personnel. Stationery. Private odds and ends.'

Gore got up and came round to Ian's side of the desk. He opened a drawer. Ian sat dumbfounded. Gore shut the drawer, opened another. There was a bottle of Scotch in it.

'What is that?'

'A bottle of whisky.'

'Can you account for it?'

Ian got up. He reached into the drawer and brought the bottle out and stood it on the desk. He shut the drawer with deliberation.

He said to Gore, 'As a matter of fact I can.' He brought his cheque book from his inside pocket. His hands were trembling but he flipped through the cheque stubs till he found it, and held it out to Gore. 'My cheque, to the licensed grocer up the road, who will witness to it, I'm sure. The whisky,' he said, 'is for my father . . .'

Gore took the cheque book. Ian pulled it back. 'That is my private cheque book.'

Gore eyed him. 'Let me have these detailed expenses, Kaydan. Send them over tomorrow. I'm only asking what is my right to know.'

'Do you want my resignation?'

'Are you offering it?'

The silence was sharp and stiff.

'No,' said Ian as if he had debated the matter and was putting his considered opinion. 'You can sack me if you've any grounds.' Gore said, 'Yes, I can.' He took up his books and went out, shutting the door behind him.

Ian was left standing. He picked up the phone and dialled

a number at the top of his pad. Then he spoke. 'Pharmaceutical Society? Could I have a word with the Secretary, please?' Trembling overcame him and he had to sit in his chair to take the call.

That night, the whisky level in the bottle dropped steadily. Ian and Moshe sat alone at the kitchen table.

'He can't sack me,' Ian recited. 'The Society would back me up for wrongful dismissal. But he's a bugger.'

'His father was all right.' Moshe remembered being hospitably received by the elder Gore.

'The son is an army officer. Anti-Semite.' He sounded the word with the stress at the end, making it the warning-call to all Jews, the call to fear and hatred. 'Chazzer.' The loathed pig-animal. 'He's goading me to resign. It's no good, Pa. I can't fold my arms and sit it out and wait for my pension.'

Moshe took his cigarette-holder from his mouth. 'You should have had your own shop.'

'I've done all right,' said Ian.

'You'll look for von.' And as Ian grimaced at the suggestion, he said 'Vy?' with an emphasis that meant 'Why not, there's no reason why not.'

'Pa,' said Ian in his whisky-tiredness, 'I'm too old to take on a mortgage. I'd never pay it off. What a load to carry.'

'Vot vill you do?'

'I don't know . . . Go to Israel.'

That was something different again. A new road to travel. But they were fighting in Israel.

'They'll win,' said Ian. 'America's recognised it. Russia's recognised it. Bernadotte's there as mediator. There is a State of Israel. I'm too old to fight but they'll need pharmacists. What's the good of me staying here?' He felt the old man's unease. 'I'll go and I'll take you with me. Pa, you'll see Jerusalem. They need clocks and watches, they tell the time the same way there as here.'

267

Father and son sat in silence. Moshe plucked a cigarette paper from his packet and sprinkled his Turkish tobacco over it, and rolled it, licked along the edge and sealed it. 'I've tought about it,' he said. He lit up and the loose tobacco at the end flamed for a second, then quieted. He puffed. 'You cannae go yet.'

'When it's peace,' said Ian.

24

The sideboard drawer was open, crammed with watches, and all the time in Moshe's world was ticking away as he picked over them, fondled his favourites and said his prayers. He was in tephillin and tallis, but God knew about his watches.

He heard the sound of the key in the front door, and listened as he muttered. He shut the drawer and held on to the edge of the sideboard as he swayed in prayer.

Mrs MacPhee came in with her basket.

'Good morning, Mr Kaydan!' A cheery greeting. He waved his response as he muttered on. It was a ritual that they both accepted, as natural a way to communicate in the morning as any other. She went on, 'I called in at the Yiddishy shops, I've got a nice bit of vorsht for you.'

This was too much communication and he waved at her to stop interrupting him.

'All right,' she said. She looked back along the hall. 'There's a letter in the box.' She went out and fetched it.

While she was gone Moshe brought his key-bunch out from his trouser pocket, locked his watch drawer and tested it, and put the keys away. Who was like unto the Lord among the mighty ones? Who was like unto Him, glorious in holiness, revered in praises, doing marvels?

'It's for you,' said Mrs MacPhee from the hall. She came in with the letter. 'It's got an American stamp. It's from Queenie. But it's no' her writing.'

Moshe waved at her to put it down and leave him.

'I'll put it here.' She propped it on the mantelpiece. 'And I'll get on. See you later.'

She went out. Moshe prayed and swayed.

Mrs MacPhee was surprised to find Ian in the kitchen. He sat at the table with the breakfast not yet cleared away. He had his feet up on another chair, and his collar open outside his jacket, and his cigarette dangling the way he dangled it from a corner of his lip. He was in great spirits.

'Hello, Mr Kaydan! What you doing at this time? Have you got a holiday?'

'No, Mrs MacPhee.' Meaning her guess was good, but it wasn't the right one. 'But I'm taking it easy.'

'So I see.'

He became lyrical, almost conducting his words with his arms. 'Mrs MacPhee, the State of Israel has been ad-mitted to the United Nations. It is the fifty-ninth nation of the world.' And all the pennies and all the halfpennies and all the farthings that had dropped with a clink down the years into the blue tin box in the house of his father had become a miracle.

'Oh ay?' said Mrs MacPhee.

'Ay,' said Shlomo Kaydan, wee boy and middle-aged man. 'So last night, all the Jews in the world were celebrat-ing. And I feel fine this morning. And safe. And I'm going to go in to the shop when I feel like going in. Just this once.'

She could see he was pleased, and she was pleased for him. She went about her business of taking off her turban hat, and brown felt coat and buckled shoes, and putting on her apron and bauchles, those old shoes that had become slippers over the years with the toes hanging out and the heels off them.

Ian talked to his audience. 'It's been a long time coming. Do you know how long? Nearly two thousand years.' He told her about the wee blue tins in every Jewish house, and how, no matter how hard the times were, a farthing at least had to go into the box. They'd been buying land with it, and planting trees, and now they had a state, a home. The Wandering Jew no more. 'Mrs MacPhee, my father will actually be able to fulfil the dream of a lifetime. He can go to Jerusalem. And I can go. As citizens.'

Moshe was at the kitchen door, still in his tephillin, with his tallis trailing on the floor behind him. He was holding the open envelope, with the letter half out of it.

'What's the matter, Pa?' said Ian.

'Kveenie . . .' was all the old man said.

Ian took the letter and read how Queenie had been wasting away, with her cough, and how she had had a bout of coughing and had died, Israel or no Israel.

So that left the two Kaydans. In April, of course, came the Passover, and they couldn't not have a *seder* night (the Passover family service at home) because of the old man; and he could not go to someone else's house to have it, although they were invited very kindly. They brought in Hannah, because she was the last of her brothers and sisters too, and she knew how to do it. And David was there. His mother had passed on last year, and Shirley had gone out to Australia to be a nursing Sister and maybe to find a husband: she ought not to have had all those boyfriends when she was younger – but anyway, she was at the other side of the world.

Hannah's hand stretched out to the two candles in their brass holders, and said the blessing in Hebrew with a strong Edinburgh accent, to bring in the Festival. She said it with satisfaction, and afterwards, 'There, your Mrs MacPhee couldnae dae that! Now come to the table and sit down, and we'll have our seder.'

She had set the table for the ceremony, with the covered matzos, and the neck and the egg and the parsley, and her *charoushes* was delicious; David had dipped his finger in before the table was set.

The three men came to the table in their suits, and all three wearing yamulkehs.

Hannah talked on at them, a vocal accompaniment to the action. She pointed out all the things on the table, and named them. 'It's how my mother used to do it. There's the wine. Nu! Maybe next year in Jerusalem, but this year, we're here.' She sat. 'It's Pesach,' she told them. 'You can begin, Moshe.'

They accepted the domination because of her unself-consciousness, and they could smile at her and this was all right too.

So they opened their thin old tattered Haggadahs with the medieval woodcuts and the bad Polish–English translation on the facing pages, and the four wine-glasses were filled with sweet, heady Palestinian wine, Kosher for Passover, and Moshe said the sanctification. They sipped the wine and made the annual rude comments on it. Then Hannah came round with a basin and a jug of water and a towel. First Moshe, then Ian, then David had a trickle of water dripped over their fingers, and dried off. Then they said the blessing for vegetables and ate the parsley dipped in salt water, which symbolised, for David anyhow, only the arguments and the jokes they had every year about what exactly it did symbolise.

Moshe broke the middle matzo of the three under the cloth at the head of the table. He put one piece under the tablecloth for the Afikomen, to be eaten as the last morsel of this Passover night. Was this really the symbol of the Paschal Lamb, whose blood on the door caused the Angel of Death to spare the first-born within, because this was a Jewish household? David thought it a far-fetched symbol, even allowing for the distortions of time: a piece of baked flour and water, made by machinery, in place of a sacrificial lamb that bled to death?

But Moshe was reciting the ancient liturgy, in the Aramaic tongue, raising the platter of symbols, and inviting all who were hungry to come and eat and celebrate the Passover. This matzo was the bread of affliction that their fathers ate in the land of Egypt. Now they were here, but next year they would be in the Land of Israel. Now they were slaves but next year they would be free men.

David, as the youngest present at the age of twenty-nine, asked the four questions that he had learned by rote when he was five from the teacher in the cheder, Mr Rubinstein. He still had an image of the man's bowler hat and hacking cough, spitting into his fingers and sticking it under the desk in Sciences School that they used every evening.

Why was this night different from all other nights? *Mah nishtanoh hallailoh hazeh micol hallailous?* Hebraic-Scottish; at least he hadn't had Auntie Hannah's nasal sing-song.

Moshe muttered and chanted his way through the book. Ian joined in piously from time to time, then looked at the woodcuts and made jokes to David and Hannah. Hannah read laboriously from the English translation and sighed and said, 'Oh, my.'

Then Moshe was silent and they realised he had come to the end. He had even muttered his way through *Bourai Pri Hagophen*, the one-line hymn-blessing of God for creating the wine in their glasses, which every other Jew gave all his relish to saying, or singing.

So Hannah asked what came next, because you forget from one year to another, and it was another ritual washing of the hands. And then the other blessings and eating of the bitter herb, and Hannah was able to 'Service the Meat' as it said in her haggadah.

There was chicken soup with alkies, then brisket with boiled potatoes and mashed turnip and some of the bitter herbs, horseradish grated with beetroot – delicious. Then lemon tea and Hannah's Pesach honey-cakes, dry as dust and her own specialty.

The men reclined satisfied, with their yamulkehs on. Moshe had eaten little, but Ian and David had heartier appetites.

'Was that a good Pesach meal?'

'Lovely, Auntie Hannah,' said David.

'Very good,' Ian said as if he really meant it.

'And you Moshe?'

'It vos all right.'

Hannah explained to him, because he couldn't have understood: 'It's what I used to do for all my brothers. And Rivka used to do for you, and your mother' – this to David – '*alevasholoum*, used to do for you.'

'It vos all right,' said Moshe.

'Yes,' said Hannah. It certainly was all right.

Ian said, 'Hannah, Pa's seen a good few seders. He's eighty-two. He must remember at least eighty.'

Hannah paused to accept that, in some wonder at the passing of time. 'Well, I remember a few as well. I'm fifty-nine. I was born in Lithuania but I came over as a baby so I don't remember, Moshe, what a seder night was like there.' She spoke to him loudly, because he was old, and also gestured her meaning in case her words were not clear enough.

Moshe humoured her. 'Lituania vos de same as dis, Hannah, vit a family.'

'The family!' Hannah grasped at it. 'That's what we are. And the table, the wine, the prayers. That's what it's about. That's why we're Jews.'

David said, 'Is that why you're a Jew, Uncle Ian? What's it mean to you?'

A fair question for a Passover night. 'Being a Jew?' echoed Ian, reviewing his life. 'Working hard. Being educated. Being harassed and having to stand up. Kids threw stones at me when I was a boy, because I was a Jew. Being different. Being part of a tribe. It is a tribe. Being able to talk to strangers, say *Sholoum Aleichem*, and talking about mutual relatives. Being always on guard.'

That was the beginning of his list. 'Nothing about religion?' asked David.

Ian hesitated. Tonight was not the night for that kind of argument.

Moshe pronounced it. 'It's about God.'

And David, being a scientist, had to come in on that one.

'Other religions are about God, Grandpa. I think ours is about life.' He raised his wine-glass and said the blessing about the fruit of the vine, and drained his glass. 'Other religions are about the after-life, Judaism is right now. What's the greatest tragedy to a Jew? Death.' He told them his memories of his father's death, stamped for ever on his mind – the stark black coffin, no flowers, old clothes and a man who cut their jerseys with a knife. And the whole ceremony saying 'That's it.'

'It's vot God is saying,' said the old man because he knew.

'But God says different things to different people, Pa.' Ian had joined in. 'Jesus was a Jew. This is the same seder as he had, and look what God said to him.'

'I am a Jew,' said Moshe with no force needed, no emphasis, a simple statement. 'God has chosen de Jews from all de peoples. And gave us de law. And I do de commandments dat God commanded me.' He reached over to the dresser and opened the top drawer and brought out an envelope.

'What are you doing, Pa?' Then Ian recognised the envelope. 'Oh, it's the photo.'

'What?' said Hannah loudly; then whispering even more loudly, 'What's he getting?'

'A photograph,' said Moshe.

Ian asked David if he'd seen it. David hadn't.

'Who's it of?' demanded Hannah. 'What photo?'

'Lituania,' said Moshe.

'Lithuania!' She was amazed.

Ian told her it had been sent from Israel; a cousin had sent it to him.

Moshe took out the photograph and studied it. 'Vere I come from. Vere I ran avay from. It's de grave.'

David took it from him. An excavated mass grave, with bodies in heaps, still recognisably human.

'In de vor,' said Moshe, 'de concentration camp. Dey're all here.'

All their relatives were there. And all Hannah's relatives.

She took it and peered at it. 'Oy veh!' she said and put her hands to her head.

Moshe said, 'Eighteen-eighty-five I came. I vos a Jew. All de Jews are here.' He took the photo again.

'Put it away!' pleaded Hannah, but it sounded like a command from her. 'It's Pesach! We're free!'

'We are, Grandpa.'

'Vot?'

'Free.'

'I ken,' said old Moshe Kaydan. He put the photograph back in the envelope.

'Think of nicer things,' commanded Hannah. 'When are you going to Israel, David?'

'I don't know if I'll go, Auntie Hannah.'

'What?' She was scandalised. 'You'll find yourself a wife there. You need a wife, a handsome lad like you.'

'I need a wife,' David agreed. 'But I don't know if I'll find one there.'

Moshe was sharp. 'Vy?' he demanded.

David hesitated. Then he said, 'My mother said to me three times a day, every day of my life, "It's all right, David," she said, "it doesn't matter what you do as long as you marry a nice Yiddishy girl." '

Moshe looked at his only grandson. 'It's a lot of telling.'

Hannah explained to the old man loudly and with a twirl of her arm, 'But he hasnae fallen in love yet.'

'No, I haven't,' said David.

'You vill. Rivka, your grandma, loved your father. And he gave de love to you. So you'll love, and you'll pass it on to your children.'

The inheritance of love was a strange idea.

'I never had love,' said Ian, and turned to Hannah. 'Did you?'

'What?'

'Did you get loved, Hannah? You probably missed out when you were a baby, like me.'

'Ian, what you've never had, you don't miss.' She got up.

276

'Now give me those plates. I'll wash up in the sink, you get on with the second half of the seder. It's the boring half so I'll be over here. I'll come back for the songs.'

She cleared the plates and cutlery over to the sink. David took up the wine bottle and asked his Grandpa if he should fill up the glasses.

'Yes,' said Moshe, 'and von for de Angel.'

'Oh yes,' nodded Hannah.

David fetched an empty glass and stood it in the middle of the table and filled it with the dark red wine. 'For the Messiah – Jews don't think of the Messiah.'

'Elijah,' said Ian.

'I thought it was for the Angel of Death,' said Hannah.

'No,' Moshe said.

'Well,' said Hannah, who'd hedged her bets long ago, 'We've been talking about him, so he might hear and come to see who it is. So he can have his wine and go away again.'

One for the Angel. Moshe picked up his envelope with the photo, and laid it down.

Later that evening David sat with Ian in the parlour, with the fire blazing. They had taken off their yamulkehs and sprawled in the easy chairs. After the second half of the service, the praise, the 'Next year in Jerusalem!' and the songs, David had walked Hannah home, and Moshe had gone to bed. It was a cold April night and David was glad to get back to the Kaydan house where he was staying for the Passover.

It was a time for putting their feet up.

'I'll give it another year,' David was saying, 'and then I'll either be Chief Chemist, or I'll go elsewhere.'

'Where? Not Israel?'

'England probably. A good-sized plastics firm.'

'Research.'

'No,' said David firmly, 'industry!' The little research that he'd done was too slow-moving for him, bringing an occasional result after months of plod.

But to Uncle Ian the word 'Research' was filled with romance. He scoffed at the idea of industry. 'Factories!' he said, waving them away.

'Throbbing with life, Uncle Ian. I love it.'

Ian wished he could say the same. He was at the top of the tree but it was a rotten tree. He poured out his woes to David. 'When I was a kid, in our slum, we had a doctor, a Theosophist. He used to amaze my mother and father with his knowledge of Jews and Judaism. He said that the Scots were one of the Lost Tribes of Israel. It could be. People like us coming to Scotland over the years. And I look at my chazzer boss. And I wonder if he could ever have been a Jew.'

He took out his cigarettes and lit up. He offered the packet to David, but David shook his head. It was *Yontiff*, a Holy Day. 'Aren't you afraid to smoke in Grandpa's house?'

'He's asleep,' said Ian. 'I need a cigarette. I'm thinking of taking the old man and going to Israel. Seriously. It's a big jump.'

He got up and went to the sideboard. He tried the watch drawer but it was locked.

'What's he got in there?' asked David.

'Watches. Some money, cash for his buying and selling.' The old man was still in business, still went to the far corners of Edinburgh, still ran for the tram. Ian made a guess that he had a hundred pounds in the drawer. One thing about his old man, he had kept his independence.

Ian opened the other drawer. It was filled with rubbish. Envelopes and table-mats, string, nutcrackers, old papers, bills and notices. He found what he wanted, the bulging envelope of the family photographs – snapshots, mounted cards, faded sepias.

He brought them to the fire and went through them, handing them to David. There was David on the sands, aged three. And Shirley as a schoolgirl. Lala . . . Ian paused in great fondness over that one. Then Queenie, poor

Queenie. And his mother. His own graduation photograph. The Burma snaps. He passed a wad of them over to David. Then there was the thick card sepia one: his father. Moshe Kaydan aged, what, twenty? In a lum hat, carrying a coconut, behind a rustic bench. He was going back to Lithuania to fetch his bride and he had to show them that he'd made his fortune.

'He hasn't had much change out of life,' said Ian. 'He's feared God, and God's just shrugged at him. Maybe he'll die happy in Israel.' He got up. 'C'mon and have a cup of tea.'

David pointed out that a cup of tea would also be against the law. They'd had the Afrikomen, and were forbidden to eat or drink any more.

Ian led the way through to the kitchen, and switched on the light. The candles had burnt out. He lit the gas under the kettle. 'Here,' he said to David lounging in the doorway, 'd'you fancy the dogs tomorrow? Powderhall?'

'Right!'

'It's a date.'

David came to the table and contemplated the full glass of wine standing alone in the middle. Ian saw him. 'Now don't drink that!'

It was the One for the Angel. David remembered that in his father's house they always left it after the seder, and in the morning, when he looked, it was empty. He had never known if the Angel had been, or if his Dad had drunk it. He asked Ian what he did with his.

'If you offer me a cigarette,' said Ian, 'yes, a cup of tea, yes. I'm not superstitious, David, but when it comes to the Angel, he might drop in tonight, and he might fancy it.'

They left the wine as it was.

Whether the Angel of Death passed their way that night, David didn't know, but he came before the year was out, painfully. Ian's cough came back, his smoker's cough that woke him up every morning. He assumed, when it got worse, that his dormant tuberculosis had become active again. He took to shouting at Moshe, blaming his father for the illness and for his unfulfilled life; but when he realised that he was failing, he became loving, forgiving, and lay in bed holding hands with the old man.

He was taken to the Infirmary and died of cancer of the lung. David's abiding memory was of a man with a twinkle in his eyes, a smile on his lips, and a cigarette dangling.

They buried him (the Edinburgh Hebrew Congregation Burial Society) at Piershill Cemetery, in the Jewish Sector. Hannah remarked loudly to the others in the thin crowd that that was Ian gone. Shlomo he'd been called: Solomon. A man in his prime.

And Moshe wept to see the last of his children to the grave. Six he had had . . . all six.

Hannah blew her nose, and said that she'd always had a soft spot for Ian. Him and her, they might have . . .

The simple black coffin had its trestles removed, and was lowered into the grave.

'Slowly, slowly,' commanded Cyril Simon, the President of the Society. He should know how to do it by now. But the coffin jammed. There was an intake of cold breaths by all present.

'What . . . ?' said Cyril. 'The grave's too wee! It won't go in!' Then there was such an argument between him and the gravedigger, who produced his bit of paper with the measurements and compared it with Cyril's notebook, and they agreed, so the grave was measured and it was two inches too short.

Mrs MacPhee, on the outskirts of the crowd, was shocked. David said to her that she knew, and he knew, that if Uncle Ian had been here he would have laughed his head off.

25

Sunshine spilled over the sideboard drawer where old Moshe Kaydan fondly rootled. Mrs MacPhee came in in her apron.

'That's the blackcurrant jam made. I've put it in the jars but it's still hot –'

Moshe had become aware of her, and he shut the drawer, keeping one watch in his hand. Mrs MacPhee went on, 'So I've left some in a saucer for you to have with your tea.'

'Yes,' said Moshe.

'You understand?'

'Yes. You ken vot today is?'

'Yes.'

'It's my birthday.'

'I know.'

'I'm eight-eight.' He was pleased with himself. He turned, opened the drawer, put the watch in and shut it . . .

'Many, many happy returns.' She'd said it to him before but she was happy to say it again.

'Tenk you.'

She asked him if he knew who was coming to see him. He didn't know vot. Mrs MacPhee reminded him.

David was thirty-four. He came along the street to his Grandpa's house with his wife Elizabeth beside him, and pushing the pram in front of him. He took a glance at Elizabeth – blonde, blue-eyed, upper-class, to match what he called his own lower-middle class, or ghetto-class: she was nice, but decidedly not a Yiddishy girl.

Elizabeth caught the look. 'I'm frightened,' she said.

'So am I. It's daft, he's a nice old man.'

Elizabeth looked straight ahead. David said, 'You're not the first blue eyes in the Kaydan family. There was a cousin on my Grandmother's side. Blonde as well. And some ginger ones.'

'Hanky-panky below stairs,' she surmised.

David told her there weren't any stairs in Lithuania. It took place behind the hen-house. 'And you mean hunkel-shmunkel. Get your Yiddish right, darling.'

'Hunkel-shmunkel,' she said. 'What about him?'

The baby in the pram was catching his toes. 'No trouble,' David told her.

'I bet there is. Your grandfather's going to ask to see his willy.'

David became uneasy. He had tried to rationalise things. The law was, you were a Jew if your mother was Jewish. Grandpa knew he'd married out; he knew that the son of the marriage wasn't a Jew. He wouldn't even ask.

They crossed to the house, and went up the garden path to the front door.

When the bell rang, Mrs MacPhee went to open it. 'Master David! Come away in!'

'Hello, Mrs MacPhee. Good to see you.' And he introduced his wife Elizabeth, and his son Anthony.

'Well,' said Mrs MacPhee, peering into the pram, 'the wee soul! Oh, what a bonny bairn!' And didn't it look like its mummy?

Hannah advanced along the hall to meet them. 'Is that David?'

'Hello, Auntie Hannah. Nice to see you.'

'My, it's been a time!'

'How are you?'

She was fine, fine. She was fit and strong and well. David introduced Elizabeth, and Hannah was pleased to meet her. Elizabeth mentioned that David had told her a lot about Auntie Hannah, and Hannah beamed at that.

'And this is Anthony.'

'Aw, look at that!' cooed Hannah. 'Isn't he just the thing!'

'Isn't he?' echoed Mrs MacPhee. She told David that his grandpa was in the kitchen.

David decided to go in first. Elizabeth was to give him just a moment, then follow in. Hannah and Mrs MacPhee were oblivious, two Scots buddies cooing over the baby in the pram.

Moshe sat at the table, little and wispy. 'David? Vos machs du?'

'I'm fine, Grandpa. How are you?'

'All right.'

So there was a smiling silence in the look of affection between them. Then Elizabeth came in and David said, 'This is Elizabeth, my wife.'

Moshe was perfectly charming. He stood up and held out his hand.

'How do you do?'

'How do you do? David's told me so much about you and the family.'

'Dat's good. Please sit down. Sit down, David. And ve'll hae a cup o' tea.'

In came the pram wheeled by Mrs MacPhee and Hannah.

David said, 'This is my son, Grandpa.'

'Ve'll put de kettle on,' said the old man. 'And dere's cake.'

Hannah enunciated loudly to the old man, because she thought he was as deaf as she was: 'Your great-grandson, Moshe!'

'And biscuits, and jam,' said Moshe.

Elizabeth told him that the baby was called Anthony, and the baby gurgled for joy. 'D'you hear him?' asked Mrs MacPhee. 'Laughing? Go and say hello.'

'Mrs MacPhee made jam,' said Moshe, 'it's good. Sit and

you'll tell me vot you're daeing in your factory. Please have a biscuit, and butter, and jam.'

The baby gurgled again. Moshe went to the door without giving the pram a look. 'And I forgot something in de sitting-room. Mrs MacPhee, make tea for dem – von moment.' He went out.

David caught Elizabeth's eye and exchanged a glance. Hannah was in wonderment. 'He didn't look at the baby!'

Mrs MacPhee couldn't understand it. 'Why did ne no'? He's had wee children here, he's good wi' bairns!'

'Maybe,' said Hannah, 'he thinks he's no' . . .' She looked to David. 'Is he no' . . . ?'

David shook his head, and Hannah understood. She gave a great, whispered, 'Oh . . .' and explained to Mrs MacPhee, 'It's – you know – circumcision.'

Mrs MacPhee, not understanding, said 'Oh ay . . .'

David went out after Moshe.

Elizabeth was distressed.

'Not tae worry,' said Mrs MacPhee. 'He'll have forgotten, whatever it was.' She poked the baby, 'He's forgotten you,' and the baby promiscuously gurgled. 'You're the winner,' she said, 'you're a' right son, you're gaun tae break a' their hearts, aren't you.'

In the parlour, Moshe had his tallis round his shoulders, and he was putting his tephillin on, and muttering. David came in.

'Grandpa? What are you doing? It's afternoon. That's for morning.'

Moshe put his hand to his head and felt the black leather box.

David said gently, 'Come and sit down.'

'No. I'm all right.'

'Come and have a cup of tea.'

'Soon. David –'

David looked at the old man fearfully, across the years.

'Leave me,' came Moshe's commanding quiet voice.

*

In the kitchen, Elizabeth was sitting at the table. Mrs MacPhee was at the stove, dealing with the kettle. Hannah was loudly holding forth.

'I've been to Israel.'

'Really?'

'Last year. I got to Israel at last. I saved up and I beat you all to it. I went to Tel Aviv, and Haifa, and a kibbutz, and Jerusalem –'

Mrs MacPhee said, 'She keeps telling me.'

'Yes, I keep telling her. Jerusalem, me!'

'It must have been fascinating,' said Elizabeth, who was fascinated.

'Oh yes,' brayed Hannah. 'I looked around, and I thought, there's been things going on here . . . over the years, you know. But I'll tell you, Elizabeth, when I arrived back here, it was awfy guid tae be back hame.'

David stayed outside the parlour door. He heard his grand-father say '*Sh'ma Yisroe'el*', then stop.

They called the doctor that evening. Moshe had been lifted up to his bed. What was there for the doctor to say? What was there for him to do?

Moshe fought for breath, fought to keep his life, for two days. They got a nurse for him. Relatives came and went, the few who were left.

Then a final struggle and stillness. David came in and looked down at him. The nurse left with a swish of her apron, and shut the door.

David took the old man's tallis from its red velvet bag. He shook it out, the well-worn woollen shawl with dark stripes at each end and fringes, that he had brought with him from *der Heim*, and covered him with it.

At the cemetery, the only mourning relative was David. There was a sprinkling of old men and a few women. The black coffin was lowered into the grave.

Cyril Simon handed David the spade, and David knew what to do. He turned the spade over and dug into the heap of earth. Once, twice, thrice he dropped earth from the back of the spade on to the coffin far below, and thrice came the hollow thud of the earth on the box.

He handed the spade back. Someone handed him a prayer-book and he cleared the tears from his eyes and took it. But he remembered what to say, without the book.

Yisgadal v'yiskadash shmai rabboh . . .
And they all said '*Omain!*'
B'olmo divro chirusai . . .

Afterwards David shook hands with everyone and exchanged the greeting, 'Long life!'

He kissed Hannah. He shook hands with the weeping Mrs MacPhee. He went to the pathway where Elizabeth waited with the pram. They embraced tightly.

They walked through the pathways with the pram, to the main drive. They bent to the baby and cooed at it, and raspberried its tummy. The baby gurgled back at them and kicked his little feet and laughed with life.

They went out through the main gates, turned left and walked up the street with the people until you could no longer pick them out.

If the shofar had sounded the '*T'kiyoh g'douloh*', the final and great trumpet-call, they would not have heard; the walls had fallen, they were in the promised land.